INVASION: UPRISING

INVASION UK SERIES BOOK 2

DC ALDEN

FOREWARD

There are thousands of books out there that dive deep into political sociology, religion and military strategy. *Invasion: Uprising* isn't one of them.

It's a military thriller set in an alternate future where the political and cultural landscape has shifted dramatically, an imagined stage on which this tale is set. Nothing more.

I hope you enjoy it.

DC Alden

2IC - Second in Command
ACOG - Advanced Combat Optical Gunsight.
AFB - Air Force Base
AFV - Armoured Fighting Vehicle
ARV - Armoured Reconnaissance Vehicle (LAV-25 replacement)
ATC - Air Traffic Control
CASE-VAC - Casualty Evacuation
CID - Criminal Investigation Department
CO - Commanding Officer
Common Purpose - Alleged Marxist social engineering cult posing as Leadership Development Charity
CQB - Close Quarter Battle
CSM - Company Sergeant Major
DEVGRU - Navy Special Warfare Development Group (formerly SEAL Team Six)
DMR - Designated Marksman Rifle
GMLRS - Guided Multiple Launch Rocket System
Haji - Slang term for anyone wearing the caliphate uniform
HEAT - High Explosive Anti Tank

HVT - High Value Target

IFF - Identify Friend or Foe (aviation transponder)

JAASM-XR - Joint Air Surface Stand-Off Missile (Extreme Range)

KIA - Killed in Action

LAV - Light Armoured Vehicle

M27 - Infantry Automatic Rifle

M-ATV - Mine Resistant-All Terrain Vehicle

MIA - Missing in Action

MTVR - Medium Tactical Vehicle Replacement

NSA - National Security Agency

NCO - Non Commissioned Officer

OC - Officer Commanding

QRF - Quick Reaction Force

RNLI - Royal National Lifeboat Institution

RSM - Regimental Sergeant Major

RV - Rendezvous

SAW - Squad Automatic Weapon

SLS - Space Launch System

UAV - Unmanned Aerial Vehicle

UGV - Unmanned Ground Vehicle

UFV - Unmanned Fighting Vehicle

"If ye love wealth better than liberty, the tranquility of servitude better than the contest of freedom, go home from us in peace. We ask not for your counsel or your arms. Crouch down and lick the hands which feed you. May your chains set lightly upon you, and may posterity forget that you were ever our countrymen."

Samuel Adams

PROLOGUE
SEMPER HIGH

SPACE MARINE.

Colonel Jon Kramer still found the term mildly improbable, like something you'd hear on a TV show or read in a sci-fi novel. The president had called him that very thing six days ago in a private ceremony at Vandenberg AFB, and even then, it had a ring of unreality to it. The Congressional Medal of Honor the commander in chief had pinned to Kramer's chest had been real enough, even though he'd done nothing to earn it.

Not yet, anyway.

Purdy's voice hissed inside Kramer's helmet. 'Quite a view out there.'

Kramer turned his head and glanced out of the viewing port. Flashes of lightning flickered across a vast cloud formation that stretched across the dark earth below. With every passing orbit, that earth was getting closer. Kramer looked up to the blackness above, and the marine corps aviator felt it again, that overwhelming sense of awe and wonder. The universe was just one of millions – *billions* – that existed out there beyond their own sun, an unexplored

1

reality so vast that Kramer struggled to imagine its size and complexity. Was its creation nothing more than a random collision of atoms, or God's work? He'd find out soon enough.

'*Sixty-seconds to separation.*'

The voice was automated, like everything else about their brief excursion into space. Back down at Vandenberg, they'd covertly boarded the SLS rocket, their Penetrator stealth re-entry craft piggy-backed onto a telecommunications satellite. The launch had been scheduled for several months, and to the curious eye (and there were many this far into the global conflict), the SLS was just another private enterprise venture about to fire yet another orbiting hunk of junk into an already crowded atmosphere. No biggie.

Except for the first space marines in the history of the United States Armed Forces on board.

Thirty-six hours ago, the SLS had blasted off the pad in California and the newly commissioned military patch on their spacesuits had been duly earned. In the following 60 hours they'd made 28 low-earth orbits of the planet below, still attached to the satellite as it hurtled predictably around the globe. Other eyes would've tracked the launch, the separation, the established orbit. By now, curiosity would be satisfied. Nothing to see here. Move along, folks.

Kramer felt a vibration through his seat.

'*Internal systems checks are complete,*' the she-computer warned them. '*Thirty seconds to release.*'

He leaned forward, inspecting the underside of the satellite through the narrow slit of the observation window. It was a pilot's instinctive gesture, a visual check, like during a mid-air refuelling. Kramer knew it was pointless, but he did it all the same.

'*Ten seconds.*'

'Going down,' Gunny Purdy warned, his gloved fingers curling around the handgrips on his seat.

'Five seconds.'

Kramer did the same. They were pilot fish, swimming beneath the belly of a whale. But not for much longer...

'Three, two, one...detach.'

They felt the metallic *clunk* of releasing bolts, and then the satellite was drifting away. Within seconds, it was lost in the darkness.

'Re-entry program initiated.'

The nose of the Penetrator dipped, and the earth filled the cockpit windows, its surface still blanketed in cloud. Kramer glanced at the altimeter; still over 200 miles above the surface but they were already dropping fast. Ahead, somewhere beyond the terminator line, daylight beckoned, but the spacecraft would avoid the intrusive glare of another dawn. Its mission would be completed long before then.

The hull shook, and Kramer watched as the nose of the ship glowed. The Penetrator had been originally designed as an escape craft for astronauts on board the Deep Space Gateway until the developers at Lockheed Martin envisaged another role for the vehicle. Not life-saving. Life-taking.

The ship shuddered, the control panel blurring as it bullied its way back to the planet. Kramer gripped his handles tight as the ship carved through the thermosphere.

After several long minutes, the buffeting eased. The ionised air beyond the viewing port cleared and the ship's surface temperature cooled. Terrestrial video and navigation systems booted into life. Behind them they could feel the whisper-quiet, ram-air engine coming on-line, a low-output system designed to give the pilots aerodynamic control all the way to the surface.

'On-board power-plant is initiated. All systems nominal.'

'Flight control check.' Kramer's hand reached out for the auto-pilot override. 'Switching to manual.'

'Switching,' Purdy confirmed, his hands now gripping the throttle and mini flight-stick.

Kramer flipped the override. 'Your aircraft.'

'My aircraft.'

'Deploying wings.' The ship vibrated as the small delta wings fanned out from the fuselage. Kramer watched another light on the systems panel blink green. 'Wings deployed.'

'Roger that. Flying like a bird.'

Kramer smiled at that and looked forward to taking control himself, but right now he had other tasks to perform. The Penetrator was flying at 68,000 feet above Pakistan, with just under 1,000 nautical miles to target. At their current speed and angle of descent, it would take approximately 45 minutes to reach ground zero.

They'd drilled this a hundred times in the simulator, even when Purdy was sick, in case Kramer became incapacitated during the flight and the gunny had to complete the mission. The radiation they'd absorbed during their low-earth orbit couldn't have done the 22-year veteran much good.

'How're you doing there, Ron?'

The gunny smiled. 'Better than I've felt in months.'

Kramer gave his fellow Medal of Honor recipient a reassuring pat on the arm, then got back to work. He brought up the checklist on the screen in front of him. He knew the fusing sequence intimately, could start it in his sleep, but he stepped through it methodically, line by line, until the list was complete and he received the computerised, cold-as-ice confirmation.

'Fusing subsystem routine verified.'

'Setting barometric trigger.' Kramer turned to Purdy and said, 'What d'ya say, Ron? You wanna see the whites of their eyes or go by the book?'

Purdy smiled again. 'Best we go by the playbook, Colonel.'

'One-fifty it is.' Kramer winked, dialling in the required altitude. He punched the *execute* key.

'Trigger set,' the Ice Maiden confirmed. *'Initiating lockout sequence.'*

Numbers scrolled down the screen as the computer randomly selected a 24-digit, alpha-numeric lockout code. Physically entering that code was now the only way to disarm the weapon, but neither marine had any intention of doing that.

'Arming sequence complete,' Kramer confirmed.

'Okay then,' Purdy said, matter-of-fact.

Kramer turned his head and looked out of the side window. Through a break in the cloud below he glimpsed civilisation, a tiny cluster of lights that the nav system told him was Islamabad. Less than 30 seconds later it disappeared beneath a weather system that stretched all the way out to the Pakistan border.

Not long now.

He thought about the road that had brought him to this point, a road paved with God's good blessings; a wonderful childhood, a private education, then the Marine Corps, just like his pops, and his pops before him. Unlike them, he'd earned his naval aviator wings through the strike pipeline, eventually piloting an F/A-18 Super Hornet. During his stellar career, he'd been attacked with SAMs four times and evaded every one. He'd crashed once (hydraulic failure), but he'd got his bird down off the deck of a rolling aircraft carrier with minimal damage. He'd married the girl of his dreams and she'd borne him three children, two girls and a boy. Every day since, Jon Kramer had thanked God for his good fortune.

Until four months, twenty-two days and eleven hours ago.

That's when the truck driver, who'd pulled a brutal overnighter from Vancouver, closed his eyes for just a second—

The state police figured it was longer than that, but it didn't matter. The 42-ton 18-wheeler was travelling downhill at 60 miles an hour in Fresno County when it veered across the centre line and ploughed into Jackie Kramer's SUV, severing the vehicle in half and dragging a mangled fusion of twisted metal and ruptured flesh a further quarter-mile before the driver stopped his rig.

And in that one, awful twist of fate, Jon Kramer lost his wife, his children, and both his parents, who were making a surprise visit for Thanksgiving. Without Karen and the kids, he was nothing. His soul had been ripped from him, his reason to exist, gone. The nightmare of watching his dead children being lowered into the dirt had haunted him every night since. He couldn't go on. The only question that remained was how it would end.

The US secretary of defence had solved that question for him, and in person. The conversation was respectful, short, and blunt. Kramer didn't hesitate for a second and answered in the affirmative. Purdy had received a similar visit from the SecDef, although his was conducted at the Walter Reed Hospital in Bethesda, Maryland, where Purdy, a Seahawk pilot, was undergoing treatment for a particularly aggressive and incurable form of pancreatic cancer. Purdy was divorced with four kids. The SecDef assured the Gunny that all four would go to college, courtesy of Uncle Sam.

The training was brief and intense. Experimental drugs kept Purdy's cancer at bay but the respite never lasted more than a few days. As they'd orbited the earth, Kramer saw it in the gunny's eyes, telegraphed by the recurring spasms of pain, although now they were heading back to earth, that burden appeared to have lifted.

'Passing 40,000 feet,' he told Kramer. 'Your aircraft.'

'My aircraft,' Kramer confirmed, his hand gripping the control stick, his booted feet stamping the pedals, feeling the Penetrator buck in the night sky. He tamed her with a little throttle and a minor pitch adjustment. They were still above the clouds, still 300 nautical miles from their target, but the time would pass quickly now. He pitched the nose down a little, increasing their airspeed. The clouds below flickered with lightning pulses, a dying tropical storm that would provide them with some cover. The Penetrator's stealth capabilities would do the rest. They were an invisible dart, plummeting towards earth.

They plunged into the cloud, the turbulence causing Kramer to grip the stick a little harder with one hand and reach for the autopilot with the other.

'Primary flight control test complete. Switching to autopilot.'

'*Autopilot engaged.*'

Kramer let go of the flight stick. The Ice Maiden was in control now. She'd take them all the way in. There was nothing left to do now except enjoy the ride.

The world outside the viewing ports was grey and violent. The Penetrator bucked and shuddered through the storm. Kramer's helmet thumped against the fuselage as the aircraft began a series of steep banking manoeuvres, slowing its forward air speed. He checked the altimeter; 8,000 feet and dropping fast. He watched the nav display, saw they were descending over the mountains of Kashmir, the western anchor of the Himalayas. In a mission fraught with a multitude of dangers, both Kramer and Purdy had agreed that this would be the most nerve-wracking moment of the mission, not because of the perilous proximity of the many jagged peaks that towered above them – neither man worried about the prospect of a violent death – but because they were so close to completing their mission. To fail now would be unthinkable.

The aircraft banked hard to the right. Outside, the grey had turned to white, the rain to snow. The cloud swirled and shifted, the terrain outside taking shape. The ship ceased its violent passage, and the ride smoothed out. They were gliding through a narrow, snowy valley surrounded by magnificent granite walls, and Kramer felt the Penetrator making minor corrections to its course as it threaded its way through the mountain range. Soon, the peaks fell away, and as the last of the cloud cleared they saw a bright cluster of lights in the distance.

'Fifty seconds to target.'

'Showtime,' Purdy muttered inside his helmet.

The Penetrator lost altitude. Below the nose, the Yarkand River snaked towards the city of Yarkant County, still sleeping in the pre-dawn darkness. Kramer took a deep breath; it wasn't nerves that made his heart beat fast. It was anticipation, the knowledge that soon – in less than 20 seconds – he'd be reunited with the family he missed so desperately.

The Penetrator banked, gliding under minimal power,

turning away from the city and towards the sprawling military base three miles beyond. This close to the Pakistan border, the Chinese were in a perpetual state of alert, but that didn't matter to the Predator. She was invisible to all eyes, both human and electronic. And she was close, so close now...

'*Ten seconds.*'

Kramer twisted his glove and took Purdy's outstretched hand. 'It's been an honour, Gunny.'

'Likewise, Colonel.' Purdy winked. 'See you on the other side.'

Kramer nodded and turned back to the instrument panel; the altimeter showed 160 above ground level. Kramer's last glimpse of the world was a vast parade square, devoid of human life but filled with Chinese armour.

The nose dipped.

The barometric trigger fired—

THE FIVE-KILOTON TACTICAL NUCLEAR WEAPON detonated in a blast of white light, obliterating the sprawling People's Liberation Army base below. The shock wave destroyed buildings, vehicles, and every biological entity in a two-mile radius. Of the Predator, there was nothing left. The ship, along with America's first combat space marines, had vaporised to nothing. All evidence of US involvement erased in a nanosecond. The weapon, however, had left its own mark.

It took the Chinese nuclear investigators some time before they discovered the truth. Initially an accident was suspected – the base at Huangdizhen also housed a battalion of the PLA's Rocket Forces equipped with their own tactical weapons – however, after a detailed analysis of the fissile material discovered at the blast site, it was confirmed that the nuclear weapon was of Pakistani origin.

That made sense to Beijing.

For years the caliphate had protested against the treatment of Uyghur Muslims, and despite strongly worded denials from the Wazir government in Baghdad, the Chinese were convinced that the nuke was in retaliation against such treatment. In reality, the ageing president and general secretary of the Chinese Communist Party had longed to unleash his vast army against an aggressor before his life ended. He'd always had the means. Now he had the motivation.

The People's Liberation Army mobilised on land, at sea, and in the air. Half a million soldiers marched towards the caliphate border in western China. Ten thousand Chinese Muslims were rounded up, put on trial, and imprisoned or executed. A million more were deported en masse in cargo ships bound for the caliphate. It didn't take long for the missiles to criss-cross the Himalayas, but thankfully the warheads were conventional. Nuclear exchanges left no winners, both sides knew.

And so, a new front in the global conflict opened.

Elsewhere, it would change the course of the war forever.

[1]

JUDGE DREAD

EDITH SPENCER WAS 68 YEARS OLD WHEN SHE KILLED her first human being.

The man had robbed and beaten a uniformed caliphate clerk who'd recently finished his shift at County Hall. The clerk had been making his way home through a dark and deserted Borough Market when his assailant, Bradley Quinn, had struck him from behind with a metal bar. After leaving him unconscious and bleeding on the cobbles, Quinn rifled the clerk's pockets and stole the rucksack he was carrying. By the time Quinn was arrested, a week had passed and the young clerk's life support had been switched off due to extensive and irreparable brain damage.

Edith Spencer remembered the first time she'd laid eyes on Bradley Quinn, a pimply, sour-faced 22-year-old who'd slouched in the dock as she'd taken her seat on the judge's bench. Edith always tried her cases in Court Number One at the former Old Bailey, renamed after the Great Liberation as the British Central Criminal Court. Determined to make an example of Quinn, Edith remembered the slight tremor in her hands as she'd read her decision to the court.

With no jury and a less-than-enthusiastic defence counsel, the criminal's fate had been sealed long before he'd set foot in Edith's courtroom.

The former lord chief justice of the United Kingdom remembered the shiver of power as she'd announced Quinn's sentence: death by hanging. Quinn himself had sniggered, and his eyes had darted around the courtroom, seeking confirmation of the prank. The anguished wails of his ill-educated brood crowded into the public gallery confirmed that he'd heard correctly.

Afterwards, in the privacy of her chambers, Edith had reflected on her decision and discovered she was untroubled by it. Her liberal outrage against such ghastly legal mechanisms was a matter of public record, but that was before the Great Liberation. Since then, she'd seen things differently. Later that day she'd taken a phone call, from the chief judge of the Supreme Judicial Assembly of Europe, Abdul bin Abdelaziz. He'd congratulated her on her decision, and she'd been extraordinarily flattered. After his kind and wholly supportive words, she'd decided to attend the execution in person, in order to appreciate the gravity of her jurisprudence. It was not the experience she imagined.

What she *did* imagine was watching a hooded Quinn dropping through a trapdoor, the thick rope around his neck snapping taut and instantly ending the boy's life. She'd imagined the corpse dangling out of sight, and her solemn pronouncement about justice being served.

The reality had been very different.

After being driven to Wormwood Scrubs in her official Mercedes, Edith had been escorted to a fenced-in exercise yard. There she'd been invited to stand facing the rusted steel scaffold frame that dominated the yard. Edith remembered thinking it resembled an oversized climbing frame, the kind one would see in a children's playground. How wrong she'd been.

A large group of people stood off to one side; the clerk's family, Edith had assumed, and she remembered their angry yells and distraught wailing when a phalanx of guards had appeared, marching towards the yard. In their midst she'd recognised Quinn, wearing an orange jumpsuit, his hands and feet shackled in chains. What Edith wasn't expecting were the other two orange-clad prisoners shuffling awkwardly behind him.

She'd steeled herself, not knowing quite what to expect. The crowd had wailed and cursed as the guards herded the prisoners beneath the scaffold. Quinn had looked right at her as a short steel wire was looped over his head and tightened around his neck.

'Please,' he'd spluttered, his eyes locked on Edith's, but she didn't respond. Instead she'd concentrated on keeping her expression impassive. There had been no master of ceremonies present, no official proclamation; Quinn was simply lifted off his feet by two of the biggest prison guards Edith had ever seen, and his wire noose looped over a hook. The other two were similarly dealt with, and within thirty seconds of them appearing, all three men were dangling from the scaffold.

The small crowd had fallen silent. None of the prisoners wore hoods, and Edith recalled summoning every molecule of self-control to keep from turning away. She'd watched Quinn as he'd kicked and twisted, his head cocked to one side as the wire dug deep into the flesh of his neck, his face purple, his eyes bulging, his tongue protruding from his mouth. The others were no different, bucking and twisting violently, their strangled chokes competing with the violent rattling of their shackles. Quinn was the last to die, and Edith imagined it was his comparative youth that had kept him going longer than the others. Finally – thankfully, in Edith's case – his legs had stopped kicking and his body hung limp. His mouth and chin were covered in snot and blood, his eyes wide and bulbous, his jumpsuit damp with urine. Then the shouts drifted down from the black walls of the prison that surrounded them, the other prisoners hurling abuse, screaming and protesting. The guards stepped back as the families surged forward and began clubbing and raking the corpses with their shoes and bare hands. Edith would never forget the spectacle. Both appalled and fascinated, she'd stood her ground until the warden had intervened with an invitation to his office for refreshments. She'd declined of course. Bearing witness to an unexpectedly barbarous execution was one thing, but drinking cheap tea and engaging in pointless small-talk with a lowly prison warden was quite another.

'Is anything the matter, Edith?'

She looked over the rim of her glass, realising she'd drifted away from the surrounding conversation. She smiled and shook her head. It was time to reengage with her guests. She was the host, after all.

'I'm sorry, a memory distracted me. My first execution.'

The chatter faded around the table. All eyes turned towards her.

'His name was Quinn, a distinctly repulsive individual. He'd beaten a young clerk half to death, and the poor boy had never recovered. Sentencing Quinn was a decision I didn't take lightly, and the execution was a ghastly affair, but these things are necessary if we are to maintain a sense of order.'

'It couldn't have been easy,' said the wife of the Berkshire assemblyman. 'It's not something we're used to seeing in Britain.' Her eyes wandered across the faces of the other guests. 'Has anyone else seen one?'

'I saw a beheading in Trafalgar Square,' Timothy Gates admitted, taking a deep breath. 'I was working at the National Gallery organising the salvage of artworks damaged during the liberation when I heard this frightful hullabaloo outside. There was a young man on his knees near where old Nelson used to stand, surrounded by a group of soldiers. A crowd had gathered, and there was a lot of shouting and cat-calling, then a big, bearded chap with a bloody great sword swiped the poor bugger's dome off his shoulders. Damnedest thing I ever saw.'

The other diners chuckled, and Edith smiled. Timmy was one of her oldest and dearest friends, which is why she hadn't denounced him as a homosexual during the purges. Others hadn't been so lucky.

She looked along the table, at the great and the good of British society, their faces lit by soft candlelight and flushed pink by the splendid food and excellent wines that Edith, in her capacity as Britain's foremost judge, had provided for them. With the royal family brooding in exile across the Atlantic, a new Republic had risen in their departure, and Edith and her dinner guests now represented the pinnacle of Britain's elite, a status they enjoyed by the good graces of the caliphate.

'I'm not convinced the death penalty works,' the white-haired Victor Hardy chipped in. He was Edith's closest ally, and as judge advocate, second in line to her legal throne. 'Especially with these resistance thugs. It can often lead to a wider resentment against the ruling classes.'

'I'll let you take that up with the chief justice.' Edith smiled. There was laughter around the table, and Victor held up his hands in mock defeat.

Edith swirled the 74 Burgundy around her glass. 'Quinn was a common criminal, and an example had to be set. As for these resistance people, well, I think it's important we show our support for the administration. They're here to stay, and it's incumbent on us, as the new establishment, to lend that administration the breadth of our experience and wise counsel.'

At the other end of the table, Victor raised his glass. 'Well said, Edith.'

The conversation moved swiftly on to other matters, primarily the reopening of the Globe Theatre on the Southbank, where pre-approved productions were scheduled for the coming summer. Edith and her guests were looking forward to the resumption of cultural life. She'd missed the theatre desperately; however, her courtrooms continued to provide their own drama, something she was always thankful for.

After dessert the party drifted away from the table and into the magnificent drawing room for coffee and brandies. She sat in her usual seat by the fire, enjoying the conversation and regaling her guests with amusing anecdotes from her long and illustrious career. As the chimes of midnight echoed through her elegant and sprawling Edwardian residence, her guests left. Soon she found herself alone with Victor and Timmy, her inner circle, her true confidants and friends. Trustworthy, discreet. Qualities that Edith favoured above all others.

Timmy stretched his legs out, teasing his brandy around the enormous balloon glass in his hand.

'A splendid evening, Edith. Most enjoyable.'

'Agreed,' Victor echoed between puffs of his Monte Cristo. 'I have to say that the food has been markedly excellent these last few months. Please pass along our compliments.'

'I will.' Edith chuckled. 'He's a former TV celebrity, a rather gruff and foul-mouthed individual, but once very successful, I'm told. He lives below stairs now.'

'That'll teach him.' Victor sneered, exhaling a fog of cigar smoke. 'Nothing more satisfying than seeing the nouveau riche toppled from their gaudy pedestals.'

'Quite.'

Edith's eyes were drawn to the fire, where the flames danced hypnotically in the hearth. She shifted in her favourite wingback chair, smoothing the material of her oriental silk dress as she crossed one leg over the other. Her fingers caressed a large spider brooch pinned to her breast, the firelight reflecting its myriad crystals. She was content, she decided. The political circumstances were not ideal; however, she had embraced the liberation as if she herself had been freed like a common slave.

She recalled that fateful night, the power cuts, then the distant gunfire and the rumble of explosions that had shaken the city. She'd ventured from her house, gathering with her neighbours in their affluent, leafy backstreet of Hampstead. There was frightened talk of plane crashes and terrorist attacks. There was no Internet, no mobile phone service, no police, no help. London had descended into anarchy, and that terrified Edith. As the days of uncertainty had worn on, visions of lawless, angry mobs had plagued her, and it was an enormous relief when order was finally restored. That military rule had replaced Prime Minister Harry Beecham and his administration was neither here nor there to Edith. What mattered was stability and the rule of law, the bedrock of her own life and her raison d'être. In its absence, humanity quickly descended into savagery.

A month after that terrifying night, Edith had finally summoned the courage to step out of her gated mansion, one that offered impressive views over the city, views now transformed into a disturbing vista of black smoke and shattered towers. A living tapestry of the chaos that Edith despised.

She'd persuaded Bertie, her regular black cab driver and part-time handyman, to take her into the city. She'd dressed conservatively and had the foresight to cover her head with a chiffon scarf that matched her pale green trouser suit. The only concession to accessorise was a beetle brooch, fashioned from jade and pinned to her lapel. First impressions were paramount back then, and her attention to detail had paid dividends.

The first roadblock was situated outside the Royal Free Hospital and had been manned by a swarm of heavily armed caliphate troops and local militia. There was a small queue of traffic ahead of Bertie's taxi, and one by one the vehicles inched towards the checkpoint, watched over by a frightening six-wheeled vehicle with an ugly, long-barrelled gun mounted on its turret.

Devoid of the correct papers, Bertie was swiftly dragged from the vehicle and beaten. Edith, projecting as much authority as circumstances allowed, had explained to the ring of beards surrounding her that she was a respected judge in both the UK *and* the European Union, and she wished to speak to someone in authority. She'd provided judicial papers with impressive seals and royal warrants written in old English, not because the men surrounding her would understand them, but the gravitas they implied might make them think twice.

The gamble had paid off. A month later, Edith found herself working as a legal adviser to London's interim military council. When the soldiers were replaced with civilian administrators sent from Baghdad, Edith's former roles of lord chief justice and supreme court justice were finally acknowledged and given the respect they deserved.

As English common law was reformed, Edith grappled with the complexities of Sharia Law, tenets of which had been quietly adopted in Britain long before Wazir had cast his conquering eye west. The British Territories, as England, Scotland, and Wales were now known, formally adopted a new rulebook, a rigid book of laws that would serve as a compass to navigate the choppy waters of the Great Liberation. Edith had been instrumental in that adoption and was promoted to chief justice of the British Territories. The *Lord* had been dropped of course, and the honorific title of *Lady* bestowed on her many years ago by Queen Elizabeth was no longer recognised by the new regime, but Edith could live with that.

Yes, she'd come far, had made the most of a seismic shift in international power. Victor had also adapted to the new state of affairs. Like Edith, Victor was a titled individual and used to a lifestyle of status and privilege, and Edith had duly appointed him as her judge advocate. Neither of them would allow a military invasion of the former United Kingdom to disrupt the lives they'd become accustomed to.

'Would anyone like a refill?'

Timmy's voice cut through Edith's reminisces, and she was glad of it. The past was the past. What mattered was the future and her role in it. She shook her head.

'I've had enough,' she told him, tipping back the warm liquid at the bottom of her glass. She set it down on the table by her chair and pressed the buzzer to summon her manservant. 'Time for these old bones to find their bed. Please stay, relax. Bertie will see you out when you're ready.' She got to her feet.

'Wait. I have news,' Timmy stuttered. 'Important political stuff.'

'Political?' Edith frowned. 'What d'you mean?'

Timmy stared at his beige loafers like a guilty schoolboy. Victor was the first to join the dots. He crushed out his cigar and leaned forward in his chair.

'You bloody idiot!' he spluttered. 'You said you'd ended it months ago!'

'This isn't a fling, Victor. We're in love—'

'Oh please.' The judge snorted, reaching for the brandy. He poured himself a large measure and swallowed half in a single gulp.

Edith felt a shiver of fear prickle the back of her neck. 'I warned you, Timmy,' she said, still struggling with what she'd heard. 'You promised me it was over.'

Timmy jabbed his chest. 'He came to me, Edie! I tried to break it off, but he was insistent. We meet once a week, that's it. No phone calls, no emails, nothing. We're being careful, I swear. He knows what he's doing.'

'Idiot!' Victor slumped back in his chair, the red leather creaking beneath his ample backside. 'I should flog you myself!'

'You're overreacting—'

'Enough.'

Edith sat down, her legs feeling dangerously hollow. It was several moments before she could think clearly. 'Timmy, you are my oldest friend, and I love you dearly, but Victor is right. You've been very foolish. Faisal is an intelligence officer at the caliphate's military headquarters. *When* your affair is discovered – not *if* – you will be rigorously interrogated, and before you are sent to the gallows, you'll have told them who knew about your illegal affair. Anyone with prior knowledge of that relationship will also suffer the consequences. It will be the end of us, do you understand?'

'We couldn't help ourselves,' Timmy explained, gulping his brandy. 'This is the real thing, Edie.'

'Spare me.' Victor scowled.

Edith held up a hand for silence. 'You said you had important news,' she pressed.

Timmy nodded. 'Something Faisal told me, and it's pretty bloody scary. Long story short, Wazir fired a nuke across the border into China. Thankfully they didn't retaliate—'

'He did *what*?' Victor's face paled in the firelight.

'When?' Edith asked him.

'A few weeks ago. Wazir pleaded ignorance but Beijing launched a retaliatory strike on Islamabad – non-nuclear, thank God – but tens of thousands have been killed on both sides. The Chinese are building up a significant force on the Kashmir border and Wazir is sending an army east. They're pulling troops in from all over the caliphate. Faisal might be shipped abroad.'

'Never mind your bloody boyfriend!' Victor snapped. 'Are we in any danger, here in the UK?'

The art historian swallowed another mouthful of brandy. 'I don't know. He never said.'

'And you didn't think to ask?' Victor shook his head. 'War with China will cause Wazir a lot of problems. He's got all sorts of deals with Beijing; oil-for-weapons, precious metals, technology, you name it. This is going to throw a serious spanner in Baghdad's works.'

Edith opened her mouth to respond, then caught a movement in the shadows across the room. She snapped to her feet. 'Bertie? I didn't hear you come in.'

'You *r-r-*rang for me, Lady Edith?' Bertie spoke with an occasional stammer, a legacy of the beating he'd received that day. Continued employment was something she felt she owed him, and he addressed her as *Lady Edith,* which she liked to hear, especially when she entertained.

'Of course I did.' She tutted. 'My guests are leaving. Please show them out.'

Victor and Timmy stood and finished their drinks. They took it in turn to peck Edith's flushed cheeks.

'We shall reconvene soon, in the next few days,' she muttered gravely.

The men left the room, and Edith was finally alone. She picked up the brandy bottle then set it down again. It was too late, and she was too tired. She would sleep, allow her subconscious to process Timmy's troubling news. She was no expert, but she knew China had a massive army and thousands of nuclear weapons. This could go very bad, very quickly. If that should happen, an exit strategy would be required. She would consider her options, talk to Victor. Alone.

As for Timmy, the man was a foolish romantic, an endearing quality in pre-liberation London, but tonight she realised he'd become a selfish, dangerous liability, and he'd placed them all in serious danger. For that, there would be consequences.

Edith cursed his name as she stared into the dying fire.

[2]
IRISH EYES

EDDIE NOVAK KNELT BEHIND THE ROUGH STONE church wall, his lungs heaving, M27 jammed into his shoulder, eye pressed against the optics, the warm barrel sweeping the unlit houses across the road.

Digger and Steve knelt either side of him, catching their breath, watching the ground ahead. Steve was swapping out a mag and Digger was still bitching about losing his NVGs. Eddie's were gone too. Around them, the rest of Nine Platoon was spread out along the wall or lying dead in the field they'd just sprinted across. The Hajis who'd opened up on them were dead too, shredded by half a dozen grenades and a couple of hundred rounds. Their remains were somewhere behind them, scattered across the churchyard graves.

No longer a place of peace and reflection, Eddie knew. The church's stained-glass windows were gone, the door blackened and twisted off its hinges. Old wounds, inflicted long before the Second Massachusetts Battalion had arrived. It wasn't the first they'd seen. Nor the last, probably.

Lance-Corporal Rab McAllister loomed out of the darkness and dropped to his knee.

'Gaffer's down,' he told them. 'Took a round through the leg. He'll live, but he's out of the game.' He pulled a small Tac-Tablet from his webbing and shielded the light. He ran a gloved finger across the screen. 'Bravo Company has cut the town off from the north, and Alpha's got all routes south sewn up tighter than a nun's chuff. They're holding Fire Support in reserve until we get an idea of opposition, but the drones are seeing a stampede down to the harbour. Hajis are on the run, but there'll be a few martyrs amongst them, so don't get complacent. You see one, send him to Paradise, even if he's waving a white flag.' He tapped the tablet screen. 'We're moving up to the corner of the high street. We'll hold there and link up with Bravo, then we're going house to house.'

'What about the Hajis?' Digger asked him.

'Ain't you done enough killing?'

Digger winked. 'Not yet.'

'Lunatic,' Mac muttered. He jammed the tablet into his assault pack and gripped his M27. 'Right, prepare to move.'

Then he was gone, working his way down the wall. Eddie watched the road ahead, the houses that flanked it, the potential dangers. The windows were dark, the curtains open. Some of them had white sheets and Irish Tricolours hanging from them. *Could be a ruse*, Eddie thought. It wouldn't be the first time they'd lost people that way, but as a designated marksman, Digger would cover their advance with his M38. Anyone showed themselves in those windows, the youngest member of Nine Platoon would end them.

Mac's voice hissed over the radio. 'Nine Section, move!'

Eddie scrambled over the wall and moved fast and low,

rifle up, eyes moving left and right. He was aware of the others behind him, their quick breaths, the familiar rattle and rasp of clothing and equipment. The houses loomed on either side. Eddie led Three Section along the wall towards the corner of the high street. He stopped short, mindful of booby-traps. His eyes searched the pavement ahead, the corner of the street. There were no road signs or lamp posts, nothing to secure a tripwire to. He crept up to the corner, crouching low, and looked to his left. Whatever shops and businesses they had in this town had been ransacked. The high street was littered with all sorts of debris, clothes, furniture, books, papers, broken glass. A couple of shops were burning fiercely, the smoke partly obscuring the road to the north. There were bodies lying out there too, civilians. That was nothing new either. Two klicks back they'd discovered a ditch full of corpses, all locals, all men, some of them young lads. It was hard to deal with sometimes—

Movement.

He squinted through his ACOG, saw armed men moving down the high street towards their position. Then he saw the faint glow of their IR flag patches and knew it was the boys from Alpha Company, moving south. He watched them pause 50 metres away and Eddie signalled with his hand, saw his gesture acknowledged. He called it in over the net.

'Come on, let's go,' Digger muttered, re-joining them.

'Take it easy, nipper,' Steve cautioned. 'No sense in getting killed, not now.'

Not this close to the end, Eddie echoed silently. *Not the end,* he reminded himself, *the end of the beginning.* At least, that's what older, wiser heads were saying.

He heard boots on the road and glanced over his shoulder. What remained of Nine Platoon crouched against the wall behind him. Then he saw Mac moving up the line towards him. He crouched down next to Eddie, his breath ragged.

'Strykers are inbound and Fire Support are moving up from the south. HQ wants the high street swept clean, so you'll be clearing everything south of this position and east of the high street, got it?' He slapped a hand on the wall they crouched against. 'Start with this one and work your way south. Sections will leap-frog as you go. And watch for IEDs, got it?'

'Roger that,' the boys whispered.

'We're moving in zero-two minutes. Steve, launch the bug.'

Mac disappeared back into the darkness. Steve swung his assault pack off his back and extracted the Black Hornet mini-drone from its padded pouch. Within seconds, the palm-sized drone was flying over their heads and disappearing around the corner.

'Get in there, ya little beauty.' Steve watched the mini-screen as he flew the tiny drone through the shattered shop window on the high street. 'Downstairs is a mess, but it's clear. No trip-wires, no targets. Going up...' Another few seconds passed. 'Jesus, I thought my house was small. Okay, looks clear.'

Seconds later the drone was settling back on the pavement next to them. Steve packed it away. The order came a moment later.

'Three Section, move up!'

'Moving,' Eddie responded, and then he was turning around the corner, gun sweeping the high street. In the darkness ahead, he heard a door crash open, and a dozen enemy troops bolted into the road, spraying wild rounds back up the street.

'Contact!'

Eddie fired as he moved. *Fire, hit, switching target, fire, fire, hit, switch...*

Everyone else was firing too, suppressors coughing like a doctor's waiting room in winter. Brass sang as it hit the road. Most of the Hajis went down hard. Others swerved the fusillade and disappeared around the bend in the high street.

Eddie ducked into the first shop, a bakery, mashing pies and pastries beneath his boots. They cleared the ground floor, and Digger and Steve did the same upstairs. Back outside, they leap-frogged their way along the high street, clearing buildings as they went, reclaiming the real estate. Alpha Company were doing the same across the street. There were a lot of hand signals and voice chatter on the net, but no shouting and no gunfire. They found only two people, both middle-aged, both dead, lying behind the counter of a gift shop. The lady had a rosary clutched between her fingers. Both had been shot in the back of the head.

When Digger saw them, he cursed and marched back outside.

'Digger, wait!'

Eddie saw him swing his M38 behind his back and pull his Sig pistol, heading for the Haji runners lying in the road. Some of them were still alive, moaning, twisting in agony, begging for mercy. Digger shot two of them before Eddie pulled him away.

'Alpha Company OC is coming up behind us,' he lied. 'Move, go! Before he sees you.'

Digger said nothing, just jammed his Sig home and grabbed his rifle. He'd been doing that a lot lately, killing in cold blood. The first time Eddie and Steve had tried to stop him, Digger had turned the gun on them. They'd left the kid alone after that.

It took 30 minutes to clear the high street. Alpha and Bravo held their positions while Charlie Company moved down towards the harbour. Three Section took up position behind the wall overlooking the narrow road that curved down to the sea. It was shrouded in darkness, but they all heard the desperate shouts carried on the cold night air. The sound of panic, Eddie knew. *Good.*

Then they heard something else; powerful diesel engines.

'Recce Platoon,' Steve observed, pointing. 'Inbound, three o'clock.'

Two 8-wheeled Stryker armoured vehicles charged out of the darkness to the south. They turned right onto the harbour road in a squeal of rubber, and almost immediately the lead Stryker opened fire, its 20-millimetre mini-gun lighting up the night. Eddie couldn't see the targets but he could imagine the carnage. The other Stryker opened up too, their short, brilliant-white strobe bursts ripping the air. Then the vehicles moved out of sight, down to the harbour. The firing went on for several more minutes, and Eddie didn't hear any return fire. That didn't surprise him.

The Strykers reappeared and rumbled past them along the high street. More troops from the Second Mass were pouring into the high street, most of them on foot, muddied and bloodied. Other than the small harbour, there was nothing special about the town of Bally Cross. It had no strategic importance, except for the Hajis, and the boats they could use to escape in. Now the place was ruined, scarred for life, along with the lives that lived here. Eddie thought about the couple in the gift shop, executed for nothing, probably. He wondered if they'd known their murderers, living as they had under caliphate rule for over two years. Maybe. In the end, it didn't matter. They were still dead.

Eddie heard Mac's voice on the radio. The platoon, or what was left of it, double-timed it to the road junction above the harbour. Mac was waiting for them.

'We're securing this area. Eddie, Steve, Digger, get down to the water and see if anyone's still alive. The rest of you, spread out and cover them.'

'The Hajis could have gunboats out there, Skip,' Steve said. 'We won't be able to see 'em, not with our gear.'

Mac scowled. 'Yanks have got a missile team inbound. Should be here within the hour. That make you feel better? Or would ye like a hug and a big sloppy kiss too?'

Steve grinned beneath the rim of his helmet. 'I could do with a cuddle, but no tongues, mind.'

'Move!' Mac snarled.

They doubled down the harbour road, keeping to the stone wall. There were no boats in the harbour, Eddie observed, none that would float again. The Stryker's had seen to that, chewing the fishing vessels, pleasure cruisers, and wooden pontoons to pieces. Same for the Hajis. Limbs, heads, and torsos bobbed on the harbour's dark, oily surface. It was carnage.

Covered by the rest of the platoon, Eddie and the boys headed out along the harbour wall for another hundred metres until they could go no further. They got down on their stomachs and scanned the horizon. The sea pounded the harbour wall below them. More wreckage and bodies drifted through Eddie's low-light scope.

'Like shooting fish in a barrel,' Steve muttered.

'Lucky bastards,' Digger said.

Eddie turned to look at him. 'Who?'

'The guys on those mini-guns. I would've loved to chop them fuckers up.'

'So go join Recce Platoon then,' Steve told him.

'I've tried. No deal.'

'Stuck with us then, eh?'

'For now,' Digger grumbled, eye pressed to the scope of his M38 as he scanned the sea.

Eddie did the same. The only thing visible were the white horses that galloped across the dark swell. Digger's mental health worried him. He was the youngest in the platoon, just 18, and both him and his dad had joined up, but Barnes senior had been posted to the First Battalion, to split up the family members, just in case. Digger's dad was on board a supply ship when it was struck by a hypersonic ballistic missile and blew like a nuke. The *MV Barnard Fisher* had been transporting thousands of tonnes of ammunition, as well as men and vehicles. Of the handful of survivors, none of them was Digger's dad. The kid had never been the same since.

They'd tried to counsel him, even send him back home to New London, but Digger had refused, fooling the shrinks he was fit to serve. And he was, pretty much. Except for the killing. Eddie didn't know what Digger's personal body-count was, but it was more than the rest of the section combined. The kid was an assassin who operated on a hair-trigger. He'd also saved their lives more than once.

The bitter wind howled, driving the waves onto the harbour wall and dumping spray all over them. Eddie stared into the darkness. The Welsh coast was out there some-where, less than a hundred kilometres away. There was nothing to see, no distant lights, no slow, steady sweep of a lighthouse, but they were close now, closer than they'd ever been. Taking back Ireland had proved to be a long, bloody slog, but they'd made it this far. It wasn't over yet, though, and Eddie told himself to stay sharp. He gave Digger a nudge.

'See anything out there?'

Digger twisted his more powerful 56-millimetre Leupold scope. He swept the sea for a moment, then his body stiffened. 'Wait a minute...I've got something. Yep, it's definitely a mermaid. Nice tits too. Ooh look, she's waving—'

'Bollocks to this,' Steve swore, getting to his feet. 'Come on, let's go. We're wasting our time here.'

As they headed back to the harbour, Eddie felt the adrenaline draining from his system, leaving a crippling tiredness in its wake.

'Anyone got any kickers? I'm out.'

'Me too,' Steve moaned. 'I'm almost on my arse.'

Digger glanced over his shoulder. 'Stop whining. They're pulling us back from the coast, anyway. In case the Hajis counter-attack with missiles.'

'How d'you know?' Eddie prayed it was true. He was flagging fast.

'I overheard Mac talking to a couple of HQ bods. We'll be gone before sun up. You girls'll be able to get your beauty sleep after that.'

Eddie shook his head. 'We've been on the move for 36 hours. I've slept for maybe four hours, tops. How d'you do it, Digger? How d'you stay so sharp?'

'He's running on pure hatred,' Steve told him.

Digger grinned. 'Fucking right I am.'

Eddie grinned too. He was too tired to know why.

[3]
TOM & JERRY

EIGHTEEN MONTHS PRIOR TO THE INVASION OF Ireland, the 72,000-ton transport ship *MV Tonberg* had bullied its way across a turbulent Atlantic Ocean, escorted by a US navy cruiser and a Royal Navy Type-45 destroyer. Their highly-classified mission was to ensure the safe and undetected passage of the *Tonberg* to the Scottish port of Thurso, the northernmost town on the British mainland. Thankfully, that mission had been a successful one, and the port and its harbour, unlike many to the south, were still intact.

When the massive Roll On-Roll Off vessel had finally docked, several thousand British and US troops of the new Atlantic Alliance had already arrived in Scotland, bringing with them their Linebacker and Stryker mobile missile launchers, as well as Rapier anti-aircraft systems to secure the airspace and protect the steady stream of troops, supplies, and munitions that were finally trickling back into the country, a reality that didn't go unnoticed in Baghdad.

Aware of his strategic inability to secure the North Atlantic or threaten the US-Iceland-Scotland air corridor, the Caliph Wazir had concluded that the dark, mountainous region to the north of Hadrian's Wall was unworthy of annexation. Instead, he emulated the strategy of those early Romans and secured the border against a future invasion.

Safely docked in Faslane and protected by a passive SAM envelope, the *MV Tonberg* unloaded her cargo, two important passengers, *Tom* and *Jerry*. Donated by their tech billionaire owner whose love for his country was equalled by his passion for innovation, both *Tom* and *Jerry* had been previously dismantled into sections and wrapped in thermal shield skins. When they finally left Thurso, they did so in two separate convoys, as quietly as their Oshkosh M1070 heavy transporters would allow.

One convoy was despatched to Gretna on the west coast, the other east, to the town of Morpeth, and it took almost 48 hours of careful route-planning across the dark and damaged country for the convoys to reach their destinations. Security was paramount.

At Gretna, *Tom* was delivered to an abandoned sewage plant east of that deserted settlement. *Jerry* was driven inside a giant car warehouse on Morpeth's only industrial estate. Both locations lay just three miles to the north of the caliphate's frontier, and as promised, Wazir had redrawn the maps, abandoning almost 1,200 square miles of English territory to form a new border that ran from the Solway Firth to the decimated town of Blyth on the east coast. The new frontier now ran in an almost straight line that was now only 63 miles long. And probably the deadliest 63 miles on earth.

The caliphate's engineers had been busy since the British evacuation, creating a no-man's-land that stretched two miles across at its widest point, and at its narrowest, just over a mile. Bulldozers, giant excavators, and the liberal use of high-explosives had levelled everything in between. Every field, every wood, every forest, every village and town, every commercial building, every tree, telegraph pole and lamppost, every abandoned vehicle, every road and pavement had been cut down, crushed, broken up and bull-dozed into a vast no-man's-land of broken earth, timber, brick concrete, and twisted metal. A kill-zone, watched over by a vast network of surveillance towers and observation posts, by snipers and heavy machine-guns, by mortars and rockets, and drones that buzzed across the man-made desolation, hunting for anything that moved.

The frontier was a scar across the landscape, a wound that still bled, and many had attempted to escape across its dangerous desolation. They believed that they could outrun the guns, avoid the countless mines and man-traps, and hide from the CCTV towers and surveillance drones. The bodies of the desperate and deluded lay where they fell, their corpses riddled with bullets or shredded by antiper-sonnel mines. Some unfortunates had died slow deaths out in the fields of wire, mud, and rubble. The bodies were left to rot, not as a cruel reminder to others but because the ground was too dangerous to recover them. Other corpses littered the wasteland, the bullet-riddled skins of balloons and parachutes, the broken wings of light aircraft, buried in the mud and concertina wire.

The frontier was a no-go zone in every sense of the phrase.

Yet in Gretna and Morpeth, the dark, nightmarish vision of the frontier had been duly ignored. Instead, prepa-rations for *Tom* and *Jerry* had begun in earnest. Below ground, Alliance engineers had improved airflow and installed thermal shields, had broken the earth with heavy plant equipment, had ensured that the abandoned towns were covertly patrolled and the specialised labour force and their excavations remained undetected. By the time *Tom* and *Jerry* arrived at their respective sites, the enemy to the south was none the wiser and preparations had been completed.

At Gretna, *Tom* was lowered into a giant concrete shaft and assembled below ground. In Morpeth, *Jerry* had been put together on the floor of the warehouse, then driven down a steep ramp to a giant wall of mud and dirt. Inside their respective control rooms, *Tom* and *Jerry*'s technicians had completed their final checks, and a message had been relayed to the military command centre at Fort William, and from there via satellite to the ground station at the NSA's Fort Meade complex in Maryland.

The reply had come back in short order because everyone had known that time was of the essence and that the top-secret operation would be a slow one. The NSA had responded in due course, and the much-expected order for the teams controlling *Tom* and *Jerry* had finally been received. The encryption code deciphered the message which had comprised only two words:

COMMENCE DIGGING.

[4]
LAW AND ORDER

EDITH SAT BEHIND THE JUDGE'S BENCH, THE EVIDENCE laid out before her.

There were photographs and CCTV footage, and the men featured in them were the same four men who now stood in the dock, staring balefully at her. There was other evidence too, statements from the police and witnesses, most of which would've been dismissed by any competent defence lawyer in a pre-liberation courtroom, but those days were long gone.

The target of the conspiracy was a senior police chief, a woman known personally to Edith for many years. And like Edith, the commissioner had overcome her post-liberation circumstances and established herself as a senior figure within the new administration. The plan was to shoot her on her doorstep as she left for work. Edith wasn't fully abreast of all the details, but that was neither here nor there. The accused had dared to challenge their new masters, and that was unforgivable.

She looked over her glasses at them, slouching in her dock

in their garish prison overalls. The architect of the plot was a 52-year-old civil servant called Gordon Tyndall, a man whom Edith would have expected more from, who'd enjoyed an unblemished career, both before and after the Great Liberation. He was part of the establishment, a cog in the machinery of government, but reading his personnel file she noted that he'd never been invited to attend Common Purpose training. That told Edith everything she needed to know about the man.

Tyndall stared back at her with cold narrow eyes, with an arrogant jut to his unshaven jaw. As he stared up at her, his chest rose and fell rapidly, but it wasn't fear Edith saw in those hard eyes. It was hate. She dropped her gaze back to the papers arranged across the bench in front of her, then turned on her microphone.

'The evidence laid before me is both irrefutable and damning,' she announced, her voice echoing around Court Number One. 'The accused have been charged with the attempted murder of a senior police officer, a charge that the defence counsel has failed to answer adequately. The law therefore compels me to pronounce judgement...' Edith cleared her throat, more for effect than anything else. This was a death-penalty case, and the public gallery was packed with relatives and friends of the accused. 'Gordon Tyndall, Rupert Lovejoy, Henry Lovejoy, and Lynton Fairbanks, you are hereby sentenced to death—'

'Traitor!'

Her head snapped up. In her 36 years as a judge, no one – *no one* – had ever interrupted Edith Spencer, especially during a summation. She felt her blood boiling, staining her cheeks with angry red blotches. And to compound the outrage, the miscreant was still speaking.

'That's right, I'm talking to you, you dirty, stinking traitor. You and your kind will get your comeuppance, mark my words.'

Edith brought her gavel down several times, its sharp crack reverberating around the room. 'Silence in court!'

'You'll pay for this in blood!' one of the Lovejoy brothers bellowed. 'All you cowards and collaborators, you're dead, all of ya! Especially you, you vicious old cunt! And when they get you, I hope they do you slowly—'

A prison guard struck Lovejoy with a club, sparking a brawl in the dock. Family members roared defiance from the public gallery and the courtroom erupted into violence. Missiles and punches were thrown with furious abandon. It took a moment for Edith to snap out of her stunned immobility. She barked at the security officer guarding the narrow staircase to her bench.

'Clear the court, idiot! And arrest everyone in the gallery!' She saw a flicker of hesitation in the man's eyes. 'Now!'

Edith hurried back to her chambers. She closed the heavy door, shutting out the last echoes of disorder, sealing herself inside the quiet, comforting embrace of her private domain. She crossed the room and dropped into a Chesterfield couch, removing her black chiffon headscarf and clutching her black robe around her spare frame. She closed her eyes, her emotions swirling; anger, outrage, embarrassment, and yes, humiliation. The Tyndall creature had threatened her in her own courtroom, Lovejoy too. *The sheer gall of it!* Her heart pounded, and she struggled to compose herself. She had to take action.

She got to her feet and snatched up the phone. 'I want the defence counsel in my chambers, now!' She slammed the phone down without waiting for an answer. She opened the drinks cabinet and poured herself a finger of Scotch.

She swallowed it in a single gulp and poured another. That one didn't last long either. She put the glass back and sat behind her desk. The alcohol warmed and soothed her, and her heart rate slowed. She plucked a mint from the jar on her desk, just in case. After several deep, cleansing breaths, she was in better shape. Her head was clear, her emotions safely under control.

Except for one.

Word of the courtroom shambles would spread. The loss of Edith's precious order could not be condoned. She sat at her computer and typed up the execution orders herself, printing them out and laying them across her desk in a neat row. She signed each one with her antique Mont Blanc fountain pen, a gift from the former president of the European Union. Her signature was a confident flourish, the official stamp of her office underpinning the authority that Edith considered a birth right. And soon the insubordinate creatures who had defiled her courtroom would bear witness to that power, and they would tremble.

The defence counsel arrived moments later, and the young man was clearly intimidated. Edith handed him the execution orders. He skimmed the four sheets of cream paper emblazoned with the crossed swords of the British Central Criminal Court. Then he looked at her.

'Crucifixion, your honour?'

'Is there a problem?'

The barrister shook his head. 'No, not at all. My apologies.'

'Make sure you file those with the clerk. Good day.'

And tell your clients to rot in hell, she wanted to bark at the departing barrister. Instead she imagined the faces of the convicted, the initial confusion, then horror. A biblical death, slow, barbaric, under the grey skies of the country they'd all professed to die for. *And so they shall.* It was a fitting punishment, Edith decided, and the caliphate administrators would approve, she was quite sure of that.

She spent the rest of the afternoon poring over legal papers and case notes. The judicial load was becoming heavier, and she believed that a significant percentage of cases being brought before the Central Criminal Court could be dealt with by less prestigious bodies. Perhaps a position paper would be in order, a prescriptive text that might persuade Congress to streamline the system in order that justice may be served more efficiently.

She was on her way home when the call came. The Mercedes was heading north towards the checkpoint at Euston when her mobile phone warbled somewhere in the bowels of her Louis Vuitton. When she saw the name on the display, she quickly swiped open the call.

'Hugh, to what do I owe this—'

She swallowed the indignity of being interrupted for the second time that day and listened. When the call ended, she ordered her driver to turn around. Twenty-six minutes later, the Mercedes glided to a stop outside the former War Office building on Whitehall Place. The damage inflicted to its Edwardian Baroque architecture during the liberation had been repaired and the building restored to its former splendour. Edith was met in the lobby by an assistant and escorted to the well-appointed office suite on the fifth floor.

Hugh Davies, governor of the British Territories, was the man who'd summoned her. As she followed the assistant into his spacious office, she saw Davies standing at the glass wall looking out over Whitehall. His hands were clasped behind his back, and he rocked gently on the heels of his highly-polished brogues as Edith's presence was announced. The assistant closed the double doors on her way out, and Edith saw Davies' mouth move in the glass' reflection.

'Crucifixion, Edith? Don't you think that was a bit of an overreaction?' His head tilted to the sky as a swarm of military helicopters clattered overhead, barely audible through the thick glass.

'I believe it was justified,' she told him.

'Perhaps, but there's a bigger picture to consider.'

'The law has no grey areas.'

Davies turned away from the window. 'The whole bloody world's a grey area.'

He waved Edith into a chair and sat down behind his huge, polished walnut desk. Fixed to the wall behind him was The Great Seal of the Caliphate, framed by two flags, the Union Jack and the black flag of the Shahada. The Union flag was a concession, a show of good faith by the Islamic Congress of the Western Territories. Davies folded his arms on the walnut monstrosity's smooth surface.

'You had the families arrested. Forty people, now languishing in Pentonville prison. Some of them children.'

Edith tapped her chin with a bony finger. 'Yes, I'd forgotten all about them. There was quite the hullabaloo in court. Threats were made, Hugh, not just to myself, but to our authority. I can have the recordings sent to you if you wish.'

Davies shook his head. 'That won't be necessary.' He took a breath and exhaled slowly. 'But crucifixion, Edith? That isn't going to play well with the public. To be blunt, it's pretty bloody barbaric.'

'It's common across the continent.'

'We do things differently here.'

Edith gave him a frosty stare. 'They intended to shoot their victim on her doorstep. In front of her partner.'

'Be that as it may, people will be horrified. It could drive many of them into the arms of the resistance. That's the last thing we need right now, especially with the—' Davies stopped himself.

Edith raised an eyebrow. 'With what?'

Davies picked up a pencil and rolled it between his fingers. A nervous gesture, Edith suspected. 'There's news. From abroad.'

'You mean the nuclear strike in China?'

Davies frowned. 'Where did you hear that?'

'It doesn't matter. Are we in danger?'

'I don't know. Congress is playing its cards very close. They informed me as a courtesy.'

'So, there's nothing to worry about. China's halfway across the world.'

Davies winced, the lines around his eyes deepening, as if he were in pain. 'There's more. Ireland has fallen to the Alliance.'

Edith felt her heart skip a beat. 'So, it's true?'

'You've heard?'

'Only rumours.'

'Well, they're rumours no longer. A task force landed on the west coast a month ago. Congress tried to explain away the flashes and thunder across the Irish Sea as *military exercises*, but that cover story quickly fell apart when caliphate soldiers began washing up on Welsh beaches.'

Edith's shoulders slumped. Harry Beecham and his American puppet-masters had vowed never to put the people of Europe in harm's way. They'd suffered enough, he'd declared publicly. A political solution would be found, he'd promised, because the truth was the Alliance had no stomach for a bloody campaign on their own soil. They'd been fooled. *She'd* been fooled.

'Didn't anyone see this coming?'

'You can't hide a task force, Edith. Yes, Baghdad knew, and they ordered a huge arms shipment from Beijing to counter the threat, but then came the nuke and the deal collapsed. It made the difference. That, and the military superiority of the invaders. I heard the caliphate's withdrawal was a complete shambles.'

Edith plucked nervously at the loose flesh beneath her chin. 'Does this mean Britain is next?'

'I've no idea.'

'But you're a former military man. You must have an opinion.'

Davies offered a wry smile. 'I was a squadron commander in the Logistics Corps, so I'm no expert I'm afraid. What I *can* tell you is that getting squeezed on two fronts never ends well. I suspect that's why they've sent General Mousa here.'

Edith felt icy fingers brush the back of her neck. '*The* General Mousa?'

'The very same. He's taken charge. And he's reinforcing.' Davies glanced towards the double doors. 'Baghdad is shipping half a million troops to these shores.'

Edith's jaw slackened. 'Half a million?'

'They're gearing up for war, Edith.'

She didn't answer straight away. Instead she got to her feet and crossed to the glass wall. Darkness had fallen outside, and she looked south, towards the distant lights on Lambeth Bridge. The view still unsettled her. Everything was gone now; Downing Street, Horse Guards Parade, the Ministry of Defence, Westminster Abbey, the Houses of Parliament, all demolished, a thousand years of history bulldozed by the caliphate's engineers and architects, transforming the cultural heart of London into a desolate, muddy landscape criss-crossed by dumper trucks and lit by clusters of harsh white lights.

Not everything is gone, she reminded herself. Number Ten was still standing, a forlorn and fragile brick and masonry shell supported by scaffold poles and wrapped in protective sheeting. It was being preserved as a monument, the spot where the Great Liberation of Britain had begun, and Edith was reminded of Albert Speer's ambitious vision for a post-war Berlin. It was all for the greater good, Edith often scolded others.

'So, the Caliph, *peace be upon him,* is preparing for war and has sent his beloved general to take charge. These are encouraging signs, Hugh. It means Baghdad is invested in us. That they're prepared to defend caliphate territory.'

Davies joined her at the window, his hands thrust into his trouser pockets, watching those same dumper trucks rumbling across the muddy moonscape.

'Or they intend to reinforce temporarily, lay waste to the entire country, then pull back across the channel.'

Edith looked up at him. 'Don't talk such nonsense.'

Davies' eyes narrowed. 'They destroyed hundreds of Irish towns and villages as they retreated. Dublin has been levelled, there's almost nothing left.'

Edith swallowed. 'Have we chosen the wrong side, Hugh?'

The governor took a deep breath and stared out through the glass wall. 'On the night of the invasion, Molly wasn't feeling well so I'd left Westminster early to pick the girls up from school. When things went to hell, we took shelter in the cellar. Molly and the girls held me so tight I could barely breathe. I told them I should do something, try to help maybe, but they wouldn't hear of it, wouldn't let me go. So, I stayed, and waited, because like you I'd already seen the writing on the wall. So, I made a decision, not just for me but for the girls too. Embrace the new reality.'

In the reflection, Edith saw him shake his head.

'I found out later that everyone in the office had either been killed or was missing, which made my decision to hide rather more bearable. And because of that, here I stand today, a former ministerial bag-carrier in Rural Affairs, now governor of the British Territories.' He fell silent for a moment, rocking on his polished heels. 'So, in answer to your question, all my eggs are in the caliphate's basket. I placed them there. My decision. Now I have to see it through.'

Edith turned to look at him. She'd never heard of Hugh Davies before the Liberation, but as one of the few surviving ministers of Beecham's government, he'd made the best of a bad situation. He'd cooperated fully and denounced his own. Like her, Davies was a survivor.

'My thoughts exactly,' she echoed. 'We could've sat back, said nothing, abandoned our previous achievements and queued with the common folk for bread and milk. Our lives would've been lived in obscurity, but you and I were born for better things, Hugh. In your case to lead, in mine, to apply the law as our new masters see fit. For you and I, for our colleagues in the National Assembly, it's vital that we keep a firm grip on things.' She paused for a moment, then said, 'It's why I ordered the crucifixions. To crush any suggestion of rebellion. We cannot afford to lose control, not now.'

Davies nodded, watching the crowds below hurrying home. 'To use a gambling analogy, you're doubling down, right Edith?'

The chief justice's thin lips cracked a rare smile.

'Yes. That's exactly what we must do.'

[5]
FIGHTING IRISH

A FINE DRIZZLE SWEPT IN FROM THE SEA OVER BALLY Cross, falling through shattered rooftops and across debris-strewn streets. From the bluffs beyond the settlement, visibility was down to two kilometres, but there was little chance of an enemy counter-attack. With each passing day, the coastline was being reinforced with mobile missile batteries, radar targeting systems, and surveillance drones. In the last 48 hours, the tactical situation had transformed, which was all good news for Eddie and the lads.

Ireland was back in the hands of the Atlantic Alliance, and every day transport aircraft were touching down at the airports of Cork, Knock, Donegal, and Shannon, all loaded with troops and supplies. Ships were on their way too, steaming out from the eastern seaboard, laden with armour and aircraft, fuel, and munitions. *Operation Rampart* the brass had named it, the mission to build up the country's defences. Maybe in a few years they could start rebuilding again.

Belfast and Dublin had both been razed to the ground.

The Irish hadn't taken occupation lightly – *never fucking had,* Mac observed – and long-buried weapons caches were unearthed and put to use. It had started with ambushes and roadside bombs, until eventually entire areas of Belfast and Derry had risen against the caliphate, resulting in some of the fiercest fighting of the campaign. Tens of thousands of lives had been lost. It had been an ugly and brutal liberation, and Eddie was glad it was over.

He refocused his mind back to the patrol, leading Three Section south along the high street. They hadn't been back since the fighting ended, and the cold, damp light of day threw a new, jarring perspective on the damage inflicted. Not a single shop had avoided serious damage, and many had been burned out. Despite that, there were lots of civilians around, townsfolk wrapped up against weather, picking over the wreckage of their lives and livelihoods, trying to salvage what they could.

As he weaved a path through the destruction, he saw entire families, mums, dads, kids, all mucking in, their hands and clothes wet and filthy, yet despite the hardship, there were a lot of smiles and some laughter. Living near Boston, Eddie knew the Irish were a tough lot, and he saw that now in their faces, in the winks from the old codgers, the motherly smiles from the ladies. Eddie tipped his helmet in response, raindrops tumbling from its rim.

He turned, walking backwards, watching the rest of the patrol, their spacing, positions. He wasn't expecting trouble but neither could he relax. None of them could. He watched Digger, Steve, and Mac weaving around piles of burnt timbers, their foul-weather gear slick with rain, gun barrels held low. They'd been patrolling for almost two hours now after the MTVR had dropped the section off a klick short of the village. They'd looped north on foot, hugging the hedgerows, scanning the route ahead with Black Hornet drones, checking abandoned farmhouses and outbuildings. They saw a lot of slaughtered animals, and that upset all of them. War was one thing, but killing defenceless cows and sheep for fun was something else.

They steered clear of the missile batteries on the bluffs north of town. They were a juicy target for the enemy, and they used their own perimeter security, US Marines with itchy trigger fingers. Eddie didn't blame them.

'Hey!'

The shout was loud and urgent. Eddie ducked into the nearest doorway and crouched, bringing his M27 up. Some civvies, men mostly, were hurrying away down the road. Eddie squinted through his optics. A commotion, towards the harbour. A crowd was gathering, urgent voices carried on the chilly breeze. Not urgent, Eddie realised. Angry. He looked back down the street where Mac and Steve were sheltering in a shop doorway. Digger was out of sight, no doubt watching through his scope. Eddie heard Mac's voice in his ear.

'Talk to me, Eddie.'

'Trouble down the hill. Looks local.'

'Women and kids have held fast,' Mac observed. *'We're heading down there. Rest of the section can watch over the civvies while we take a look.'*

Mac jogged past him, and Eddie followed. Steve and Digger were strung out behind him, weaving through the debris. Up ahead, a sizeable group of men were pushing to get inside a pub. Whatever good humour he'd witnessed earlier had disappeared.

Mac ordered the crowd to make a hole. Inside, the pub was a scene of destruction. Everything was smashed, the optics, mirrors, pictures on the wall, all of it now churned into a filthy, razor-sharp mash beneath their boots. And the smell was awful. Stale booze, burned timber, and something else, something foul.

A group of civvies stood around a trapdoor, rough blokes with clubs, knives, and hammers in their hands. Must be the cellar, Eddie assumed. Mac zeroed in on the meanest-looking one, a burly, dark-haired farmer-type with bushy sideburns and big gnarly hands. The look on his face was one of pure hatred, and Eddie wondered if it was his cattle that had been machine-gunned in the fields outside of town.

'What've you got?' Mac asked him, nodding at the hatch.

The man didn't seem the least bit intimidated by soldiers. 'Got a couple of heathens hiding out down there.'

'I heard whispers,' said the man next to him, a kitchen knife held in his hand. 'They weren't speaking English, that's for sure.'

Mac held a finger to his lips and backed everyone outside. The big man held his ground until Mac quietly reminded him that whoever was down there probably had guns and grenades. That didn't seem to bother him either but he left with the others. Steve moved them all back across the street and stayed outside with Digger, covering the trapdoor through the broken windows.

Mac leaned close to Eddie. 'I'm going to crack it open an inch. Any sudden movement, empty your mag.'

'Rog.'

Mac stood behind the hinges and rapped his gloved knuckles on the wooden door. 'You down there! Listen carefully. I'm opening the hatch! Don't do anything stupid!'

Mac twisted the rusted metal ring and lifted it a couple

of inches. A muffled voice in broken English stammered, 'Don't shoot, please! I have wounded men here.'

Mac grabbed the lip of the trapdoor and threw it backwards. It landed against the tavern floor with a loud thud. Eddie's trigger finger tensed. Hands shot out of the hatch, empty. Voices pleaded, but Eddie wasn't fooled. The Hajis were full of tricks, most of them deadly. He kept his gun trained on the greasy black head of hair he could see. He glanced to his left, saw Digger and Steve aiming their own weapons.

Then the smell hit him, a rank odour of human shit and rotten flesh. The man who clambered out of the cellar was an officer, quickly followed by two others, Africans, their ebony skin glistening with sweat, their bulbous eyes darting with fear, both of them patched up with bloody field dressings. Digger and Steve hurried inside and slammed the prisoners against the wall. They were cuffed with plastic ties and searched thoroughly.

'They're clean,' Steve announced.

Mac swept the cellar with a torch. Eddie peered over the lip, saw a body lying face-down on the concrete floor. He also saw four rifles propped against the damp brickwork, magazines unloaded.

'He's dead,' the Arab officer explained, glancing over his shoulder. Mac lifted his rifle and fired two suppressed rounds into the corpse. The officer swallowed hard.

'Call it in,' Mac ordered. 'Three prisoners, two wounded.'

The Africans had their heads down, eyes glued to the floor. One had a leg wound, the other an injury to the head. Digger stepped close to the officer and sniffed the surrounding air.

'You fucking stink,' he told the man. Then he turned

his attention to the Africans. 'You two scumbags got anything to do with the bodies we found in the ditch outside town?'

'Digger...'

He jabbed his rifle into the ribs of the closest one. Eddie saw him flinch. 'You, fuck-face. What d'you know? Who did it? You? You kill all those animals too?'

'Stand down, Barnes,' Mac warned. 'Get yourself outside and wait for the transport.'

Digger didn't move, his eyes boring into the prisoner, gun barrel still jammed against the man's guts. 'I say we let the locals deal with 'em.'

'I won't tell you again,' Mac warned. 'Outside. Right now.'

Digger turned on his heel without another word. Mac watched him go then spread the prisoners' confiscated possessions out on the bar. 'There's fuck-all here. ID cards, a couple of personals, nothing of any intel value. HQ will squeeze 'em.'

'Taxi's here,' Digger yelled from outside.

Eddie heard it then, the familiar whine of a Land Rover. It squealed to a halt directly outside, triggering an excited murmur from the crowd of civilians. When the Land Rover's occupants stepped inside the pub, Eddie realised why. Soldiers from the Irish army, probably troops from the initial invasion force. The giveaway was their US military uniforms and weapons, but that's where it ended. They wore Tricolour flag patches and no helmets, and their kit bristled with spare mags, knives, and grenades. They were older guys too, thirties Eddie guessed, but he couldn't see any rank. One of them wore a ghillie suit, the stock of his sniper rifle carved with more scratches than Eddie could count. They were bearded and bleary-eyed with exhaustion, and their uniforms were caked in blood and mud. *Still in combat mode.*

The leader was a big guy, six-two maybe, with red hair that was cropped to the skull and receding fast. He had a boxer's nose and sunken cheeks that sprouted a few days of rusty growth. And his eyes missed nothing. He glanced at the hatch, then the prisoners. Finally he looked at Mac, offered his hand.

'The name's Dee, First Irish.'

'McAllister, Second Mass.'

The First comprised mostly Irish refugees from New York and Massachusetts, and their reputation for ferocity had reached everyone's ears. No one had a beef with that. This was their country. Dee turned to his men.

'Take them out back.'

The prisoners were frogmarched through the wreckage of the pub. An excited cry went up from the crowd outside and the next minute they were pushing and shoving through the bar, following the soldiers and their prisoners.

Mac watched them piling out back. 'I guess you're not the prisoner escort we're waiting for.'

The big Irishman shook his head. 'Sorry to disappoint you, lad.' He looked at each of them and said, 'There's not going to be a problem here, is there?'

Mac shrugged. 'As far as I'm concerned the prisoners did a runner.'

'God bless.' Dee winked, then sauntered out towards the back of the pub.

Mac watched him go, then said, 'Time to leave.'

They filed outside into the rain. It was falling heavily now, and all Eddie wanted to do was get back to the firebase, get some hot food, and a kip.

'Where's Digger?' Steve asked.

Eddie spun around. The kid was behind him as they left the pub. Now he was nowhere to be seen.

'Fuck,' Mac swore. 'Eddie, get out back and grab that wee fucker. We can't be involved.'

He ducked back into the pub and marched through the bar, drawn by the noise of the crowd. There was a cobbled courtyard out back, the walls lined with metal kegs and crates of empties. The mob had formed an unruly semicircle, cursing and spitting, baying for blood. The prisoners stood against the wall, facing the crowd. They'd been stripped naked, their hands cupped around their genitals, shivering in the rain. Dee stood in front of them, a pistol in his hand. Some people were filming the whole thing on their phones, but Dee didn't seem to care. The gunshot made Eddie jump, and he saw the Arab officer fold to the ground, blood pumping from his head.

'Kill them fuckers! Kill 'em!'

The English voice was unmistakable. Eddie saw Digger through the mob, craning his neck to see over their heads. Eddie pushed through them, grabbed Digger by his webbing and dragged him backwards. Free of the mob, Digger turned on him.

'Take your fucking hands off me,' Digger snarled.

'We can't be here for this, you fucking idiot! Mac's waiting. Go!'

Digger pushed past Eddie and headed back through the pub. As Eddie followed, he heard two more shots, two more cheers. He was glad to be back out on the street.

'Let's move,' Mac ordered. 'Eddie, take point, lead us the fuck away from here.'

Eddie trotted across the street and headed towards the harbour road at a brisk pace. They'd continue their patrol as planned, a route that would take them south, away from the village and into the surrounding countryside.

Away from the madness.

Another hour and they'd be back at base. Eddie couldn't wait.

So far, it'd been a lousy day.

[6]
RESISTANCE IS NOT FUTILE

ALBERT 'BERTIE' PAYNE TURNED THE WHEEL OF HIS Toyota hybrid and pulled into the vehicle checkpoint on Pancras Way. Access into the city was still tightly controlled but not as it once was. Gone were the rolls of concertina wire, the soldiers and armoured vehicles, gone were the signs that screamed *Stop! Use of deadly force authorised!* Many people had lost their lives to the trigger-happy soldiers who'd manned them, but that was in the old days, the uncertain days. Now the checkpoint was more like a customs check, with hydraulic vehicle traps and well-marked lanes, but it didn't make them any less dangerous than the earlier ones. Like the one outside the Royal Free Hospital, where he'd been dragged from his taxi and savagely beaten. Where he'd almost died.

Soldiers still manned the checkpoints, but these days they were run by British coppers, men and women who'd taken their 30 pieces of silver. Bertie had a name for them too – *dirty, treacherous, horrible cunts*.

As the Toyota idled, Bertie's eyes drifted over to the glass and steel entrance of Kings Cross tube station, and he smiled. The station always reminded him of his footballing days as a supporter of his beloved Tottenham Hotspur. Back then he'd often travel out of Kings Cross with the firm, visiting grounds all over the country, packing the away ends, making their voices heard, letting the locals know that the Yids were in town and up for it. Naturally it didn't always go their way, either on or off the pitch, but that's what made football the drug of choice for men like Bertie, the fleeting highs and the crashing lows that often lasted for entire seasons. Mid-table mediocrity was all the average football supporter could expect, and Bertie knew that adopting such a mindset was a valuable life lesson; enjoy the good times while you can, because things always turn to shit, eventually.

And lo, it had come to pass, Bertie mused, as a bearded copper waved him forward. He stopped at the security barrier and powered down the window, handing over his City Pass to the butch-looking plod squeezed into the security booth. She snatched and swiped, watching her terminal, and then she brightened. A familiar reaction once the traitors discovered Albert Payne was in town on business for Chief Justice Spencer. She handed his pass back.

'Thank you, sir. Have a good day.'

Bertie smiled and powered up the window. The security barrier lowered, and he sped away with an electronic whine, glancing in his mirror, cursing the reflection. 'Rot in hell, you traitorous fucking dyke.' That made him feel a little better.

He turned right onto Euston Road and remembered a time when he'd driven his black cab, when he'd sit for hours in slow-moving traffic, stopping at lights every hundred metres, waiting for pedestrians, for cyclists, then cross-traffic. The city was a bloody nightmare. It was different now.

Traffic lights were a thing of the past. Instead, cops with coloured wands marshalled the big junctions, making sure the traffic kept moving and VIPs travelled unhindered. That was one of the perks of working for The Witch, Bertie knew. Wherever he went, he was left alone.

He drove south to Chancery Lane and collected two boxes from Ede & Ravenscroft, legal attire for The Witch, then he drove further into town. He parked the car on Goodge Street and walked the rest of the way, enjoying the crisp air and the unseasonal blue skies. The view, not so much. Much of central London, *the West End* as Bertie has always referred to it, had either been destroyed during the initial invasion or bulldozed by the caliphate.

Soho was a case in point. The entire area had been demolished during the religious purges, the demolition teams and wrecking balls knocking over several blocks of buildings between Oxford Street and Shaftesbury Avenue. Nothing remained of London's gay Mecca except a couple of square miles of a fenced-off building site. Bertie couldn't care less about the cultural eradication of London's gay scene. No, what bothered him were the changes going on in his city. The past was being erased, the culture, history, all of it. It was like that old film *The War of the Worlds,* but instead of the creeping red stuff, they were knocking down beautiful architecture and replacing it with mosques, government buildings, and loads of modern glass and steel shit. London wasn't being rebuilt. It was being *transformed.*

Leicester Square and Chinatown were gone too, courtesy of the airliner that was shot down on that fateful summer evening nearly three years ago. Bertie had seen it too, the giant Airbus trailing smoke as it thundered over Mile End Road, wings dipping and swaying. The size and noise of the stricken aircraft had frightened him, and he'd kicked the punter out of his cab and drove straight home to his dingy flat in Kentish Town. It had been a wise move. London had gone to shit after that. The Witch had saved him, though. A couple of weeks into the invasion, they'd come for him, the feral hood rats, and as they'd attacked his barricaded door, Bertie had dropped out of his first-floor bedroom window and fled into the night. He'd known it was coming, because he'd seen them do it to others around the blocks, so he'd prepared himself. With his bags in the boot of his black taxi, he'd driven up to Hampstead, to one of his regulars, the lord chief justice herself, and begged her for refuge in return for his services. She had the room, that big old house where she lived alone, and to Bertie's surprise and relief, she'd welcomed him inside. The trade-off was his servitude; gopher, waiter, butler, the works, 24/7. Bertie didn't mind. He lived a decent life compared to most, but sleeping under the same roof as The Witch was often difficult, knowing what she'd become.

He turned into Great Russell Street and saw the cafe further down the pavement. He stepped out of the cold and into a warm, bustling eatery, the tables filled with construction workers and office types eating lunch, chatting, buried in their phones. Behind the counter, white-aproned staff serviced a queue of hungry punters while chefs worked the grill in clouds of sizzle and steam.

He glanced at a group of construction workers sitting nearby, chewing their food like cattle, their faces drawn and sullen, their clothes crusted with mud. Bertie didn't envy them one bit. It wasn't a good earner like the old days. Now it was low-paid, dangerous, and crazy-long hours. The fact was, most of them didn't have a choice. They could work like a slave or starve to death. Simples.

At the counter, Bertie ordered a cup of coffee and a

pastry. He made a big deal of searching for a spare seat, working his way over to a window booth occupied by three construction workers. He gestured to the empty space.

'Mind if I sit here? Busy today.'

'We're leaving,' grumbled a younger guy with a thick Eastern European accent. Him and his pal grabbed their bright yellow coats and left. Bertie thanked them and sat down. The man opposite wore a chequered shirt, sleeves rolled up to the elbows, his thick forearms folded on the table as he read a newspaper. His grey hair was cut short and parted to one side, and the nose on his flat face had been broken more than once, the bridge twisted like a knuckle. He peered over his glasses as Bertie took a careful sip of his coffee.

'Got a light?'

Bertie dug into his coat pocket. He slid a disposable lighter across the table and the man fired up a self-rolled cigarette. While there was almost nothing positive about what had happened over the last few years, Bertie had to admit that being able to smoke in a café or coffee shop felt good.

'Want one?' The man offered a pre-rolled cigarette from an old tin.

Bertie plucked one out. 'Very kind. Cheers.' He lit it, blowing a thin column of smoke towards the yellowed ceiling.

George Jacobs muttered under his breath. 'So, how are you, Bertie?'

'Fine, George. You?'

'Bearing up.'

'How's work?'

'Tough.' George scowled. 'I had to let a bunch of blokes go this morning. Labourers, most of them. Couldn't hack the work. Most of 'em had never seen a site before let alone worked on one. They were office bods mostly, IT workers, teachers, that sort, all of 'em middle-aged. Working the shovels all day is no picnic, let me tell you. The job slipped, so I had to let 'em go. Broke my heart.'

'What about you, George?'

The big man's cigarette glowed. 'I'm safe for now. Good gang-masters are worth their weight, and I've earned my stripes. They'll leave me alone.'

'That's a relief,' Bertie said, flicking his ash into a metal tin.

Across the table, George took a pen out of his shirt pocket, the felt tip hovering over the crossword puzzle on the paper in front of him. 'Go ahead, Bertie. I'm listening.'

'The Witch had a dinner party the other night,' Bertie began, taking another drag of his cigarette. 'All the usual traitors were there, no one special. Later, after most of 'em had left, she summoned me. When I slipped into the room, they were having a heated discussion.'

'Who's *they*?'

'Victor Hardy, judge advocate, sits in the Criminal Court with The Witch, and Tim Gates, an art historian or something. Both are regulars at the house...'

Bertie glanced over his shoulder. The café was still buzzing, the staff still jabbering away, the barista machine belching steam like the Flying Scotsman. No one could hear them.

'Gates said that Wazir dropped a nuke on China. It's all kicking off out east. They're pulling troops in from all over the caliphate.'

'Jesus,' George whispered, cigarette smoke leaking through his yellowed teeth. 'And you heard this first-hand?'

'They didn't even know I was there. The Witch seemed

a bit riled when she saw me but I just played dumb.'

George chuckled. 'Still faking that stammer, eh? Well, it's interesting, but China's a long way away. Doesn't really affect us. I'm more concerned with Ireland and what's happening over there.'

'That's not all,' Bertie pressed. He stubbed out his cigarette, flicking ash from his fingers. 'Gates is queer, bent as a boomerang. He got that stuff about the nuke from his boyfriend, a military intelligence officer, Faisal Al-Kaabi. Works at the big military base in Northwood.'

George's eyes widened. 'Holy shit.'

'That's not all. Guess who else is in Northwood? General Mousa.'

'*The* General Mousa?'

'The very same. Fresh in from Baghdad, according to The Witch. I heard her on the phone talking about it. *Rising tensions* is the phrase she used. She also used the word *liability*. With all the increased security and whatnot, she's terrified Gates will get caught and tell all.'

'So?'

'So, they want me to get rid of him.'

It took a moment for George to react. 'Seriously?'

Bertie bobbed his head. 'She sat me down last night, her and Judge Hardy. They called Gates *emotionally reckless*. If he's outed, we'll all hang. Guilt by association, she reckons.'

'The old bitch is right. I'd grass her up myself if you weren't involved. What did you tell her?'

'I told her I'd do it. That I *w-w*-would do anything for her.'

George grinned. 'Very convincing, Bertie.'

'I do my best.' Bertie winked. 'Besides, it's not like I have a choice, right? My neck's on the line too.'

'What about this Al-Kaabi? Gay or not, he's still military

61

intelligence. If he finds out Gates was killed, he could cause serious problems.'

'They want it to look like suicide. They're going to fake a letter, implicate lover-boy too. Out him to the authorities.'

George raised an eyebrow. 'They're playing for keeps. They'll hang Al-Kaabi for that, no question.'

'Two birds with one stone, they said.'

'Evil fuckers.' George leaned a little closer, his hard eyes flicking over Bertie's shoulder. 'You were careful, coming here, right Bertie?'

'I'm on official business. I've got the old slag's shopping in the boot of the car.'

'No chance she's setting you up for something? Like this meeting, for example?'

Bertie shook his head. 'She's scared, George. She wants Gates gone.'

George's cigarette had gone out. He re-lit it with the disposable, puffing tiny glowing embers across the table. Bertie recognised that familiar frown; George was thinking, weighing up the options, figuring the angles. He was good at that kind of thing. That's why he was an organiser in the resistance.

A stiff wind barrelled around the café as the door banged open. Four big soldiers barged through the door, heavy-looking beards with body armour and submachine guns. They wore black berets cocked to the side, the crossed gold swords cap badge catching the strip lights. Shuffling in their wake, four traitors in scruffy uniforms, batons and handcuffs dangling from their belts. They stared around the room, emboldened by their gun-toting masters. Bertie's heart thumped in his chest. *Have we been fingered?* He wasn't armed, and neither was George, so fighting their way out wasn't an option. Bertie sipped his coffee, eyes fixed on the café window. George buried his nose in his crossword. Bertie could hear the soldiers jabbering away in Arabic with the guys behind the counter. He heard the rasp of Velcro and the crackle of radio traffic.

They've stopped for a coffee, that's all. Probably get it for free here. Relax...

'We're sweet,' George muttered as he scratched letters on the paper. 'They're leaving.'

The sounds of the street filled the cafe, and Bertie felt that wintry wind swirling around his feet again. The door closed, and then the guns were strolling past the window, faces blurred by condensation, passing out of sight.

'Time to go,' George said, standing. 'Let me have a think about this, see if there's an angle here. I'll be in touch.'

George squeezed out of the booth and yanked on a heavy winter coat. He pulled a beanie from his pocket and pulled it down over his ears. A moment later he was gone.

Bertie waited for another 15 minutes before leaving. He made his way back to the car, bent against the strengthening wind, and was grateful to get behind the wheel of the Toyota. As he drove through the checkpoint and headed north towards Camden, Bertie realised that things were about to change. Edith Spencer had always been a target for the resistance, and Bertie believed that one day he'd be called upon to murder her, or at least be an accessory. He had no problem with that. He was all too aware of the pain and terror she'd inflicted on the British people.

But now there were others involved, Gates and his lover, Judge Hardy, the infamous General Mousa. Things were about to get interesting, and probably dangerous.

Bertie smiled as he eased the Toyota along Camden High Street.

Payback was coming, and it would be a proper bitch.

[7]
THE GUNNER SLEEPS

THEY HELD THE SERVICE JUST BEFORE LAST LIGHT IN A field outside the small rural town of Carrickmoor.

A large pit had been excavated by military engineers, and the surviving ranks of the Second Mass, the Third Maine, and the First Irish had gathered in close order around three sides of the grave. There were other units there too, US Marines; Rangers; assorted Canadian, Aussie, and Kiwi infantry, all packed tightly together. Above the graveside, a colourful assortment of national and regimental flags rippled in the chilly breeze, yet they were all fighting for the same cause, for liberty and freedom. This conflict wasn't like those of the recent past, predetermined by powerful groups with vested interests and dangerous ambitions, conflicts that fed the voracious appetite of the military-industrial complex and often triggered by false-flag operations and suspect evidence. No, the war they were embroiled in now, *this war,* was worth fighting for. And for those being laid to rest, their deaths hadn't been in vain.

Eddie was in the front rank, standing close to the edge of the mass grave. It took over an hour for the burial party to carry the shrouded bodies to their final resting place, their names read out for all to hear. Eddie knew some of those names, good lads from the Second Mass, and he struggled to keep his emotions in check. Glancing along the tightly-packed ranks around him, he could see he wasn't the only one. By the time the burial party had trudged back up the muddy ramp to join the mourners, nearly 300 bodies had been laid to rest.

A stiff westerly scattered the cloud, and the sun made a late, brief appearance, throwing pale bars of light across the field as it slipped below the horizon. As if God himself was paying his own tribute to the men who'd fought and died this last week. When the time came for prayers, led by a military parade and joined by a group of local clergymen, the voices of the First Irish were strong and word-perfect. A hymn was sung with gusto – *Dear Lord and Father of Mankind* – followed by three volleys of rifle fire and finally *The Last Post*, its haunting notes drifting on the wind. Eddie felt the bond between him and the men around him strengthening, and as the bugler's last notes were carried away on the wind, his eyes were drawn to the flags rolling and snapping in the breeze. A lot of blood had been shed for those colours throughout history, and Eddie wondered if there would ever be a time when the fighting would stop…

'NAE FUCKING CHANCE!' MAC SAID, SLAMMING HIS beer down on the wooden trestle table. 'Money, land, natural resources, whatever. Some people would shoot their own mother to get their grubby paws on it. And don't get me started on religion.'

'It comforts people,' Eddie countered.

'Not if you're getting your napper sawn off by some

Haji executioner. Don't talk to me about religion, lad. It's done enough damage.'

Mac necked his beer and reached into the six-pack for another. Eddie did the same, looking around the community hall filled with troops from the Second Mass, their divisional flag hanging from the rafters alongside the Union Jack, their voices boisterous, the tables jammed with bodies and beer, their first since they'd waded ashore all those weeks ago. Six-a-piece, that's all they were allowed. Mac had downed four of his already. Eddie was trying to pace himself, but he was feeling the buzz.

'So, what now?' Steve asked.

Mac shrugged. 'Who knows? As long as the war with China rumbles on, Wazir will focus most of his attention there.'

'Think it'll go nuclear?'

'There'd be no point. Both sides have got enough warheads to irradiate the planet. Besides, that first nuke was one of those battlefield jobs. Decent punch but localised.'

'And Baghdad is still denying they did it,' Steve added.

'Course it was them,' Mac scoffed, 'had their reactor fingerprints all over it. I reckon it was some rogue Pak general with a beef.'

'Did us a favour though, the timing an' all.'

'Aye.' Mac took another swig of his beer and stared across the table at Digger. He'd barely spoken since the funeral service. 'What about you, nipper? What d'you think?'

'About what?'

'About crop rotation in the 15th century, ya daft cunt. Have ya no been listening?'

Digger stopped peeling the label off his bottle. His eyes narrowed. 'Get off my back.'

'No. I won't. I'm gonna ride you like a fucking Grand National winner, ya miserable wee prick.' Mac leaned closer, jabbed his finger across the table. 'You think you're the only person to lose someone? Take a good look around. Everyone here has suffered because of this bullshit.' He pointed to Steve. 'He's not seen his wife and kid since the invasion, doesn't even know if they're still alive—' He glanced at Steve and said, 'No offence, mate.'

Steve shrugged, but Eddie saw the words had landed below the belt.

Mac gulped his beer, smacked his lips. 'I get it, your dad's gone, and it hurts like fuck, but you've got to let all this hate and anger go, son. It's not doing you any good...' Another swig. 'In fact, you're becoming a liability.'

Digger glared across the table. 'You've got some nerve. I've got us out of more jams than the rest of you put together. I've saved all your arses.'

'And how many times have you gone MIA?' Eddie shot back. 'How many times have we risked our necks to go find you? Bally Cross was a perfect example. All because you wanted to watch those guys getting slotted. For what?'

'Mind your business, Novak.'

'You need help, mate. You should speak to the shrinks—'

Digger shot to his feet. Empties toppled and rolled across the table. Eddie stood too. Mac dragged him back down.

'Sit, the pair of ya.'

'Fuck this.' Digger stepped over the bench and stormed away.

Steve called after him, 'Come on, son, don't be stupid!' But Digger was already threading his way through the packed tables.

Eddie shook his head. 'He's gonna get us killed.'

'Aye. One of us, at least.'

'Kid's got a death wish,' Steve chipped in.

'Truth? He scares me,' Eddie told them.

Mac chewed his bottom lip. 'He's got a point, though. Remember that APC that chopped us up outside Kilkenny? He took it out, saved a lot of lives.'

'He shot the prisoners too,' Steve reminded him.

Mac took another long draw on his beer and cuffed his lips dry. 'Boo-fucking-hoo.'

Eddie cracked open another bottle. 'I'm not saying he hasn't got us off the hook, but there's something else going on with Digger.'

'Aye, the nipper's got something loose in his skull,' Mac agreed, 'but now we've had time to catch our breath, let's cut him some slack for a few days. Might do him the world of good.'

'And pigs might fly.' Steve grimaced. 'If you ask—'

'Get on your feet!'

The voice boomed around the hall. The battalion scrambled upright, tables and benches screeching in protest. Bottles toppled and tumbled, and some shattered on the floor. An enormous cheer went up, and Eddie and the boys cheered too. It was good to see so many smiling faces. Eddie saw the RSM standing by the main doors.

'Quiet down!'

The laughter died away as the blackout curtains were swept back and the Battalion CO strode in, accompanied by the 2IC and a gaggle of battalion HQ officers.

'A full house,' Mac muttered. 'Something's coming.'

'Sit down, please,' Lieutenant-Colonel Butler told them, stepping up onto the stage at the back of the hall. Of the 600 men of the Second Massachusetts Battalion, Fourteenth Infantry Brigade Combat Team, Kings Continental Army Division, only 487 men remained. It had been a tough war so far, and they all knew it. Even Butler had lost an eye, during a furious Haji counter-attack in the first week of the campaign. He'd stayed at his post though, issuing orders even as the medics worked on him. That's why Butler wore an eye patch, and why the battalion had nick-named him *Colonel Cyclops*. The man was already a legend, and the hall waited in silent anticipation for his next words.

'How's the beer?' he opened, smiling.

'Fucking awesome,' a voice yelled from the back of the hall. There was laughter, but it was subdued, more of a *ha-ha-just-get-to-the-point* type deal. Eddie took a nervous swig of his beer as Butler continued, his eloquent baritone filling the room.

'Well, you've earned it, all of you. This has been a hard-fought campaign against a highly motivated and determined enemy. It hasn't been easy, for any of us.' Butler paused, his good eye sweeping the expectant faces around the hall. 'Some of our friends and comrades will never leave Ireland, and their families will soon receive the King's letter, thanking them for their sacrifice. Unless Baghdad recon-siders and pulls its troops out of Great Britain, many more letters will be written, because this war won't end here, in this fair country. It will be waged elsewhere, and it will continue, until we are victorious. And believe me, gentle-man, we *will* be victorious.'

There was a rumble of agreement around the hall. Mac muttered something dark under his breath. Butler continued.

'A few short miles across the Irish Sea, word of our victory will spread, and that news will bring joy to the hearts of our fellow countrymen who have suffered for too long under the yoke of tyranny...'

Something was coming, Eddie could feel it, could feel the electricity crackling around the hall.

'Reinforcements are pouring into the country,' Butler continued, 'which means we will be rested and resupplied. That means downtime, gentlemen, an opportunity to let off a little steam, to decompress, to speak to the support teams should you feel the need. And we'll use this opportunity to come together, to mourn our losses, to welcome their replacements into our family, and to celebrate our friendships.'

Butler took a moment to study the faces around the room, the soldiers who were hanging on his every word...

'And then we will put recent events behind us and get back to work. We will prepare ourselves, get our heads where they need to be, and look to the future, to the mission ahead.' Butler took a breath and said, 'Gentlemen, the Second Mass is going to Scotland—'

The hall erupted in a deafening roar of defiance, of desperate joy and fevered anticipation. Mac was already on the table, his arms raised, fists clenched, as others scrambled up to join him. Bottles tumbled to the ground and boots stamped the floor in a thunderous wave of celebration.

'Silence!' The RSM roared from the stage, although he struggled to suppress the grin on his own face. The cheering soldiers fell silent, and trestle tables creaked with the weight of the men standing on them.

'Tonight you will enjoy yourselves,' Butler told them, 'that is an order, but don't forget that we are guests in this country, one that has suffered greatly. Remember that, all of you. Am I understood?'

'Sir!' boomed nearly 300 voices in unison.

'Thank you, gentlemen. Have a pleasant evening.'

Butler stepped down off the stage, and the officers fell in behind him. As soon as they'd left the hall, trollies full of teetering six-packs were wheeled in through the doors.

'Look at that.' Eddie grinned. 'I'm gonna get proper slaughtered.' He felt almost delirious, and not because they'd just been given a much-needed break. No, it was because they would set foot on British soil once more. They were going home.

Up on the table, Mac was hugging and shaking hands with a couple of the other Scottish lads. He caught Eddie's eye and jumped down.

'Glorious news, eh lad?'

'Brilliant.' Eddie beamed.

Then they saw Steve, sat on the bench, tears rolling down his face as he tipped back his beer. Mac sat next to him and gave him a hug.

'We're going home,' Mac told him, 'and that means Sarah and Maddie will know that you're not far away. That you're coming for them.'

Steve couldn't speak, could only nod his head as the tears rolled. Eddie felt the emotion too and sat by his side, snaking his own arm around Steve's shoulders. Then Mac was moving, swaying from side to side, bringing Steve and Eddie with him as he started to sing...

'Here we go, here we go, here we go...'

Others around them joined in, and then it spread like wildfire around the hall, every voice bellowing out the chant, accompanied by the pounding of boots on the floor and fists on the table, threatening to lift the roof off its rafters.

The Second Mass were on their feet now, even Steve, his arms raised, a beer clenched in his fist, singing with the rest of them, their voices filled with an unfamiliar joy and a lungful of sheer defiance. Eddie sang too, with all his heart, and in his imagination, their voices lifted into the night sky and were carried on the wind, across the sea to the shores of Britain, where oppressed and terrorised ears would hear them.

And fill them with hope.

[8]
LEWD BEHAVIOUR

BERTIE WAITED PATIENTLY IN THE MAIN HALLWAY. He was dressed in a black coat, trousers, and shoes, and the keys to the Toyota were in his pocket. He was ready.

The venerable grandfather clock chimed on the half-hour. Outside, night had fallen and the squally weather would keep the streets clear of traffic and pedestrians. Conditions were almost perfect, Bertie observed. A stair creaked, and he saw The Witch stepping down towards him, a bony claw squeaking on the bannister. She stood in front of him like a small bird, frail in the soft light of the hallway. Bertie could reach out and snap her neck with one hand if he wanted to.

'I've just spoken to him,' she said. 'He's having a quiet night in alone. Use the tradesmen's door at the back of the property. Apparently it's always open, and you'll avoid the concierge.'

'What about CCTV?'

'Hasn't worked for some time, he tells me. You're clear on the story?'

'Yes, ma'am. I'm worried about your mental health,

73

which has deteriorated of late. I'm there to ask Mr Gates for advice.'

'Yes, very good. Timmy can't resist a good gossip. You have what you need?'

Bertie pulled a clear plastic freezer bag out of his pocket and held it up. It contained a small brown pill bottle. 'Powdered barbiturates. Enough to kill an elephant, apparently.'

The Witch's nose wrinkled as she handed over an envelope. 'The suicide note. Leave it somewhere obvious.'

Bertie dropped it in the bag, wrapped it all up and pocketed it. He slipped on a dark flat cap. 'I'd best be off then.' He walked back down the hallway towards the basement stairs.

'Bertie?'

'Madam?'

'I don't want him to suffer.'

Bertie nodded. 'I understand.'

'We're doing this for all our sakes. You have a good life here. Remember that.'

'Y-y-yes, Lady Edith.'

The Witch opened her mouth to say something else then decided against it. She crossed the hall without another word and closed the reception room door behind her.

Bertie made his way through the basement. As he exited the house, the wind almost snatched his hat away. He clamped it on his head and strode across the manicured gardens to the high wall that bordered the rear of the property. He unbolted the heavy gate and stepped out onto the pavement on the other side. The road was lined with trees and set deep in shadow. Above his head, skeletal branches creaked and swayed in the wind, smothering the sound of the van door swinging open. Bertie climbed inside the waiting vehicle. George dropped it into gear and pulled away.

'Everything set?'

'We're good to go.'

George kept the speed and the chatter down, skirting west around Hampstead Heath which was now a militarised zone. The woods up there bristled with anti-aircraft batteries, and Bertie had heard the *whoosh* and thunder of launching rockets many times, especially in the early days. It had been quiet for months, however, and that frustrated a lot of people. Like the Alliance had given up or something. Still, at least the resistance was active.

Soon they were rolling through the empty streets of Golders Green. George's van was electric and had ladders secured to the roof. There was so much work going on in and around the capital that builders' vans were two-a-penny these days. George's wouldn't attract any attention.

'There.' Bertie pointed. Up ahead, set back from the road in well-kept gardens, was an art déco mansion block. Lights glowed in most of the windows of the eight-storey building. 'Drive past. There should be an access road that leads around to some garages at the back.'

George saw it, took it, and parked in the shadows. The back door was unlocked as promised, and they stepped into the gloom beyond. They took the stairs, and less than a minute later, Bertie and George were standing in the residents' hallway on the second floor, where the carpet was plush and the air was tinged with something sweet. Wood-panelled doors with brass numbers stretched along the silent hallway. As George stepped out of sight, Bertie tapped gently on the door of flat number 16. A moment later it opened. Timothy Gates was wearing a striped chef's apron over a pale pink shirt. The expectant smile melted.

'Bertie? What are you doing here?'

'Sorry to disturb, Mr Gates. I'm here about Lady Edith. Urgent business, sir.'

'Well, you'd better come in,' he said, holding the door open. Bertie stepped inside and George pushed in behind him. Before Gates could protest, George closed the door and held a finger to his lips.

'Be quiet, Timmy, there's a good boy.' He towered over the petrified art historian. 'Are you alone?' Gates nodded, wide-eyed. 'Good. Let's have a chat, shall we?'

Bertie followed them into a large and exquisitely decorated sitting room. Artworks lined the walls, and there were sculptures and figurines arranged on antique sideboards, tables, and cabinets, most of them male and nude. *If the cops saw all this, they'd have a field day*, Bertie reckoned.

George ordered Gates onto the couch and sat opposite. Bertie remained standing. Gates looked at him, his expression torn between outrage and anxiety.

'Bertie, what the hell's going on? I've got guests arriving any minute. Important guests.'

Bertie glanced into the adjoining dining room. The table was set for two, and candles flickered seductively. The penny dropped. 'It's Faisal, isn't it?'

Gates swallowed. 'Who?'

George wore a broad smile. 'That's a stroke of luck, eh? What time are you expecting him?'

'Right about now,' a voice from the hallway said.

Bertie spun around. The man who pointed a small-calibre pistol at them was in his early 40s, with wavy black hair, light brown skin, and a six o'clock shadow. He was dressed in a dark blue hoodie, jeans, and running shoes, and he spoke in perfect, accented English. He waved the pistol at Bertie. 'On the couch.'

Bertie obeyed and sat next to George. Al-Kaabi stepped into the room as Gates scuttled behind him. 'Timmy, who are these people?'

'The one in the cap is Edie's man, Bertie. I don't know the other one.'

'My name's George. And we come in peace. In fact, we're here to help you.'

Al-Kaabi's pistol waved between them. 'Help with what?'

'Perhaps Bertie should explain.'

Gates and Al-Kaabi waited. Bertie eased the plastic bag out of his coat pocket and dropped it on the coffee table. 'Judge Spencer isn't your biggest fan right now, Mr Gates. The truth is, she sent me here to kill you. Because of your affair.'

Gates' jaw dropped open. 'What?'

'She believes you've put her in danger, so she wants you got rid of. She wanted it to look like a suicide. I agreed to do it, but I had no intention of seeing it through.'

That was a lie, of course. Gates was as bad as the rest of them. He'd turned a blind eye to the persecution, condoned the barbaric judgements of Spencer and her kind, and often mocked the victims. He was weak, shallow, and self-centred. If it was a simple choice between the hangman's noose or killing Gates, the man would already be dead. Except now, things weren't so simple.

'You'd better start talking,' Al-Kaabi ordered, rattling the gun at him.

So Bertie talked. The education of Timothy Gates and Faisal Al-Kaabi took less than 15 minutes, and by the time he'd finished, Gates was a broken and terrified man. Al-Kaabi dropped the suicide note back on the coffee table.

'They're telling the truth, Timmy.'

'How could she?' Gates said. 'She's my friend, for God's sake!' He dropped onto the couch, his head in his hands.

Al-Kaabi still had the gun pointed at Bertie. 'She plays a dangerous game, your mistress.'

'Mr Gates is compromised and you're a threat. That's how she sees it.'

'You know what they do to gays,' George said. 'Why take the risk?'

Al-Kaabi shrugged. 'You can't help who you fall in love with.'

George's nose wrinkled. 'I suppose not.'

Al-Kaabi finally lowered the pistol. He sat next to Gates and gave his hand a squeeze. 'So, I assume you haven't come here out of compassion for your fellow man.'

'Not entirely,' George conceded, 'but I think we can help each other.'

'How?'

'Because you're done, finished. Now that you're on Spencer's shit list, your days are numbered. You *and* Timmy.'

'I could have Spencer arrested, charged with attempted murder.'

George nodded. 'That's an option, but it's one that'll blow up in your face because we both know that your lifestyle choice is a far bigger crime than an attempted honour killing. You and Timmy will both go to the gallows, and given your rank and job title, I'm guessing the Islamic Congress would sweep the whole thing under the carpet.'

Gates looked horrified. 'Are you saying she'd get away with it?'

'He's right,' Al-Kaabi said. He got to his feet and crossed to the drinks cabinet. He poured four brandies into heavy crystal tumblers and passed them around. No one refused.

Gates smiled, teary-eyed, and offered Al-Kaabi a silent, dejected toast. The intelligence officer sat down again, teasing the dark liquid around his glass.

'There's a place called Yabreen, an old mining town in the desert south of Riyadh. It's a prison now, and at its centre lies a huge, deep shaft. It is said that the caliphate's worst transgressors are lowered into that shaft and left to die. A hundred metres deep, no food, no water, no room to breathe. They say it's like looking into the depths of hell.' He lifted his eyes. 'That's where they'll send me. Where they've sent others like me.'

'No!' Gates gasped, clinging to him like a drowning man. 'Don't leave me, Faisal, please!'

George frowned. 'Let's dial down the drama, can we Timmy?'

Gates detangled himself, dabbing his tears with a corner of his apron. 'I'm sorry. This is all so stressful.'

'Your options are limited,' George continued. 'We can help you, get you out of the country.'

'Or we can walk away,' Bertie added. 'I could go back and tell Spencer that Mr Gates had company. Sooner or later, she'd try again. She might even send someone else. Someone without George's connections.'

Al-Kaabi turned to George. 'So, I take it you're in this resistance movement?'

'I've got friends, put it that way.'

'And you'll get us both out?'

'It's conditional.'

'I thought it might be.'

'Quid pro quo.' George smiled. 'You know how these things work.'

'Military intelligence is heavily compartmentalised. I might not be as valuable as you think.'

'That's not my call.'

Al-Kaabi squeezed Gates' hand again. 'Spencer is expecting a body. How will you get around that?'

It was Gates himself who answered. 'Since Faisal and I met, I've discouraged all visitors. It'll be weeks before anyone comes knocking.'

'By which time you'll both be long gone,' Bertie told them. 'The Witch will assume that the whole thing has been quietly dealt with and just move on.'

'The Witch,' Gates echoed with a tired chuckle. 'It suits her.'

'So, what happens now?' Al-Kaabi asked.

George got to his feet. 'First, we need to get Timmy somewhere safe. And you need to go back to work.'

'No!' Gates said, and Al-Kaabi held a finger to his lips.

'He's right, Timmy. It would look odd if I just disappear, especially now. It's not a good time.'

Bertie watched as George and Al-Kaabi ironed out their contact details and then shook hands. Gates showed the soldier out, and Bertie heard tender whispers in the hallway before the door closed.

Gates stepped back into the room, his eyes red and puffy. George pointed back down the hallway.

'Why don't you go and pack your things, Timmy? A small bag, essentials only, okay?'

Gates looked around the room. 'I'm never coming back, am I?'

'At least you'll be alive.'

'Where will we go?'

'Does it matter?'

Gates' eyes took on a faraway look. 'I suppose not, as long as we're together.'

'I'll pop to the kitchen,' Bertie told him, 'make us all a nice cup of tea.'

Gates offered a tired smile. 'You're a darling, Bertie. And turn everything off on the cooker, would you? Safe to say that dinner is well and truly ruined.'

Bertie gave him a wink. 'No problem at all.'

He arrived home almost three hours later, re-entering the property the same way he'd left, locking the gate behind him and re-crossing the manicured gardens. Shutting out the frigid wind, he hung his coat on a hook by the basement door and listened. The kitchen had closed, and the staff had retired to their rooms for the evening. Bertie passed unnoticed and went upstairs.

The Witch was waiting for him in the drawing room. A fire burned in the grate, and Bertie wondered who'd set it in his absence. *Maybe The Witch herself*, he thought. Idle hands and all that. She closed the book she was reading and to Bertie's surprise, gestured for him to sit opposite her. He eased into the wingback chair and waited for her to speak.

'Is it done?'

Bertie nodded sympathetically. 'He didn't feel a thing.'

'You're sure?'

'I watched him slip away, ma'am. Very peaceful.'

'Poor Timmy,' she said, wringing a balled-up tissue in her hand.

Bertie studied her dry eyes and felt a rush of anger. How many people had she sentenced to death without a shred of sympathy? Too bloody many. The Witch removed her glasses and let them dangle from the chain around her neck.

'And the suicide note?'

'I left it on the pillow next to him.' Bertie paused, then said, 'It might be some time before he's discovered, ma'am. It could be weeks, maybe a month.'

'The deed has been done, that's all that matters.' The Witch took a deep breath and exhaled. 'You've done this house a huge service, Bertie, and I'm very grateful. Now we must forget the sordid events of this evening and look to the future.'

Bertie feigned a puzzled frown. 'Forget what, Lady Edith?'

The Witch cackled, a sound so rare it unnerved him.

'Yes, very good, Bertie, very amusing.' The smile faded from her thin lips, like a curtain being drawn. 'Breakfast at six-thirty, please. I have a long day in court tomorrow.'

She slipped her glasses back on, picked up her book and settled in her chair. Bertie got to his feet and left. As he stepped down into the basement and closed the door to his cramped room, he allowed himself a satisfied smile. The evening had proved to be a successful one and lying to The Witch's face while she lapped it all up felt good. One-nil to the home side.

He brushed his teeth, undressed, and climbed into bed, curling up beneath his quilt. Tiredness plucked at his consciousness, and as his eyes closed and his mind drifted, he imagined a day when he would confront Edith Spencer with the truth of his deception, with his membership of the resistance, of Timmy Gates' survival...and of her impending doom.

He imagined the look of horror on her face.

In the darkness of his room, Bertie smiled.

[9]
THE NORTH WEST FRONTIER

Eddie got his first look at the frontier from the shadows of a hilltop forest. He'd seen footage on TV and videos on the Internet, but none of it prepared him for the reality of the brutal scar that carved across the undulating landscape. It was probably the ugliest thing that Eddie had ever seen.

'Jesus, look at that,' he muttered, sweeping the hi-power spotter scope across the unsettling vista. To the south, down in the distant valley, the English town of Haltwhistle had been completely destroyed. All that remained were grey stone teeth of demolished buildings jutting out of the weed-strewn rubble, as if a giant had stomped its way through the village, leaving a flattened, broken landscape in its wake. Some of the town's outlying farms and houses still looked intact, but a twist of the magnification ring revealed collapsed walls, burned timbers, and sunken roofs. Nothing had escaped the deliberate destruction.

'You could hear the bastards from 20 miles away,' their guide told them, a grizzled colour-sergeant in the reformed Black Watch regiment. Dark bars of camouflage cream divided his narrow face, and his uniform and equipment was an ad hoc mix of British and American issue, all of it well-worn and weather-beaten, a second skin that every combat vet tailored to his own spec. Eddie could relate. Like the rest of the guys who'd never fired a shot in anger until he'd set foot in Ireland, he'd adapted his set-up. Tactical vest, body armour, assault pack, weapons, nothing he wore or carried was the same as when he'd waded ashore on that darkened beach.

His right hand went to the handle of the knife he wore on his tactical vest, just to the right of his magazine pouches. It used to be lower down, on his utility belt, until that day in the abandoned house in Ennis. The guy had literally run into him, a big, bearded Haji, older and heavier. They'd both gone down, the guy on top of him, both of them grunting and cursing as they'd wrestled on the floor. Eddie's M27 was trapped against his body so he'd pulled his pistol, but the Haji had grabbed the barrel, twisting it and nearly breaking Eddie's finger. That's when the panic had set in, Eddie remembered. He'd scrabbled desperately for his knife, but he couldn't pull it because the handle was trapped beneath him. Then came the gunshot and the fine mist of blood, and Digger had dragged the dead Haji off him and screamed at him to *get up and keep moving!* It'd been a very close call. Now Eddie wore his knife where he could get to it in a pinch.

'They used the old A69 cross-country route as the line of demarcation,' the colour-sergeant was explaining, 'then they drove two massive engineering crews towards each other from both coasts. They rolled right over every town and village in-between, then dug up the road to form the vast no-man's-land you see before you.'

'Must've been big crews,' Mac ventured.

'A couple of thousand in each one,' the colour-sergeant told him, 'though half of it was slave labour, which meant we couldn't drop any munitions on the bastards. We tried sniping the architects and other HVTs, but they shot a bunch of prisoners in retaliation, so we just had to sit back and watch.'

He folded his arms and shook his head.

'Anything that stood in their way, they just bulldozed straight over the top of it. In the bigger towns, they blew up entire buildings to form giant barricades. What they left behind is sown with trip flares and anti-personnel mines, and they dammed every river along the route with rubble, flooding the surrounding lowlands. Like they did down there. Take a look.'

Eddie twisted the focus ring on the spotter scope. Beyond the flattened town, the early morning sun sparkled off a vast body of water. Partially submerged beneath it, an unending sea of razor wire and rusted metal stakes stretched all the way across the flooded fields to the dark, rising ground beyond. It reminded Eddie of a World War One battlefield. The colour-sergeant pointed to the hills.

'Up there they've got surveillance posts every quarter mile or so, plus tethered blimps, drones, CCTV, and thermal imaging, which gives them a lot of overlapping coverage. They deploy human patrols too, both foot and mounted, and the engineers are always beefing up potential weak points and re-sowing mines.'

Eddie took another slow, visual sweep. What was left of the town was also under assault by Mother Nature; grass, brambles, and blooms of purple heather sprouted through the cracks and fissures of collapsed roofs and broken roads. It reminded him of the post-apocalyptic landscapes of Glasgow and Edinburgh, two ruined and desolate cities they'd skirted on their journey south. Eddie realised he'd yet to see a single living creature down there. Even the birds seemed to avoid the area. Nothing moved in the sky except for a single, distant drone, sweeping the ground to the east. Ours or theirs, Eddie didn't know.

'Fifty miles,' muttered Steve next to him, pointing towards the enemy-held hills.

Eddie turned and looked at him. 'What's 50 miles?'

'Sarah and Maddie. I worked it out on the map. That's how far the house is. Give or take.'

'Don't think about it, mate.'

'That's like asking me not to breathe.'

Eddie didn't respond. Since landing in Scotland, Steve had lost whatever spark he had left. His smile wasn't as ready, his bad jokes now few and far between. He hadn't seen his family for almost three years. Maddie, his *bonnie lass,* would be nearly ten. How Steve had coped with the uncertainty was hard to imagine, but he wasn't the only one. Countless others had been left behind during the evacuation, but how much longer Steve had to wait until he was reunited with them was anyone's guess.

'So, when do we go over?' Digger asked the colour-sergeant.

The man's hard eyes narrowed. 'What's the rush, wee man? Had enough of life, have ye?'

Digger bristled. 'I'm not scared of dying.'

'Open your eyes, son. No one's getting across that frontier any time soon.'

Eddie glanced at Steve and registered his painful wince. Another body blow for the poor guy. The colour-sergeant whistled to the rest of Nine Platoon strung out along the tree-line. 'That's it, orientation's over. Make your way back to your transport.'

Eddie was glad to be going. He'd seen enough.

'The North-West Frontier,' Mac said, as their truck bounced and swayed back down the track on the other side of the hill. 'It's got a familiar ring to it.'

Eddie had to think about that one. 'That's Pakistan, right? Or Afghanistan?'

'Someone stayed awake at school.'

Mac was buzzed to be back home, or *hame* as he called it. He also liked to remind any Englishman in earshot that Scotland was now bigger by 1,200 square miles, courtesy of the caliphate's redrawn border. *The only decent thing them bastards have done since they've been here,* he never tired of telling everyone.

It took nearly an hour to get back to the Second Mass HQ at Otterburn, some 30 miles to the north. The military camp had been extensively damaged during the invasion, and in the months that followed, before they withdrew behind the frontier, the invaders had ransacked it for anything useful, but apart from a few burned-out buildings, most of the infrastructure had survived. The battalion's 600 men and vehicles had been widely dispersed across the installation, and on the rising ground above the camp, camouflaged beneath the trees, an American Patriot battery provided anti-missile cover. Since the Second Mass had moved in, there'd been no incoming, even though they drilled for it most days. There was always the risk of a low-level aircraft attack too, and the Royal Artillery had their backs in that regard, providing air cover from the surrounding hills with their Stormer armoured vehicles and Starstreak missiles. Eddie slept pretty well at night.

Nine Platoon spent the rest of the day in a classroom, refreshing their first-aid skills, and after six it was their turn to eat. They queued up at the temporary cookhouse and took their food – chicken curry with rice and naan – back to their accommodation. They were billeted in a small, red-brick block at the western edge of the camp, close to the vast, empty training area beyond the chain-link fences. They shared a four-man room with no beds, but they had their roll mats and brand-new US-issue cots. There was no natural light because the window had been blown out. Sandbags now filled the shell hole in the wall, with battery-powered storm lamps providing light, and down the hall, they had flushable toilets, hot water, and working showers. It wasn't five-stars, but it was pretty decent.

The curry was decent too, and no one spoke as they chowed down. It was Eddie who eventually opened the conversation. 'That was some sight today, eh?'

'Unbelievable,' Mac agreed. 'Using slave labour too. Bastards.'

Steve looked up from his mess tin. 'One of the Black Watch guys said a lot of 'em were squaddies and cops. They dressed 'em in caliphate uniforms too.'

'If we hadn't got out, my dad would've been one of them,' Digger mumbled, his mouth full.

Eddie glanced at the others. When Digger spoke about his dad, things always got uncomfortable. Mac was always quick to defuse, though. The big Glaswegian smiled and tapped the side of his head.

'A smart guy, your pa. He saw what was coming, got you and your ma to safety before it all went to shit.'

'His luck ran out though, didn't it? Only one missile got through and it had to hit his ship.'

'Aye, rotten luck,' Steve agreed. 'How's your mum taking it?'

Digger sneered. 'How do you think?'

'Take it easy, nipper—'

'Don't tell me to take it easy. You've been sulking like a bitch ever since we got to Scotland.'

'Hey! That's enough,' Mac warned them, spitting grains of rice. Digger continued the assault on his curry. Mac put his spoon down. 'Listen, we had it pretty rough in Ireland, more than others but not as bad as some. We've seen a lot of shit, and if any of us are having trouble dealing with it, there are people we can talk to. There's no shame in getting help—'

'Subtle as a brick in the face.'

Mac stared at the youngster. 'That's right, I'm talking about you.'

'I'm fine,' Digger told him.

'We're worried about you,' Eddie said.

'Worry about yourself.' In the silence that followed, Digger looked at each of them. 'I get it. This is an intervention, right? I'm angry about my dad, so what? You would be too.'

'We need to know we can rely on you,' Mac said. 'You're taking too many stupid chances. You want payback for your dad, fine, but you can't go solo on us, Digger, so I need to know right here and now that you'll think before you act. Be a team player.'

'Or what?'

Eddie felt the tension ratchet up. Mac pointed a finger at him. 'Or I'll—'

'Relax, I'm kidding.' Digger grinned, but it didn't last long. 'Stop worrying, all of you. I'm dealing with it. And I won't let you down, you've got my word on that.'

Mac nodded. 'Okay, son. But know this; if I think you're going off the rails, I'll yank you from this section without a second thought, got it?'

This time Digger didn't smile. 'Understood, boss.'

'Okay then.'

They went back to eating their food. It was Steve who broke the awkward silence.

'So, what d'you think'll happen next?'

Mac shrugged. 'Christ knows. I guess they're trying to work out how best to open up that frontier.'

'Tactical nuke,' Digger mumbled through a mouthful of curry.

'Beecham won't use nukes on UK soil,' Mac told them. 'I think we should wait it out, see what happens with China.'

'Easy for you to say,' grumbled Steve. 'When I found out that my girls didn't get evacuated, I've done nothing but hope and pray they're all right. Sarah's a smart girl, and my parents are no fools either. They'd be okay, make the right choices. I've always believed that, but now I'm here, this close to them...' Steve winced, as if in pain. 'What I'm trying to say is, I've got an awful feeling. That maybe they didn't make it.'

Mac tossed his mess tin to one side and crouched in front of Steve. He gave his shoulder a squeeze. 'They'll be fine, mate. Don't take any notice of my big mouth. I'm sure they'll find a way to get us over that border.'

'We could go around it,' Digger chipped in. 'Get the navy to kick their Haji arses all the way back to France.'

Eddie shook his head. 'You could walk from England to Norway without getting your feet wet, they've got that many mines out there. Not to mention the missile batteries around the coast. Same goes for the English Channel. The navy would get cut to pieces.'

'Air assault, then.'

'Too risky,' Mac told him, sitting back down. 'If we're

honest about it, it's gonna take time to build up a big enough invasion force to crack this nut. Months, maybe even years.'

Steve pushed his mess tin to one side. 'I can't wait that long.'

'You might have to. That's the reality.'

Eddie winced. 'I hate to say it, but we might not invade at all.'

All eyes turned to him. Mac glared. 'I didn't realise you'd been promoted to field fucking marshal, Novak.'

Digger laughed. Eddie didn't blink. 'England and Wales are living under caliphate rule, right? Buses and trains are running, people are going to work, shops and restaurants are open, they've got TV—'

'Six state-run channels,' Mac shot back. 'Same for the Internet, closed network, no Wi-Fi. And definitely no porn. Must be a real hoot.'

Digger laughed again. Steve was looking worried. Eddie pushed on.

'The cities are being cleaned up, and they're rebuilding London, right? We've all seen the news.'

'Get to the point, Novak.'

'It's simple; England and Wales are occupied like Europe was during World War Two. More than that, people have adjusted to life under caliphate rule. Whether we like it or not, peace has broken out down there. Do you really think Beecham will green-light another massive assault on the country? Drop Tomahawks on London? Risk untold collateral damage?'

'Not a bad idea,' Digger said. 'Place is full of traitors, anyway.'

Eddie shook his head. 'No mate, it's full of frightened people, just keeping their heads down and praying it'll all be over one day. And now it's kicked off with the Chinese, I just can't see Beecham risking it.'

Mac growled. 'That's bullshit. We took Ireland, didn't we? No talk of collateral damage there.'

Eddie shrugged 'Maybe there was, but the Irish were prepared to spill blood to get their country back, even if it meant their own. I don't think we're prepared to go down that same road.'

'You're wrong,' Steve muttered. 'The people I know, they see us coming over the frontier, they'll rise up and fight.'

'So will the hundreds of thousands who've come here since the invasion, not to mention the millions who were already here beforehand. You think they'll all pack up and piss off? No chance. They'll fight too, all of them.' Eddie pointed off into the distance. 'That frontier, that's not just a defensive line, that's a message. It says, *we're here to stay, so keep the fuck out.*

Digger got to his feet. 'Why bother sending us here, then? Why give us new NVGs, upgraded rifle optics, exoskeletons, a ton of other stuff? We all saw the armour at Prestwick. Tanks, APCs, mobile SAMs, hundreds of them. And thousands of troops—'

'Landing every day,' Mac confirmed.

'That's right. And now they've shipped us down here, closer to the border. We're on that training area every other day doing live-fire exercises, combat drills, first aid, map reading, right? It's Iceland all over again. They're prepping us for something, no question.'

'It might all be window dressing,' Eddie said. 'You know, political pressure. Force Baghdad to negotiate.'

Digger stared at him for a moment. 'Negotiate what? In case you hadn't noticed, they've conquered Europe. Why would they need to negotiate anything? You're talking out of your arse, mate. You don't know shit.'

Steve got to his feet, picked up his mess tins and walked out of the room. Eddie could feel Mac's eyes boring into him.

'Do us all a favour and keep your opinions to yourself, son.'

'Yeah, you've upset him now,' Digger added.

Eddie shrugged. 'I didn't mean to. I'm just trying to help him deal with it, that's all.'

'Nice job.' Digger got up and left the room.

'I'd better say something,' Eddie said, feeling guilty.

'Just leave 'em to it, let the dust settle. It's been a long day.' Mac stood and stretched. 'Right, I'm away for a shite and a shower. Alpha company is running security tonight, so we can all get a decent kip.'

Steve returned a few minutes later, his mess tins dripping water on the linoleum. Eddie half-smiled.

'Take no notice of me, Steve. I'm just trying to work it all out, that's all. I'm sorry.'

'What you said makes sense though,' Steve told him, stuffing his mess tins in his pack. 'I guess if we build up a big enough force that'll give Beecham some kind of political clout, right? So maybe they'll get around the table, do a deal. Maybe I won't have to go to the girls. Maybe they'll come to me.'

Eddie offered him a tentative smile. 'Stranger things have happened.'

'No chance,' Digger said, walking into the room. 'They've been talking for three years and Baghdad ain't listening. Sooner or later, we're gonna go toe-to-toe. And when we do, they're going down.'

Eddie and Steve shared a look.

Digger sat down and started stripping his M27.

AT THAT MOMENT, ALMOST 5,000 MILES AWAY, AN aircraft was being rolled out of a hangar at the Groom Lake military installation located deep in the Nevada desert. The hangar's interior, a vast cavern carved out of the living mountainside, had been plunged into darkness in preparation for the flight.

As the ground crew towed the aircraft out onto the deserted apron, every light across the installation had been extinguished. The air was still, and countless stars glittered in the clear night sky. Hidden by dark mountains and surrounded by an uninhabited and restricted area of the Nevada desert that covered over 1,300 square miles, the Groom Lake facility enjoyed almost complete physical secrecy, despite it being the most famous military base in the world.

Not one of the small group of men and women gathered in the shadows of the hangar was concerned with such trivial matters. What concerned them was the aircraft that sat on the concrete apron, the matte-black, teardrop-shaped machine emblazoned with the black-and-grey Stars and Stripes on its twin tail fins, a machine they'd all been working on for the past decade, and what their mystified forebears had been puzzling over for several decades before that. The culmination of all that time and effort, all the research and development – and the lives lost – had now disengaged from the tractor a short distance away. The tractor swung around and rolled back into the hangar where it was swallowed by the darkness.

Somewhere in the distance, a coyote's mournful cry echoed across the installation. The aircraft stood motionless, silent, the pilots invisible behind their black windshield that curved seamlessly around the front of the craft. They would be in contact with the tower over a mile away, seeking clearance for this, the aircraft's inaugural combat mission. It was a historic moment, one that the group of scientists, engineers, and military personnel could celebrate only with each other. One of them, a propulsion specialist from Lockheed Martin's Advanced Development Program, held a finger to the radio receiver in his ear as he listened to an incoming transmission. Then he said quietly to those around him, 'Here we go.'

They all felt it then, that familiar, mild vibration, and then the craft lifted silently off the apron and hovered 20 feet off the concrete, the only sound a quiet hiss as its three thick, black legs buckled upwards and folded into the main body. For a moment the aircraft remained there, suspended as if by magic, bouncing ever so slightly, and then, with a mild blast of dust and warm air that rolled over the gathered spectators, the craft accelerated upwards and away. In seconds it was lost to the naked eye, and to the electronic ones that had already conceded to the aircraft's groundbreaking stealth technology.

Its official Air Force designation was the MSS-2, which stood for *Multi-Mission Special Operations Aircraft*. The men and women on the ground who shook hands in the darkness and filed back inside the darkened hangar had another name for it.

They called it *The Game Changer*.

[10]

SNOOP DOG

BERTIE SAT ALONE IN THE BASEMENT KITCHEN, nursing a cup of coffee.

He glanced up at the clock on the wall, then checked his watch again. Both had barely moved since he'd last looked. He turned his chair and his back to the clock. Time was his enemy tonight.

He sipped his coffee and reflected on his role within the resistance movement. He'd always been a low-key player, serving as an information conduit between George and The Witch, gleaning whatever intelligence he could from his employer. A daily schedule here, an extract from her personal journal there, transcribed notes of conversations he'd overheard. And the names of The Witch's frequent dinner guests, of course, traitors all, cowards who'd embraced the brutal regime that continued to persecute their fellow countrymen. Bertie often daydreamed of walking into one of those dinners holding a gun, just to see their faces. He hoped that day would come in the not-too-distant future.

In the meantime, he gave anything useful to George,

and that's where his involvement usually ended. He was proud to do his bit, knowing that many others out there did so much more.

Like Gordon Tyndall for example. It was Bertie who'd copied the commissioner's home address from The Witch's diary and given it to George, so when he'd heard that the dyke had survived the assassination attempt and Tyndall and his boys had been arrested, he'd panicked. George had put him straight, though. *Compartmentalisation,* he called it. That's the way George operated; no phones, no emails, just cut-outs, hand-offs, and dead-letter drops. He was the same back in the Yid Army days, a mobile phone in every pocket, making quiet plans, organising tear-ups. George was a leader. Bertie was nothing more than a foot soldier, and that suited him just fine. He was golden.

Until he'd overheard The Witch discussing Tyndall's execution on the telephone.

Crucifixion.

Bertie's blood had run cold. It was a chillingly cruel and barbaric death, and for the first time since the invasion, Bertie feared his employer. He'd taken too many chances, he realised. He'd listened at doors, rifled her handbag, the drawers in her study, because he assumed he'd never be caught. But things had changed. What if she found out he'd been snooping? What if she made the connection with Tyndall's attempted assassination?

He'd be finished.

He'd become complacent, he realised, and the thought of a slow death hanging from a wooden cross had woken him from that dangerous slumber. Dreams of payback and sweet revenge had vanished like a fart in a gale. The only thing that mattered now was getting through the next 12 hours.

He looked at his watch again. *A watched kettle never boils,* his mum used to say. Bertie forced himself to relax. He sipped his coffee and thought back to that morning. The day had started with such promise.

He'd been driving into the city when he'd seen the first one, the huge, neon-green letters spray-painted on a wall near Belsize Park: *IRELAND LIBERATED!* He'd seen the same in Camden, twice, and the fourth one a couple of hundred metres short of the checkpoint at Pancras Way. That one was being hurriedly scrubbed by a prison gang in yellow overalls, but the sight of those defiant words made Bertie's heart sing, and he wondered how many more had appeared across London that morning. If Ireland had been truly liberated, he wondered how long it might be before British tanks rolled across the frontier.

He saw that same hope reflected on other faces as he crossed the road to Harrods. He registered a smile here, a nod and a wink there, strangers quietly united in their joy, and the knowledge that Alliance troops were not far away.

The Harrods food hall was busy, and Bertie picked up a basket and began browsing the shelves for the items on Chef's list. He hadn't expected to see George there, nor the sudden change of plan that George had whispered to him as they'd perused the shelves. Al-Kaabi's planned pickup from Northwood was in jeopardy. The driver had taken ill, a heart attack, George explained, which meant they needed someone with the right travel permit to meet him at Northwood and drive him to the pre-arranged pickup point. *It's time to step up,* George had told Bertie, dropping a carefully folded note into his basket. Right then, all Bertie could think about was being nailed to that cross.

The rest of the day had been a blur. He had no choice but to take The Witch's car without her consent, drive up to

Northwood for midnight and wait until 1 am. If Al-Kaabi didn't show, it meant he'd been rumbled. And if that happened, they'd all have to run. He packed a bag, all his worldly goods in fact, which wasn't much. He had no kids and his wife had left him years ago. *It's me or the football,* she'd told him. The memory made him smile.

He'd planned to leave for Northwood at 11.15 pm, which would get him there in plenty of time and keep his loitering in the residential street to a minimum, but then The Witch had thrown an unscheduled dinner and a giant fucking spanner in the works. As if he wasn't stressed enough.

Behind him, the clock on the wall taunted him, ticking like a bomb. He gave in and looked; 10:30 pm, and still no sign that things were winding up. It was a quiet dinner, with Judge Hardy and two others from the National Assembly. Dessert had been served, but they were taking their sweet fucking time about it. Bertie thought about going upstairs with a kitchen knife and doing the lot of them. *If only.*

Instead, he decided on another coffee, topped up with a shot of excellent brandy, and tried to stop thinking about his own crucifixion. As he unscrewed the cap, he heard Chef's muffled voice down the basement hall, swearing at the TV, and Bertie considered inviting him for a nightcap. *No,* he decided. Better to stay focussed. He topped his black coffee off with a soothing measure of *Hine Triomphe* and retook his seat. The coffee tasted excellent, and Bertie glanced up at the wall, praying for the drawing-room bell to ring, for the guests to piss off and The Witch to climb back inside her coffin.

So he could embark on the most dangerous journey he'd ever undertaken.

. . .

Faisal Al-Kaabi's eyes flicked to the row of digital clocks on the wall of the conference room. New York, Beijing, Islamabad, Baghdad, those time zones held no significance for the intelligence officer at that moment. It was only the local time that concerned him.

His armpits were damp with sweat. The subterranean basement was disagreeably stuffy and packed with bodies. General Mousa held centre stage, strutting around the table, berating, cursing, cajoling, praising. He spoke rapid-fire, jerking his finger at maps and wall-projections, at the uniformed staff officers around the low-ceilinged room. All the talk was about Ireland. Mistakes had been made, none of which had been laid at the door of the culprit, Major-General Kalil Zaki. The man was an incompetent buffoon, but he was also the Caliph's beloved nephew, and therefore untouchable.

Mousa knew it too. None of his vitriol was directed at Zaki, who stood behind Mousa glowering at the room, daring anyone to make eye contact. And to be fair, it wasn't all Zaki's fault. Their shore-based anti-ship missile defences had been taken out by *kuffar* special forces and cruise missiles long before the allied invasion fleet had sailed into range. Precious aircraft had also been destroyed on the tarmac by Irish resistance fighters, and US submarines sank 50 per cent of the French warships that had been put to sea from the port of Brest before they'd rounded Land's End. Of the four giant underground bombs in Derry, Enniskillen, Athlone, and Limerick, three of them failed to detonate. The one in Athlone exploded too soon, killing the engineers and alerting the Allies to the threat. After Zaki had fled the country to save his own skin, the defence of Ireland had collapsed.

The conference room reeked of sweat, failure, and

fear. Al-Kaabi felt anxious too, mainly because he was carrying a data drive in his shirt pocket that contained 150 gigabytes of raw intelligence and logistics information.

He glanced at the clock on the wall, and once again he cursed the Americans. He knew his defection would come at a price, and that the act of betrayal would be stressful, but he didn't imagine this. The day before he'd thrown up several times, confining himself to his quarters with a fake bout of food poisoning.

Now he was feeling trapped, acutely aware of the 30 feet of earth above his head pressing down on him, the tiny data drive bulging like a house brick in his breast pocket. Once again, he questioned his sanity. He should've broken off the affair, fled the moment he realised he'd been compromised. He could've asked for compassionate leave, flown back to Amman, asked for a re-posting. He could've done all of that, and yet here he sat, exposed, frightened, and desperate to run. To escape.

'Are you late for something?'

The man who whispered in his ear was Yosef Hassan, an intelligence officer like Al-Kaabi, but older, thinner, and bald, with cold, officious eyes behind his round glasses. Hassan's career had faltered somewhere down the line, and the man was keen to make up for lost time. He was a sycophant, eager to please his superiors at the expense of others. When he'd taken the seat next to Al-Kaabi, the younger man had cursed his luck.

'Excuse me?'

'You keep looking at the clock,' Hassan whispered. 'Is there somewhere else you should be?'

The man's breath reeked of onions. Al-Kaabi winced theatrically. 'Yes, the bathroom.'

Hassan leaned a little closer. 'You could always ask the general to get a move on.'

Al-Kaabi forced a quick smile and looked away. Now the data drive felt like a laptop strapped to his chest, visible for all to see.

He focussed as the subject turned to missiles. Hostilities with China meant no more weapons shipments, no more replacement parts or system boards. No more support of any kind. The tap had been turned off and that would hurt their forces badly. Al-Kaabi listened carefully as his colleagues discussed the dispersal of their precious missiles. Mousa wanted them split between the UK and Chinese theatres. A plan was thrashed out and agreed, and orders issued. Then, to Al-Kaabi's immense relief, the meeting was adjourned.

The fresh air above ground felt wonderful. Al-Kaabi headed back to his accommodation block, replaying the meeting in his mind, keeping it fresh. He entered his narrow room with its cheap wardrobe and single bed and dropped the blind. He clicked on a reading lamp and sat down at his desk. He ignored the laptop, snatched up a notepad and pen and began writing every word, every location, every order, and every date and time he'd just heard. He scribbled furiously, determined to get it all down. It was late, gone midnight, and he knew a car would be waiting for him at the prearranged pickup point. That was risky in itself. Al-Kaabi's escape was riskier. He had to cut his way through the chain link. He wasn't looking forward to that at all, but leaving the camp at this time of night would raise more questions. He had no choice—

The knock at the door startled him. He shoved the pad in the desk drawer and got to his feet. A smiling Hassan was waiting outside. He was alone, Al-Kaabi was relieved to see, but the man's nose twitched like a rat, his eyes peering over Al-Kaabi's shoulder.

'Yosef. How can I help?'

'I thought I'd stop by, check on you.'

'I'm fine, thanks.'

'You said you needed the bathroom. When the meeting broke up, you walked straight past one.'

Al-Kaabi frowned. 'That's none of—'

'You've been acting strange all day. I'm concerned.'

'You're not spying on me, are you?' Al-Kaabi smiled, a sudden knot of fear twisting his stomach. *Why say spying? Why use that word, idiot!* Voices echoed along the corridor. Al-Kaabi threw the door open. 'Please, come in. Let's talk.'

Hassan stepped inside, his hands clasped behind his back, looking around the narrow room as if he were carrying out an inspection. 'Something's troubling you, Faisal. What is it?'

'Nothing, really. I've not been well, that's all.' Al-Kaabi closed the door. *Now what?* He had to think of something quick, but first, he had to stash the data drive. He'd feel better if it wasn't in his damn pocket. He plucked it out, turned to the wardrobe, to hide it beneath his neatly-folded sweaters—

The tiny device slipped from his fingers.

Shit!

It hit the floor and skittered across the room, disappearing beneath the bed. Al-Kaabi cursed, knelt down, saw it lying against the skirting board.

'Do you need help?'

'It's fine. I dropped something,' Al-Kaabi grunted, reaching out and plucking it from the dust. He balled his fist around it and stood up. 'A ring,' he explained, 'a family heirloom...'

His face dropped. The desk drawer was open. Hassan was holding up his pad.

'What's this?'

Hassan's face was triumphant. He reminded Al-Kaabi of a TV detective, confronting a criminal with a damning piece of evidence. Except this wasn't TV.

'I told you, I've been ill. I'm having trouble focussing. I made some notes.'

'*Some notes*?' echoed Hassan, waving the pad. 'This is four pages of detailed military intelligence.'

'Don't be ridiculous.' Al-Kaabi reached out, but Hassan whipped it out of reach.

'You're an odd fish, Faisal. Secretive. Like you're hiding something. I'm right, aren't I?'

Al-Kaabi's shoulder's sagged. 'Yes, but it's not what you think.'

'Doesn't matter what I think. Others will get to the truth.'

'Others?'

Hassan frowned. 'Of course. I must report this immediately.'

Al-Kaabi swallowed. 'There's no need to—'

'No need? Are you serious?' Hassan gripped the notepad in his hand. 'Move aside, major.'

Al-Kaabi dropped his head. 'Fine. Do what you must.'

Hassan brushed past him. Al-Kaabi moved fast, snaking an arm around the older officer's throat and choking off his cry of alarm. He dragged Hassan backwards onto the bed, tightening his chokehold. Hassan's legs kicked wildly, knocking the lamp off the desk. The laptop followed it, crashing to the floor. Al-Kaabi redoubled his efforts, squeezing his arm tighter. Hassan struggled like a wildcat, thrashing on top of him, reaching for Al-Kaabi's fingers, for his face, clawing, spitting, and wheezing. Al-Kaabi held on, sweat pouring from his face, his muscles aching. He could smell Hassan's onion breath, the stench of his rank body odour, and it made him gag. He held on, crushing Hassan's windpipe until finally the man's breath rattled and he went limp. Al-Kaabi rolled him onto the floor and lay on top of him, his arm still clamped across Hassan's throat, terrified he was bluffing. But he wasn't, Al-Kaabi realised. Hassan lay still, his head bent to one side, his glasses twisted and broken, his disbelieving eyes bloodshot and lifeless.

Al-Kaabi staggered upright and sat on the bed panting. Killing a man with one's bare hands was harder than he'd ever imagined. He sat and listened to the world outside his room. There were no inquisitive voices in the corridor, no urgent knocking. Hassan's death, like the man himself, had gone unnoticed.

He checked his watch and stood quickly. It was approaching 1 am. He had to leave right now, before the car left without him. He pushed Hassan's body beneath the single bed and changed into dark jogging trousers, a matching hoodie, and running shoes. He snapped a security pouch around his waist containing the transcribed notes and the data drive and left the room. He locked the door and made his way out into the night.

There was one more gamble to take, one more roll of the dice. He had no time to head to the perimeter fence, to the spot he'd carefully reconnoitred, to cut his way through it, link by laborious, dangerous link. Instead, he broke into a jog and headed towards the main gate.

Beneath the wash of halogen lights, half a dozen gun-toting guards manned the high, chain-link double gates, pacing slowly, eyes alert, guns held low. There was no traffic, vehicular or otherwise, and the gates were sealed. All eyes turned to Al-Kaabi as he jogged into the bright pool of light.

'Evening,' he puffed, slowing as he approached the pedestrian security gate.

The guard looked puzzled. 'Can I help you, sir?'

'I'm going for a run. Open up.'

'A run?'

'That's right...' Al-Kaabi glanced at the man's combat uniform. 'Lance-Corporal.'

'I wouldn't advise it, sir.'

Al-Kaabi spun around. Another soldier had emerged from the gatehouse, a pistol strapped to his thigh. 'The alert level has been raised,' he said. 'Leaving the camp this late and unaccompanied is not advisable, sir.'

Al-Kaabi walked towards him, stopping a few feet away. He made sure the others could hear him. 'Sergeant, I've been sitting in a chair in the Ops Centre for the past 12 hours. I need fresh air, and I need to stretch my legs.'

The sergeant frowned, then said, 'I must clear it with the duty officer. Your name, please sir?'

'Major Al-Kaabi. Theatre Intelligence Unit.'

The soldier turned on his heel and disappeared back inside the gatehouse. Al-Kaabi thought about heading to the fence, cutting his way out. He checked his watch: 12:52. There was no time. The sergeant reappeared.

'The duty officer is calling me back. Shouldn't be too long.'

'What's his name? The duty officer?'

'Lieutenant Rasheed.'

'Tell him I'm going for a run, and I'll be 30 minutes or so. If he has a problem, he can speak to my superior officer, General Mousa. I'm sure the general will be keen to find out the names of those who have inconvenienced a member of his intelligence staff. Or would you rather make that call yourself?'

The sergeant's Adam's apple bobbed nervously.

'Open the gate,' Al-Kaabi pressed, 'or find yourself on the next flight to the Chinese border.'

The sergeant didn't blink. 'Open the gate!' he shouted at the soldiers.

Ten seconds later, Al-Kaabi was on the other side of the fence. He made a brief show of stretching his arms and legs, and then he was jogging sedately away from the camp.

Once he'd reached the darkness of the leafy lane, he broke into a run.

[11]
UBER ALLES

THE CURTAIN ACROSS THE STREET TWITCHED AGAIN.

Bertie told himself not to look, but it was the second time in 15 minutes that someone in that house had sneaked a peek outside. An innocent adjustment of the curtains, perhaps? Or maybe that person was watching him, making a call...

Yes, a dark-coloured Toyota hybrid. No, they're too muddy, I can't read them. He's a Caucasian male, shifty-looking, certainly not a resident. You'd best come quickly...

Either way, Bertie had been parked on this quiet suburban street for far too long.

He'd arrived just under an hour ago, the journey passing uneventfully, and Bertie had obeyed the speed limits and avoided the major roads as planned. Arriving at the location, he'd driven sedately around the wide, curving crescent until he'd reached the designated pickup point, pulling silently into the curb and shutting off the engine. To his right, a row of smart, detached homes curved away into the darkness. There were no street lights, which Bertie was grateful for, and most of the windows were dark. All tucked up in bed, he'd assumed. Except for the nosy bastard across the street.

Bertie looked to his left, along the dark, narrow footpath bordered by trees and overgrown grass. It led to another suburban street, one that backed on to the camp at Northwood, the route that Al-Kaabi would use to get to him. Time, however, was marching on, and Bertie's neck was aching as his head swivelled left and right – *curtains, footpath, curtains, footpath.* One of them would decide his future.

The stress of waiting triggered a montage of dark thoughts. He saw a convoy of military vehicles roaring around the crescent towards him, lights blazing, brakes screeching, a stampede of boots, the car door wrenched open, his face on the cold asphalt as his hands were cuffed behind his back.

Then the long, slow walk up into the dock, coming face-to-face with The Witch herself, her screeching accusations and condemnation filling the courtroom, the sharp, rapid tattoo of her gavel. Then later, forced down onto that thick wooden cross, the ropes lashed around his elbows, a huge iron nail jabbed into the palm of his hand as his executioner raised his hammer to drive it home...

Jesus, get a grip, Bertie.

He banished the nightmare from his mind and sought the cold reassurance of the Ruger automatic pistol beneath his seat. It was a small weapon, but it packed a decent punch, George told him. It was to be used only in an emergency, and Bertie had already decided that if he was cornered, he'd use it on himself.

He checked his watch again. 12:58. Two more minutes, and then he'd have to leave. George was explicit; there would be no extension, no hanging around. If Al-Kaabi didn't show, he was probably singing like a canary, and Bertie wouldn't blame him. He doubted he'd last long himself.

Bertie had done a little time back in the day, punishment for a credit card scam he'd got involved in. Nothing heavy, just booze runs to France using stolen cards, then selling the goods to pubs and clubs back in the UK. They'd all been nicked eventually, and even though Bertie was barely out of his teens, he'd kept his mouth shut. Things were so much different now. There was no easy bird anymore, and the cops who'd taken the caliphate's shilling were worse than their masters. Corrupt, violent, and eager to please. A dangerous combination.

He's not coming...

Bertie peered into the inky blackness of the footpath. Nothing. Then he glanced over the road and saw that curtain twitching again, and suddenly Bertie was frightened.

This was it, he realised.

He couldn't go back to Hampstead anymore, back to his life with The Witch. Now he had to run, with all of his worldly possessions stuffed in a bag behind him, and head for the safe house in Lincolnshire, the farm that his uncle ran. Or used to. Bertie hadn't seen him in over five years, had no idea if the man was still alive, but it was the only option he had. And it was better than getting caught.

He stabbed the ignition button, and the Toyota purred into life, the instrument panel glowing in the dark. He dropped the car into gear and pulled away from the curb, keeping his lights off and his speed down as he drove carefully around the wide, tree-lined crescent. He checked his mirror one last time, praying he'd see Al-Kaabi emerge from the footpath behind him, waving frantically. But there was no one there.

'Shit!'

He yanked the wheel to the right, missing the dark figure by a hair. He stamped on the brakes and the back door flew open, the figure bundling into the seat behind him.

'Go, quickly!'

Bertie could've yelled his delight, his euphoria, but instead he kept his mouth shut and his eyes glued to the road, only flicking the lights on when he'd turned the distant corner. He sped up then, thinking about the route ahead, but this time their destination was far beyond the city where patrols and twitching curtains were rare. Still, he would keep to the quieter roads, just to be safe.

He glanced at the hooded figure of Al-Kaabi in his rear-view mirror. 'You okay?'

'Fine,' he said, panting. Then his eyes narrowed. 'Bertie?'

'Yes. The other guy got sick. Look, I'm sorry I drove off. I waited until after one, pushed it as much as I could.'

Al-Kaabi nodded. 'I'm grateful, believe me.'

'Any problems?'

'None you need to know about.'

'Understood.' Bertie passed him a bottle of mineral water. 'Here, take that, relax. The journey will take about an hour.'

Al-Kaabi took a swig of water. 'And Timmy will be there, yes?'

'George gave you his word.'

He saw Al-Kaabi deflate and slide a little lower in his seat. He turned the radio up, a classical station, the slow, soothing symphony filling the car. He glanced at the man in the mirror and thought about the journey he was about to embark on. *Lucky bastard,* Bertie stewed. He wished he was going with him, instead of that fat poof Gates.

The more he thought about it, the tougher it was to swallow. Two men were about to escape these troubled shores, one of them an enemy soldier and the other a traitor to his own people. Why did they get to sail off into the sunset? Why not him and George?

Life ain't fair, he heard his mum's ghost say. *If you want something in this world, go out there and take it.*

Mum was right, Bertie realised.

She was always right.

[12]
HURRY UP, HARRY

EDDIE FIRED TWO ROUNDS IN QUICK SUCCESSION AND saw the target drop. He twisted left as another target sprang up out of the undergrowth, then fired again. Another double-tap, another hit. He kept moving as daylight faded. It was still too light for his NVGs, but gloomy enough for the naked eye to misinterpret the data. The new EOTech holographic combat optics they had issued him bridged that dangerous gap. As the surrounding woods darkened, the world through his gun sight was clear and defined. Eddie was a good shot; not the best in the platoon, but the EOTech gave his confidence a boost. He dared the targets to show themselves.

He moved quickly along the trail at a half-crouch, weapon up, trigger finger tense, the instructor behind him keeping pace, evaluating. The soft exoskeleton he'd been issued was a dream, and Eddie hardly felt the 75 pounds of ammunition and equipment he was carrying. Another eight targets fell to his shooting before he reached the end of the CQB range and unloaded his weapon. He made his way along the safety path to the edge of the wood, where the rest of Nine Platoon were chatting in small groups. A fine drizzle fell from the leaden grey sky as Eddie strolled over to his Three Section buddies. Mac saw him coming.

'Those optics are pretty sweet, eh?'

'It's harder to miss,' Eddie admitted.

'We'll be using them in anger soon enough,' Digger said, cradling his M27 across his chest like a new-born.

No one took the bait. The road to solid intel was a dead-end, they all knew that much, but Eddie suspected Digger may be right. Soldiering was like any other skill; you had to practise it to master the craft, and since landing in Scotland, they'd barely let up. The last week, in particular, had been full-on, honing their drills, section attacks, react-to-contact, ambush and room clearance, not to mention trench clearing, breaching mined obstacles, and reorganisation procedures. They'd boned up on their comms, first aid, and casualty evacuation drills too. They were sharp, much sharper than they ever could've imagined before setting foot in Ireland.

'Did you speak to Sarge?' Eddie asked Mac.

The Scot shrugged. 'He's in the dark, just like the rest of us. The boss is still away though. Who knows where he's gone, but Sarge reckons it's some sort of top brass pow-wow.'

'They're prepping us for battle, no question,' Digger told them.

Mac's eyes drifted to the grim line of hills in the distance. 'Can't say I'm fired up about assaulting that frontier.'

'I heard someone in Six Platoon say something about a low-level para-drop,' Steve said.

Mac snorted. 'Fuck that. I'd rather take my chances tip-toeing through a minefield.'

Sarge's voice bellowed. 'Right, you lot! On the trucks!'

Eddie and the boys scrambled aboard, and 30 minutes later they were swinging through the main gates at Otterburn. Darkness had fallen, and the drizzle had strengthened into a steady rain. Sat by the tailgate, Mac pointed to the parade square.

'Looks like we've got guests.'

Eddie saw three black helicopters squatting on the tarmac, a Eurocopter, a Blackhawk, and an Apache, wheels chocked and slick with rain. Shadowy figures moved around them, and Eddie caught a flash of red torchlight.

'VIP bird, plus escort,' Steve observed. 'Must be someone special. All the lights in the camp are out.'

So they are, Eddie realised. Even the heavily guarded gate they'd just passed through was barely visible.

'Some general, come to wave us off.' Digger grinned. 'We're on the move, boys. I'll lay a year's wages on it. Any takers?' Nobody answered. 'Didn't think so. Pussies.'

The trucks rolled to a stop outside the blocks. No one said much as Nine Platoon jogged through the rain to their billet, or even later, as they sat around the table cleaning their weapons. It was apprehension, Eddie knew. The whole of the Second Mass had seen the frontier, its multi-layered defences, the undulating terrain sown with all manner of life-taking traps and munitions. Once the bullets started flying, the potential breach points would morph into kill zones of mud, blood, and guts, of that Eddie had no doubt. How any assault could be accomplished successfully was a mystery to all of them, but whatever lay ahead, he was sure they would find out what it was soon enough.

Hot-boxes were delivered to the block, and everyone took polystyrene trays of pasta back to their rooms. Eddie was just finishing his when the shouts echoed around the building.

'Get in the corridor!'

He followed the others outside, lining up with the rest of Nine Platoon along the walls. Sarge stood at the end of the hallway, his deep Welsh voice filling the void.

'I want everybody outside the block in five. Weapons and wet weather gear only. And watch your light discipline. If I see anyone waving torches out there tonight, you'll find yourselves in very deep shit. Five minutes,' he repeated, then disappeared through the doors.

Anticipation buzzed like a swarm of bees. Eddie grabbed his waterproof and beret, then slung his weapon across his chest. Nine Platoon filed outside into the rain, and Sarge marched them around the camp to the gymnasium. Inside, Eddie saw the whole of the Second Mass had gathered there, a huge cluster of combat uniforms barely distinguishable beneath the few portable lights. At the far end of the gym, rain fell through a shell hole in the roof's corner, forming a shallow lake of water on the floor. It was a shadowy, dramatic gathering, like an ancient clan assembling before their tribal leaders on the eve of war, and Eddie guessed that the dark Northumbrian hills surrounding the camp had witnessed many such gatherings down the centuries.

A low murmur rippled through the crowd. Heads turned towards the cluster of battalion HQ staff at the far end of the gym. It was Mac who saw him first.

'Holy shit. Is that who I think it is?'

'It can't be.' Eddie's eyes narrowed in the gloom.

Next to him, Digger beamed. 'See? I told you.'

Eddie's heart beat a little faster. The RSM barked, ordering everyone closer. Eight hundred men shuffled forward, and then the figure in boots, combat trousers, and a thick North Face coat stepped up onto the platform and addressed the waiting men.

'Can you all hear me?' Harry Beecham asked them.

He was answered with a low murmur of *sirs*. Beecham cupped a hand around his ear. 'Didn't catch that. I said, can you hear me?'

Yes, sir! the Second Mass boomed, their voices thundering off the walls.

'That's what I thought.' Beecham smiled as he looked around the crowd of uniforms. 'I've had the honour of meeting some of you before, on that wind-swept airfield back in Massachusetts. That feels like a lifetime ago now, and for those men and women who are no longer with us, it is a life already spent...'

Eddie glanced at Digger and saw his face cloud over. Up on his makeshift stage, Beecham continued.

'You've all seen the frontier, a daunting obstacle that separates many of us from our family and friends, from victory, and from an end to this war. Behind that grotesque scar, behind that blight on our beloved landscape, the enemy, after almost three years of occupation, has become complacent. I stand here tonight to tell you we are about to shatter that complacency.'

A buzz rippled around the hall. The RSM bellowed for silence as Beecham continued.

'Colonel Butler will brief you in due course, but I wanted to come here tonight and thank you personally, for your service, your commitment to the fight, and for the inevitable sacrifices some of you will make. Rest assured, those sacrifices will never be forgotten.'

Beecham thrust his hands in his pockets as his eyes roamed around the shadowy gymnasium.

'I've been here before, addressing British troops on the

eve of battle. That was a tough time for me, both as a Prime Minister and as an individual, talking to men like your-selves, shaking hands with them, wishing them luck, knowing that many of them would never see another sunrise. I look around this gymnasium and I'm reminded of that dark period in our recent history. Now another battle looms, one that will mean more deaths, more injuries, more lives shattered. Such are the certainties of war, but in my heart, I know we will stand victorious in its aftermath.'

Eddie swallowed as he realised that, just for a moment, the Prime Minister had looked right at him.

'You're fighting for your families, your friends, and neighbours, all of them struggling beneath the yoke of tyranny behind that frontier. You're fighting for freedom and liberty, and believe me, there is no greater cause to die for. So, gentlemen, I bid you goodnight, good luck, and may God watch over you all. Thank you.'

The RSM brought the room to attention as Beecham stepped down from the platform. Four heavily armed soldiers fell in around him and then he was lost in a crowd of senior officers. The air in the gymnasium buzzed.

'So, Digger was right.' Steve smiled in the gloom, the first for quite a while.

'See? None of you believed me.'

'Course we did,' Mac shot back. 'That's why we didn't take the bet.'

'Bullshit.'

The RSM barked again and Colonel Butler climbed up on the platform. 'Thank you, Sarn't-Major.' He adjusted his eye-patch as he looked at the faces of his battalion. 'You're done for the evening,' he told them, 'and morning parade is cancelled, so use your time wisely. Rest, gentlemen, catch up on your much-needed beauty sleep. It might be the last chance you'll get for a while. Tomorrow, after lunch, the Second Mass will be on the move. As the prime minister has just told you, we're going back into the fray, so start switching on. Understood?'

Yes, sir.

As they filed out of the hall, Eddie could feel the surrounding tension, laced with excitement, and maybe more than a little trepidation. They'd trained their arses off. They had every confidence in their weapons, equipment, drills, and each other. Whatever the future held, they'd handle it, overcome the obstacles, prevail. Still, Eddie found it hard to shake the image of that deadly frontier from his mind.

Outside, the rain was falling heavily. The whine of jet engines filled the night air, and the rising thunder of helicopters battered the surrounding buildings. A moment later they were passing overhead, the shadow of the Apache clattering above them, followed by the Eurocopter and the Black Hawk, so low that Eddie could feel the vibrations in his stomach. Then they were gone, disappearing over the hills to the north, the thunder fading to nothing.

'Show's over,' Mac said, watching the sky.

'I beg to differ.' Digger grinned in the darkness. 'It's about to begin.'

[13]
EXCESS BAGGAGE

THREE HUNDRED METRES WEST OF CHALFONT ST
Giles in Buckinghamshire, Bertie pulled the Toyota into a
narrow lay by. He powered down the window, switched off
the engine, and listened. As expected, it was quiet, and the
only sound that Bertie could hear was the breeze rustling
the high hedges on both sides of the deserted road.

They were far beyond the city now, and life in the sticks
was supposed to be pretty normal. Farmers still did their
thing, because everybody had to eat, but the village pubs
were all gone, boarded up and closed, like every other
drinking establishment in England and Wales. Country
fairs were banned too, so no more cheese-chasing or dwarf-
throwing, or whatever yokels did at those things. British
country life was dead. *No,* he corrected himself. *It is
dormant.*

Still, it was nice to be out of London. It wasn't a particularly cold night; the sky was clear and littered with stars,
and the air had that faintly sweet tang of cow shit, which
was unsurprising considering everything north and west of
their current location was a mixture of farmland, wild

meadows, and thick woods. The perfect place to carry out a clandestine hand-over, it seemed, but all Bertie wanted to do was get back to Hampstead.

'Aren't you concerned at all?'

Bertie glanced in his rear view mirror. 'About what?'

'Being traced,' Al-Kaabi replied. 'Your phone signal, for example, and the car's GPS. Your location history will be recorded, not to mention your licence plates.'

Bertie shook his head. 'The car's been modified; every time the engine stops, it wipes the sat nav's history. My phone is powered off and in case you hadn't noticed, the plates are filthy.' Bertie yanked the door handle. 'Wait here.'

To the south-east, he could see the sharp silhouettes of the village rooftops, but everything else was dark, rolling hills. He walked north along the road until he saw the break in the hedge, just as George had described. He whistled low, and a figure stumbled out onto the road.

'Oh, thank God!' Timmy Gates cried. 'I was freezing to death—'

'Be quiet!' Bertie said. He started walking back towards the car. Gates hurried behind him.

'Is Faisal with you?'

'No, he's washing his hair.' Bertie glanced over his shoulder. 'Of course he is. Just get a move on.'

'There's no need for sarcasm,' Gates grumbled.

Thirty seconds later they were back at the car. Gates scrambled inside and a moment later Bertie was behind the wheel and driving north-west towards Amersham.

'Faisal! I was so worried!' Gates gushed, hugging and kissing Al-Kaabi.

'I'm here now,' soothed Al-Kaabi, holding him.

'Did you get what they asked for?'

Al-Kaabi smiled. 'More than enough to buy us a new life, Timmy.'

Bertie's stomach churned. He had nothing against gays, but he didn't want to see them getting jiggy with each other either. 'We're not out of the woods yet,' he warned them, watching them disentangle.

Gates glanced out of the window. 'Nonsense, we're in the middle of nowhere. You're the first people I've seen since George dumped me behind that hedge.'

'Helped you to escape, you mean.' *Ungrateful shit.*

'What happens next?' Al-Kaabi asked him.

Bertie shrugged. 'I've got to drop you at a certain point. That's me done after that.'

'George says they'll take us west. Wales, probably, or somewhere up north. Then a boat to Scotland, or Ireland.'

'At least you're getting out. You're lucky.'

'Lucky?' Gates echoed. 'I'm leaving a life behind, Bertie. Friends, family, and then there's the gallery; I have important work there. I'll be missed.'

'Friends like that evil bitch Spencer, you mean?'

'I won't hear that talk, not from—'

Gates stopped himself. Bertie stared at him in the mirror. 'From who? Someone like me, is that what you mean?'

'That's enough, Timmy,' Al-Kaabi interjected.

'Listen to your friend,' Bertie warned, but his knuckles were white as he gripped the steering wheel. Despite everything he'd done, Gates still looked down his nose at him. He really was an ungrateful bastard.

'Let me ask you a question,' Bertie said, watching Al-Kaabi in the mirror. 'The word is, you've lost Ireland, and Alliance troops are massing in Scotland. So, what's the plan?'

Al-Kaabi stared out of the window. 'Believe it or not, I don't have a hotline to Baghdad.'

'You're an intelligence officer at Northwood. You must know something.'

'What I know is inconsequential. The data I'm handing over is something else entirely.'

'What sort of—'

'With respect, Bertie, just get us where we need to be, okay?'

'Right you are.'

The road twisted through the countryside. Bertie glanced at the map display, saw the turning a couple of hundred metres ahead. He slowed, flipping his lights off, allowing the Toyota to decelerate so he wouldn't have to pump the brakes. He saw the lane and turned the wheel. Mature hedgerows crowded either side. No one spoke as they drove deeper into the countryside. After several minutes, Bertie let the car roll to a stop and yanked the handbrake.

'This is it.'

Al-Kaabi twisted around in his seat. 'Here?'

'So I'm told.' He climbed out. The hedgerows had given way to a dark, rolling landscape of fields and distant woods. Bertie pulled his coat tighter against the chilly breeze.

'What now?' Al-Kaabi asked. He was almost invisible, a dark hooded figure standing by the Toyota. Gates clung to him like a limpet, his face pale.

'This is as far as I go. You need to head further up this lane. Someone will meet you.'

Al-Kaabi disengaged himself and held out his hand. 'Thank you for helping us.'

Bertie took it, gripped it. 'Good luck.'

Gates said nothing, just linked his arm through Al-

Kaabi's. As they walked away, Bertie pulled the Ruger from his pocket and shot Al-Kaabi in the back of the head. The hollow pop echoed across the field, and Bertie saw the intelligence officer drop to his knees then roll sideways onto the ground. Gates jumped like he'd been electrocuted. He spun around, and Bertie saw his eyes, wide with fear. He took aim and shot out the left one. Gates staggered backwards, but instead of falling, he weaved like a drunk towards the Toyota. Bertie was dumbfounded. *How is that possible?* He watched his hands flapping at the door handle, and it disturbed him. Bertie marched towards him and shot him again, twice, three times in the chest. Gates staggered against the door, gurgling and spitting blood, but still, he stayed upright. He stared at Bertie with his one remaining eye, his lips moving, his words jumbled, nonsensical. Then his knees finally buckled, and he fell to the ground, smearing a bloody hand across the rear window. Bertie stood over him, unnerved and sickened.

Move, Bertie!

He jogged back to Al-Kaabi. The man was lying on his side, and blood ran freely from his nose and mouth. His eyes were wide open – he never knew what hit him – and that made Bertie feel a little better. He found the security belt around Al-Kaabi's waist and checked the contents; a tiny data drive and a folded sheaf of hand-written notes in swirly Arabic. Perfect. He shoved it in his coat pocket.

He struggled with the bodies, dragging them across the road and rolling them into a ditch by the side of the road. He got into the Toyota and continued up the lane towards the *actual* rendezvous point. He drove without lights, trying to keep his speed down, swerving to avoid the fences and deep verges, until he saw the wood ahead. He pulled off the road, threw open the door, and plunged into the trees. He stumbled through the undergrowth, low branches whipping his face and snatching at his coat. He couldn't believe what he'd done, the sudden decision he'd made. It was rash and stupid and treacherous, but Bertie was convinced that eventually, the disappearance of Al-Kaabi and Gates would lead right back to the big house in Hampstead. When that happened, The Witch would give him up in a heartbeat. They would take away Bertie, question him, torture him. Then they would execute him. He couldn't risk it.

He dodged left and right, branches lashing and snapping, leaves crunching underfoot. Ahead, the trees thinned, and then he staggered out into a meadow, chest heaving, breathless. He stopped and looked around. The meadow was enclosed on all sides by the same thick woods he'd blundered through. And there was something else there too, a black object out there in the open. Bertie squinted his eyes. *Is that a helicopter?*

'Don't move,' said a voice behind him. 'Lemme see those hands.'

Bertie froze, lifted his arms. Figures appeared out of the darkness and moved towards him, black helmets, black uniforms, black weapons, their faces obscured by insect-like goggles and balaclavas. One thing was clear though; the Stars and Stripes flags on their chests. One figure looped plastic cuffs over his wrists and zipped them tight.

'There's a gun in my right coat pocket,' he told them.

They searched him, found the gun and the pouch.

'Where's the other one? The other passenger?'

'He didn't make it,' Bertie said. 'It's just me.'

'We're moving,' he heard one of them say, and powerful hands grabbed his arms and propelled him forward. Helmets bounced in the darkness in front of him, the long grass swishing beneath his feet. Ahead, the helicopter took shape, but Bertie couldn't see any rotors, any jets. It stood high on three black legs, like a fat lozenge. It was the strangest flying machine Bertie had ever seen, but he didn't care. All that mattered was getting the hell out of England.

He ducked under the twin fins, and then his feet hit a steel ramp. The inside of the craft was gloomy, lit only with thin red strip lights. Bertie saw two rows of seats, like an airliner. A figure appeared, this one in a flight suit, his face obscured with a helmet and visor. One of the soldiers handed him the pouch. He snapped a torch on, checked the contents, checked Bertie's ID card.

'It's all there,' Bertie told him.

The figure shone the light in his face. 'Where's Al-Kaabi?'

Bertie blinked. 'I told you, he didn't make it. It's just me.'

'You're not Gates.'

'He didn't make it either.'

The mouth beneath the black visor cursed quietly. 'Off-load him,' he ordered. They spun Bertie around and forced him back down the ramp.

'Wait!' he yelled, digging his heels in. 'I brought you the intel! It's all kosher!'

'Move!' one of his captors urged, pushing him down onto the grass. They marched him a short distance away and cut off his plastic cuffs. The pistol was unloaded and shoved back in his pocket. One of the black helmets jerked his barrel towards the trees.

'Get out of here.'

'Please! Take me with you! They'll kill me!' Bertie begged, but the soldiers were already backing away and disappearing into the aircraft.

A low vibration rumbled in Bertie's stomach as he

watched the ramp raise up and seal itself against the fuse-lage. For a moment, Bertie forgot his woes as he watched the craft move almost silently, the legs folding up beneath its body like a giant black dragonfly as it spun around and drifted low across the meadow. Then he felt a deeper thump, and the surrounding grass flattened as if blown by a powerful wind. The last thing he saw was the aircraft lifting over the trees and disappearing into the night sky.

Bertie stood motionless, his legs frozen, hollow, barely able to support his weight. He'd rolled the dice and lost. Now his choices were limited. He could make a run to the farm in Lincolnshire, or spill the beans to George, tell him he'd panicked and hope he'd be forgiven. Or he could clear up his own mess and bluff it out. The fact was, he was in deep shit.

A nocturnal bird shrieked, and Bertie spun around, star-tled. He checked his watch; the sun would be up in a couple of hours. He reloaded the gun, shoved it back in his pocket, and headed back across the meadow. What the next few days held in store would depend on what Bertie did now. He had to think, and he had to act, and do both decisively. Anything else was suicide.

An option that is now officially on the table, Bertie realised.

He plunged back into the wood, and into the darkness.

[14]

ALL ABOARD

THE TRAIN STOOD IDLE, PARKED DEEP BENEATH THE mountain of Monte de la Coche, 35 kilometres outside the city of Chambery. Technically, the snow-capped peak was only 25 kilometres to the east of the city, but to get there, the train had wound its way around the steep, rising ground at La Thule before turning north towards Albertville. Eleven kilometres short of the former Winter Olympic city, the train had branched left onto a highly-restricted railway spur that twisted through a thick pine forest before entering a guarded tunnel entrance carved into the mountainside.

French engineers had laid the spur back in the early twentieth century, to exploit a series of natural caverns beneath the mountain. The idea was to create a route to the city of Annecy to the north, but the engineering project, hugely ambitious for its time, ran into a literal dead end after several costly kilometres of tunnelling. Shortly thereafter, the project was abandoned.

The years passed, and the network of tunnels and caverns inside the mountain lay abandoned until the nuclear age dawned when the French military decided to put the installation to good use. Years were spent refitting the track and signalling systems, building living accommodation and enormous storage facilities for vehicles and equipment. Later, as the Cold War fizzled out, the tunnels were once again repurposed, this time as a dedicated weapons and munitions storage facility.

Henri Platt wasn't particularly interested in the history of the mountain that towered thousands of metres above his head. What concerned him was the journey he was about to undertake. A train driver with over 22 years' experience working for SNCF, the state-owned railway company, Henri had transported both freight and passengers throughout his career, driving TGVs to San Sebastian and Geneva, to Munich and Brussels, and the Eurostar to London. He'd even driven nuclear waste to the underground dump at Bure in eastern France. In fact, there wasn't a single major route on the French railway system that Henri had not travelled. Today was a first, however. Today he would transport munitions, and the prospect unnerved him.

He stood at the window of the control room and stared out at the vast cavern beyond. It was impressive, Henri had to admit, and the engineers had worked wonders to create a railway station and sidings beneath the mountain. Standing idle beneath the arc lights of the main platform was his giant locomotive diesel engine, connected to 690 metres of flatbeds, liquid tanks, and boxcars, plus another locomotive coupled to the rear car for additional power. Officially, Henri was unaware of the cargo he was due to haul, other than that it was flammable, but one of the shunting crew had told him it comprised of missiles, propellants, and munitions, much of it stamped with Chinese writing. *Basically, Henri, you're hauling a giant fucking bomb,* the shunter had said, winking.

That made Henri very nervous. He'd never transported military cargo before, but things had changed for all of them. He'd been lucky, however. Identified early on as a key worker, Henri was able to earn a decent wage and feed his family, unlike some of his neighbours whose previous jobs were deemed forfeit. They were office staff and civil servants mostly, people without transferrable skills. Some of them now worked the local farms, but others had packed up and moved on. Henri didn't know where, nor did he care to ask. It didn't pay to poke one's nose into other people's affairs, not these days.

Yet life wasn't too bad at all for Henri Platt. He lived just outside of Paris, in a small, well-kept town that had escaped much of the carnage that had engulfed France's capital city. Before the rise of the caliphate, Henri was the *train-driver chap.* Now he was respected, an important cog in the caliphate's logistics machine, a transport captain who regularly drove his train all across the caliphate. Some of his neighbours believed he was well connected within the Islamo-French military, a rumour that Henri neither confirmed nor denied. He was just a train driver, a hugely experienced one, but a train driver nonetheless.

The clanking of shunting rolling stock reverberated inside the mountain complex. Whistles blasted and men in hi-vis overalls swarmed around his train, checking couplings and air lines. Henri turned away and sat down with his crew of four. They spent the next hour checking their charts, the potential obstacles of bends and gradients, the trunk lines, spurs, and junctions they would need to negotiate. The run to Lyon was fairly straightforward but their orders were to avoid the major cities, which meant some careful route planning with the National Operations Centre in Paris. Officially, their cargo was logged as machine parts for the damaged ports of Calais and Boulogne; the French resistance might not be the force it was during World War Two, but there were still some anti-caliphate terrorists out there who were well-armed and motivated enough to derail a train like theirs.

Another hour had passed before Henri was informed that his cargo had been loaded successfully. Together with his crew, he walked the length of the train, checking mountings, couplings, safety bolts, air-lines, and running lights. There was nothing to suggest that the cargo was military, the boxcars and sheeted flatbeds were unmarked, rusted, and weather-worn, and that gave Henri some consolation. Satisfied that all was well, the crew split up. Two men headed back towards their engine at the rear of the train, and Henri and his co-driver, Jean-Michel, climbed up into the huge front locomotive.

They ran through their departure checklist and radioed the mountain controller for authority to travel. It was granted, and Henri gave the order to depart. Diesel engines roared, and an enormous thunder of steel and machinery echoed beneath the mountain before the train started to move. Through the window, far in the distance, a small pinprick of fading daylight marked the entrance to the mountain complex. That was where the mission would truly begin, Henri knew.

What he didn't know was that he was hauling every Chinese-made missile and rocket that the caliphate's western theatre had left in its arsenal. Those munitions had been earmarked for what the military planners in London were now preparing for; the assault on the caliphate's northern frontier. The train driver knew nothing of this. All he knew was that his cargo contained thousands of tons of fuel and munitions and that the journey ahead of them would be a lengthy one.

'Train is rolling,' Jean Michel reported from the seat next to him. 'Speed is ten kilometres per hour.'

'Let's keep her there until we clear the mountain.'

'Oui.'

It took another 20 minutes before the train left the bowels of the Monte de la Coche. The densely-wooded valley beyond was already dark, and the train was using minimal running lights, which suited Henri just fine. The more invisible they were, the better.

He leaned back in his chair and shook a rare cigarette from a crumpled packet he kept in the cab. The hand that lit it shook, and Henri realised that for the first time in his career, he was troubled at the thought of what lay ahead.

THEY ASSEMBLED BEHIND THEIR ACCOMMODATION block at Otterburn camp for the last time. They wouldn't be coming back, which was all they'd been told. There were so many unknowns, but only a single certainty; they were going back into combat.

Charlie Company stood on parade as a fine curtain of rain swept down from the hills and drifted across the blacked-out camp. A hundred men formed up into their designated platoons, carrying their equipment and weapons, black deployment bags at their feet. They were ready to move.

Eddie waited in the darkness alongside Mac, Steve, and Digger. Thanks to the exoskeletons they all wore, standing around with their gear and guns wasn't the strain it used to be. The skeleton didn't make them supermen, but the technology helped to distribute the weight through their feet instead of building pressure on their joints, back, and hips. Knowing what lay ahead, they'd take any advantage they could get.

Eddie spied a dangling strap hanging from Steve's rucksack and snapped it home. 'There you go,' he told him, slapping his pack. 'You're all good.'

'Cheers, brother.'

'Keep it down,' Mac warned as the CSM brought them to attention. The company commander stepped out of the building and into the rain. Like the rest of his men, his face was smeared with camouflage cream and he was loaded with gear. His voice echoed off the walls of the empty buildings around them, a last-minute pep talk that wasn't necessary. They were ready.

When the OC was done, the company fell out and headed towards the parade square where the transport waited. It was an odd mixture of vehicles, a few military trucks, but most of it was civilian; container lorries, coaches, minibuses, and civvy cars. Nine Platoon was directed to two dark-coloured minibuses with a smiling otter logo and the words *Otterburn Primary School and Nursery* stamped on the doors. They piled aboard, bunching tightly together in the cramped vehicle, their rucksacks and deployments bags secured beneath a waterproof sheet on the roof-rack. The surrounding vehicles were leaving at ten-minute intervals, and after almost an hour's wait, it was finally their turn.

The driver, wearing NVGs, fired up the minibus and headed towards the camp gates. When they drove out onto the main road they turned left, heading east. Eddie looked over his shoulder, saw another vehicle leave the camp and disappear into the darkness in the opposite direction. Ahead, there was nothing to see beyond the struggling windscreen wipers. They were running without lights, and the night outside was cold, dark, and wet, but for now, the boys of Three Section were warm and dry. *Make the most of it,* Eddie told himself, because he knew it wouldn't last long.

'Heading east,' someone up front said.

'Fucking Columbo,' Mac joked, and that got a laugh.

'It's good to be on the move,' Eddie said. 'All that waiting around was doing my head in.'

'Agreed.' Steve's face was pressed against the window, his eyes roaming the darkness outside.

'This time next week we could all be dead,' observed the joker up front.

Mac growled. 'You keep flapping your gums, you won't have to wait that long.'

The banter faded, and the soldiers lapsed into silence. Squeezed between Mac and Digger, Eddie gave up trying to watch the world outside and closed his eyes, hoping the warm air and the gentle rocking of the vehicle would send him to sleep.

The prime minister had mentioned sacrifice, and since then, all Eddie could think about was the impending assault of the frontier, of the Second Mass slogging their way through freezing mud as flares and tracer rounds lit up the night, of bogged down vehicles and incoming artillery. Of carnage and death.

And despite Beecham's optimistic words, those dark thoughts wouldn't go away.

[15]
NO JUSTICE

Edith was escorted into the governor's outer office and invited to sit. She forced a smile as Davies' personal assistant rose from behind her desk.

'Can I get you anything, chief justice? Tea, coffee?'

'I'm fine, thank you.'

She sat with her knees clasped tightly together, her Louis Vuitton handbag resting by her smart black shoes. Once again she'd been summoned to Davies' inner sanctum. She recalled their last meeting and Davies' concerns over the forthcoming crucifixions. She wondered if that was the reason she was here. Perhaps he'd had second thoughts. Perhaps he would override her decision, but in her view, that would send all the wrong signals. She might have a battle on her hands, but the prospect didn't faze her. She was Davies' intellectual superior, and if she'd been born a man, it would be she who occupied the grand office beyond the highly polished double doors, and not the former junior minister.

The PA's phone warbled, and she snatched it up. She nodded, said *yes sir*, then put the phone back down.

'You may go in now,' she told Edith.

The chief justice got to her feet. As she approached the doors, the woman told her, 'You need to cover up, ma'am. Governor Davies has a guest.'

Edith wondered who it could be as she lifted the chiffon scarf from around her neck. When she entered Davies' office, she saw the governor on a couch near the glass wall, talking quietly to another man. Only one of them stood as she approached.

'Chief justice, good of you to come,' Davies greeted her, shaking her hand. He introduced the man on the opposite couch. 'This is Colonel Al-Huda, senior criminal investigator with the CID.'

Edith felt the icy fingers of fear brush the back of her neck. The military's Criminal Investigation Department was known for hunting spies, traitors, and religious transgressors within its own ranks, but she'd never met a single member of the caliphate's notorious secret police. Al-Huda's presence unnerved her. *You have nothing to fear,* she reminded herself, forcing another smile.

'Colonel Al-Huda. A pleasure indeed.'

Al-Huda nodded from his seat. Davies gestured to an easy chair between them, and Edith perched on the edge. Al-Huda was a cross-looking man, she noted, which was no surprise given his profession. He wore a black suit and a white shirt buttoned to the neck, and the only adornment was a gold lapel pin with the crossed swords of the caliphate armed forces. He eyed her curiously, his head tilted to one side as if deciding what to make of her. Edith thought she detected suspicion in those light brown eyes, and the icy digits brushed the skin of her neck once again.

'Colonel Al-Huda is investigating a crime, Edith. He was hoping you might help him.'

Edith forced the smile wider. 'I'm happy to assist in any way possible.'

'I have unpleasant news,' Al-Huda told her without preamble. His voice was scratchy but his English was impeccable. 'Your friend Timothy Gates is dead.'

So, they've found him. It was probably the smell. 'Dead?'

'He'd been shot several times, then dumped in a ditch. In Buckinghamshire.'

Edith didn't have to fake the sudden wave of shock. 'Are you sure it's him?' Al-Huda nodded, his eyes boring into her. She felt a ripple of panic and reached into her handbag for a tissue. She dabbed at dry eyes and said to Davies, 'Could I get a glass of water?'

As Davies snapped to his feet, Al-Huda stared at her but said nothing. Inside, she shrivelled and blew her nose as a distraction. Davies handed her a glass and retook his seat. She sipped the cold liquid as the investigator continued his questioning.

'You and Gates were friends. Good friends, I believe.'

Edith nodded. 'For many years. Timmy was a well-known figure in the art world, before the Great Liberation.'

'And you knew he was a homosexual.'

It wasn't a question, Edith realised. What else did he know? 'I did, but his sexuality was something we never discussed.' She took another sip of water to slake the sudden dryness of her mouth.

'He was a regular visitor at your Hampstead home, yes?'

Edith nodded again, her heart thumping inside her narrow chest. 'As I said, we'd been friends for many years...' Her voice trailed off. She put down her glass. 'Can you tell me what happened, Colonel Al-Huda? Timmy was a law-abiding citizen. He was very careful to play by the rules.'

'Was he indeed?'

Perhaps he's testing me. As well as the unease she was feeling, there was another emotion plucking at her consciousness; anger. Bertie had lied to her. She forced herself to focus as Al-Huda got to his feet and crossed the room to Davies' drinks cabinet. He poured himself some juice and swallowed a mouthful as he stared out of the window.

'Who told you about the nuclear attack in China?'

Edith felt the blood drain from her face. She twisted the straps of her handbag, her palms suddenly damp, her thoughts tumbling aimlessly like clothes in a dryer. Her tongue was frozen in her mouth. Her eyes flicked to Davies, and he looked away quickly. *You told him?*

Al-Huda turned and faced her. 'Well?'

Edith surreptitiously pinched the skin of her finger until the pain sharpened her focus. The next words out of her mouth could be pivotal, so she went with her instinct. 'Timmy told me. I thought he was joking, so I ignored it. He was an occasional eccentric. He would often make controversial statements, to get a reaction.' She raised an eyebrow and asked, 'Is it true?'

Al-Huda ignored the question and strolled back towards them, his hands clasped behind his back. Edith felt like she was being cross-examined in one of her own courtrooms.

'Did Gates mention anything else during these outbursts?'

'Not that I recall.'

'Did you ask how he came by such information?'

Edith shook her head. 'It was late, and the mood was all very light-hearted.'

'You'd been drinking alcohol.'

'I have a permit. Besides, I didn't take him seriously.'

'Did he ever mention the name Faisal Al-Kaabi?'

Edith struggled to keep her face impassive. 'Who?'

'Al-Kaabi was a senior military intelligence officer. He was found dead in the same ditch as your friend. They'd both been executed.'

'What?' Edith's surprise was genuine, but she recovered quickly. 'Are you suggesting they were having relations with each other?'

'It would explain your friend's knowledge of the nuclear detonation.'

Edith sat a little straighter and held the investigator's stony gaze. 'Colonel Al-Huda, I've been a loyal servant of the caliphate for almost three years, and my record speaks for itself. Had I known any of this, or suspected anything, I would've reported it to the authorities immediately.' She gripped the straps of her Louis Vuitton to stop her hands from shaking. Al-Huda studied her for several uncomfortable moments, then smiled without warmth.

'Your loyalty is commendable, chief justice, yet questions remain; who killed Gates and Al-Kaabi, and why?' He reached into his jacket pocket and handed her a business card. 'My personal number. Call me, day or night, if anything comes to mind.'

'Immediately,' she assured him.

He left the room without another word, leaving the door wide open. Davies hurried over and closed it. Edith leaned back in her chair. 'Fix me a drink, would you? A proper one.'

Davies handed her a tumbler of dark liquid. Edith swallowed it and placed it on the table. The brandy took the edge off almost immediately. She plucked a notepad from her bag, scribbled quickly, then showed it to Davies.

'A bug? No,' he told her, shaking his head. 'I have a

scanner, a left-over from the minister's office. I sweep this place every day, just in case. See where I rank on the trust scale. Pretty high, it would seem.'

'Then you were foolishly indiscreet,' she scolded him. 'I told you about the incident in China in confidence. Why did you repeat it?'

'I wasn't thinking,' Davies snapped back. 'He never mentioned Gates initially. He was asking about you, if you'd ever shared anything of a delicate nature, that sort of thing. I thought he already knew, that maybe it was a test, so I told him about the nuke. Jesus, these people make you paranoid, don't they?'

Indeed. Al-Huda's grilling had embarrassed her, made her feel soiled, dirty. She was reminded of her time as a young lawyer, defending society's bottom-feeders, watching them struggle with underdeveloped thought processes, their inarticulate and expletive-riddled protestations a sordid assault on her ears. Time spent with the underclass always made her feel unclean. Being spoken to like one had brought those feelings rushing back. Davies' voice cut through her depressive recollections.

'I'm sorry, Edith. Al-Huda caught me on the hop.'

'It's not your fault,' she lied. She'd held her nerve while Davies had lost his and blabbed. Today had truly been an education.

'Did you know Gates was having an affair with this Al-Kaabi?'

'Of course not,' she lied again.

'The Islamic Congress is deeply concerned. A delegate mentioned his name in our weekly meeting. They shut him down immediately.'

'Why?'

Davies shifted closer and spoke quietly. 'Al-Kaabi murdered someone at Northwood and stole sensitive data. Al-Huda told me before you arrived.'

'What data? And what were they doing in Buckinghamshire?'

Davies shrugged. 'He didn't say.'

Edith leaned back on the couch. Ireland was lost, and the Alliance was reinforcing in Scotland. There was a de facto war with China, the secret police were trying to discover who-knew-what about Al-Kaabi, and Congress was deeply troubled. The future didn't bode well.

She got to her feet and smoothed her headscarf. 'These are troubling times, Hugh. I need to go home, rest, allow all of this to percolate.'

Davies stood. 'Things look bleaker now than when we last met. We may need to rethink our plans.'

Edith cocked her head. 'Oh?'

'We should tread water. Not do anything that might antagonise the population.'

'It's rather late for that, don't you think?'

'I mean it, Edith. Cancel those crucifixions. Don't make things worse.'

'Worse?'

Davies stepped closer. 'What if Wazir abandons Britain? Have you thought about what they'd do to us if we get left behind?'

Edith smirked. 'Really, Hugh. You're letting your imagination run wild.'

'They'd lynch us, Edith, no question. Imagine that, you and I dangling from the same lamp post.'

She did and felt a shiver. 'Nonsense. Wazir is too heavily invested here.'

'Militarily, the caliphate is no match for the Americans. If they invade, it could go badly for us. I'm going to start deleting emails, just in case. The controversial stuff. I suggest you do the same.'

Edith's nose wrinkled in disgust. 'Do you seriously think that will make a difference?'

'It can't hurt. Then it's our word against any potential accusers. *Deny, deny, deny...* isn't that what we politicians are supposed to do?'

Edith glared at him. 'I've sent hundreds to the gallows, thousands more to prison. I'm a chief proponent of the deportation program, and even I have no idea where those people end up—'

She stopped talking. Davies was making no sense. He was a rabbit, caught in the headlights of a speeding car. She nodded her head. 'Yes, maybe you're right, Hugh. We must look to the future, make plans. Save ourselves.'

Davies took the bait. 'Absolutely, Edith. It makes sense, doesn't it? Why go down with a sinking ship?'

She made her excuses and left. As the Mercedes made its way north back to Hampstead, she thought of Davies, pictured him sweating at his computer, hammering the *delete* key, force-feeding documents into his shredder, his brow spotted with a fearful sweat. Edith Spencer would not indulge in such cowardly labours, she decided. She was too long in the tooth, too committed to the cause to turn away now.

Besides, she felt no loyalty to the country of her birth, to its people or institutions. Its culture had been deliberately diluted over many decades, a social engineering process designed to divide the populace, a clandestine policy that had paid dividends for her former political allies in Westminster and Brussels. What she was doing now, as Chief

Justice of the British Territories, was merely an extension of that work.

And those that would do her harm, who sought to rebel against their betters, who would dare to dream of lynching her from a lamp post, well, they would pay too.

And she would start with the traitor Bertie.

[16]

BYKER GROVE

FROM THE COBBLED COURTYARD OF AN ABANDONED manor house, the fixed-wing autonomous drone launched off its catapult rail and into the night sky, quickly reaching its cruising speed of 100 kilometres per hour. It climbed to an altitude of 1,200 feet and headed due south towards the city of Newcastle, just under 20 miles away. The drone's black-painted carbon fibre fuselage and tiny electric motor were undetectable to ground radar as it flew south through the cloudy night sky, sweeping above the no-man's-land of the frontier and into caliphate air space.

Its pre-programmed destination was a point in the sky above the playing fields of Gosforth Middle School, a scant three miles to the north of Newcastle city centre. As the drone approached from the north-east, it lost altitude, banking low and unseen over the A1 motorway, its on board delivery software running through its pre-drop checks. Satisfied that the system was functioning correctly, it sent a command to the small cargo bay doors beneath the aircraft. They flipped open, just as the plane swept low above the playing fields, and released the cargo inside the bay. Its mission complete, the aircraft banked to the north and climbed once more, heading back towards the military drone port from whence it came.

Hidden in the trees that bordered those same playing fields, Jed Drummond heard the whisper of the unseen drone overhead, and a moment later, saw the package swaying towards the grass beneath its mini-parachute. He left the safety of his hiding place and scampered out into the open. He moved fast and low, as he'd been taught, the eyes behind his balaclava sweeping left and right. He slid to halt on the wet grass, snatched up the parachute and the cardboard box it had carried to the ground, and sprinted back to the tree line.

Lost in the shadows once more, Jed turned and looked back across the playing fields. There were no shouts of alarm, no torches waving in the darkness. He didn't expect any either, because he'd been told that the caretaker would turn a blind eye and a deaf ear to anything that might happen within the grounds that night. Still, Jed waited another minute or two until he was sure, and then he picked his way carefully back through the trees towards the hole that had been cut in the chain-link fence. He squeezed his way through it and found his bike on the other side, propped against a tree. He shoved the parachute and cardboard box inside the backpack he was wearing, mounted his BMX bike, and cycled across the deserted, overgrown golf course until he reached the corner of Salters Lane. There he waited as he watched a police car cruise slowly past him, the cops inside oblivious to the finger Jed gave them from the leafy shadows. Then he waited a little longer until their lights were tiny red pinpricks in the distance.

After 15 more minutes of furious pedalling along deserted paths and pavements, Jed cycled into the alleyway at the rear of the shops on Field Street. He bumped open the gate with his front wheel and rolled his bike to the back of the brick building. As he approached, the door opened and a figure ushered him inside. Jed obeyed, rolling up his balaclava, and was led into a sizeable sitting room where a dozen adults waited for him. They greeted him with smiles and quiet words of appreciation, and a couple of them ruffled his thick red hair.

They gathered around as he shrugged off his backpack and handed over the cardboard box, its parachute still attached. Inside the box was a small plastic tube, and inside that, a sheet of yellow paper covered in letters and numbers. An older woman, Roz, the owner of the hairdressing business out front, took the paper and flattened it out on the coffee table. Then she began deciphering the code. Jed and the other adults watched as Roz worked her magic. When she finished, she repeated the process, just to be sure. Satisfied, she looked up at the surrounding faces, silent now, expectant. When she spoke, she looked at each of them and smiled.

'They're coming.'

EDDIE PARTED THE FILTHY CURTAINS AND PEERED AT the street below. Most of the cars parked there had been torched a long time ago and were now charred, rusting shells. The rest had flat tyres and broken windows, and in sills and vents, weeds flourished. Debris lay everywhere, strewn across the road and pavements, and piled in rotting heaps in overgrown front gardens; he saw shattered TVs, broken furniture, clothes, luggage, books, papers, photographs, all of it rotted and unsalvageable. People's lives, trampled beneath the boots of the caliphate army that had withdrawn south after they'd been stopped at the border. Where Eddie's brother Kyle had died. And as they'd retreated, they'd laid waste to every town they'd passed through, pillaging and destroying town centres, tearing up roads and rail lines, blowing bridges and buildings. And killing indiscriminately.

They'd found bodies on the approaches to Morpeth, the historic Northumberland market town the Second Mass now occupied. As they'd marched across the fields towards it, they'd discovered long-dead civilian corpses, most of them hairless and shrunken, their yellowed bones poking through rotten clothing. They found 30 or so piled on top of one another in a muddy ditch, and another dozen in the woods just north of town, dangling beneath the dark canopy like macabre Christmas decorations. Most had rotted and slipped their nooses but others remained, the ropes that had killed them creaking in the wind. The victims were mostly men, but there were some women and children amongst them too. The grid references were radioed in, and the burial teams would take care of the dead. Eddie didn't envy them.

The massacres had unnerved him, but Steve had taken it much harder, and his mood had darkened. Small talk was rare now; he'd withdrawn, only engaging when he needed to. Mac had spoken to him, but it was clear he wasn't doing great.

Neither am I, Eddie admitted to himself. He let the curtain drop back into place and flopped back down onto his roll mat. The rest of Nine Platoon was crammed into a small terraced house on an estate just south of the River Wansbeck. The whole of the battalion occupied the surrounding houses, and the other estates to the north and west of them housed other battalions of the Kings Continental Army, a British force of just under 10,000 men. Eddie wondered how many of them would still be alive in a week's time.

He picked up his notepad and pen and focussed on the letter he wanted to write. *We're going old school,* Mac had joked when he'd handed the basic writing materials out. Their mobile phones had been stored away with the rest of their personals, and the only electronic devices permitted were media players. Most of the guys around the room were plugged in now, lost in their own worlds. Eddie wanted to write instead. He chewed on the end of his pen as he thought about what he wanted to say to his parents. He couldn't tell them where he was or what he was doing so it really didn't leave that much to say. He was still thinking when Steve's voice interrupted his thoughts.

'Writer's block's a bitch, ain't it?'

His friend was stretched out on a roll mat, staring up at the weather-stained ceiling. 'I'm struggling,' Eddie admitted.

Steve sat up and leaned against the wall. 'What do you *really* want to tell them?'

Eddie didn't have to think too hard. 'I want to say sorry, I guess.'

'For what?'

'For volunteering. For being here. Losing Kyle devastated them, so when I signed up they went nuts. Mum cried for days and Dad wouldn't even look at me. All I cared about was doing my bit, enlisting like all the other lads. I didn't think twice about how my folks would feel, how they must be feeling now. Every time I call home, Mum breaks down and Dad's always got a reason why he can't come to the phone. I didn't realise how much pain I'd caused them.' Eddie tapped the pen on his pad. 'I want to tell them how sorry I am, tell them not to worry, that I'll see them again soon. Something like that.' Eddie stopped talking. He could feel the emotion starting to build.

Steve shook his head. 'Just tell 'em you're fine. Tell 'em the weather's great and that you visited Kyle's regimental monument up at the old border. Tell 'em things are quiet and you're bored. Tell them anything, just don't tell them how you feel. Keep all that shit buried until this is over.'

'Maybe you're right.' There was a quiet beat between them, then Eddie said, 'How about you? You've barely said a word these last few days.'

Steve folded his arms and stared at his boots, his eyes taking on a faraway look. 'When we saw those bodies in that ditch, the others hanging in the woods, I couldn't tear my eyes away. I was looking at the clothes, see? I thought I might recognise a coat, a scarf, something like that. I kept telling myself it couldn't be them; after all, what would my girls be doing way up here? But the invasion displaced millions, right? Maybe they were sent north to work, maybe—'

'Hey, you can't think like that,' Eddie cut in. 'You have to stay positive.'

Steve frowned. 'Have I been anything else up to this point? We all know about the atrocities, but seeing it with my own eyes—' He caught himself. When he spoke again, his voice had lost its edge. 'I've always believed that my girls were okay. If anything had happened to them, I'd know. I'd feel it here,' he said, tapping his chest. 'But now I know that's bullshit. So, I *have* to get home. I can't rest until I know.'

'Might be a while before we get that far south.'

'I know. My place is an hour's drive from here, but it might as well be a million fucking miles.'

They heard the stamp of boots and creaking stair treads. Mac appeared in the doorway in full battle-order, his face smeared with different shades of camo cream. Everyone in the room stirred. Digger unplugged his headphones.

'Well? What's the gen?'

Expectant faces stared at the section 2IC. A wide grin split the Scot's green and black face. 'You've got two hours to eat, shit, and square away your personal admin, because after that, the Kings Continental Army is heading for the frontier and we ain't coming back, not until we've driven those cunts into the English Channel.'

'About fucking time,' Digger said, snarling.

'When's the mission brief?' Eddie asked.

'When we get closer. Much closer.' Mac grinned again.

Steve shook his head. 'Don't fuck us about, big man. If you know something, tell us.'

Mac's grin slipped from his face. 'You heard me. Two hours, then we're moving, so get your shit together and start switching on. The boss will reveal all when we get to the RV.'

The rest of the section began breaking out their mess tins and rations. Eddie stared at his blank notepad and realised there was nothing to say. Steve was right, he would tell Mum and Dad to their faces, if he got back home. All he could think about right now was that frontier, and it made him feel nauseous. He jammed the notepad in his rucksack and rummaged for his rations instead.

'Don't sweat it,' Steve told him. 'You'll get another opportunity somewhere down the line.'

Eddie forced a smile. 'You're confident.'

'I'll swap you a chicken curry for a beef stew.'

Digger was dangling a packet of freeze-dried curry from his fingers. Eddie handed over the stew.

'Cheers,' Digger said, then he frowned. 'You all right, Eddie? You've gone a bit green.'

Eddie noticed some of the others look his way. 'I'm sick of rations.'

'We've only been on them two days.' Digger leaned closer, kept his voice low. 'Listen, whatever happens, we'll stick together, watch each other's backs, see this thing through. Got it?'

'I got it.'

He watched the youngster walk back to his bed space. *Youngster.* Digger was 18, a year younger than him, yet he'd read Eddie like a seasoned pro. They'd aged, all of them, since this thing had started. They weren't boys any more. They were older, wiser.

The question that haunted Eddie was, how much older would any of them get?

[17]
BERTIE SMALLS

BERTIE HURRIED ALONG THE PAVEMENT TOWARDS THE café on the Grays Inn Road. It was breezy, but the sky was clear and blue, and the temperature reasonably mild. Spring had almost sprung, but they weren't there yet. Bertie preferred the summer, not only for the weather but because The Witch liked to decamp to her modest estate in Cornwall for a month. She enjoyed the sea air, the country walks, and the seclusion of her private beach. The estate had been a gift from the Islamic Congress, and the first time he went there, Bertie wondered what had happened to the real owners. He didn't dwell on it, though. There was nothing he could do about it and besides, he enjoyed being there. Or rather, he *used* to enjoy it. The future was worryingly uncertain.

Two cop cars cruised past, windows open, suspicious eyes watching the pavements. Bertie had noticed a lot more of them on the streets lately, and a lot more soldiers too. The increased para-military presence seemed to confirm the rumours trickling down from the frontier; Alliance troops were landing in Scotland, and in big numbers, so maybe that wasn't suspicion he saw in those cops' eyes. Maybe it was fear. Bertie hoped so.

The news would help pile the pressure on Wazir, which meant that they might find a political solution. Maybe they'd all pack up and piss off back to the caliphate, but Bertie dismissed that thought. There were mobile rocket launchers in every park in London, tens of thousands of troops stationed around the capital, and according to the TV, more were coming across the channel every day. They were reinforcing, getting ready for a tear-up. If war was coming, it would get ugly.

Maybe George knew more. Bertie hadn't seen him since the night of the pickup, and he was nervous about meeting him. He figured that if George knew about his treachery he'd be in big trouble, but their association went back a long way. They'd work it out, somehow.

He pushed open the door of the café, and the scent of greasy food washed over him. He saw George sitting in a booth at the back of the restaurant. He weaved between the busy tables and sat down.

'Good to see you, George.'

'Bertie.'

George was plucking at French fries and dipping them into a blob of ketchup on his plate. He stared at Bertie as he munched his food. Bertie squirmed.

'Everything all right?'

George shrugged. 'You tell me.'

'What d'you mean?'

'What happened, Bertie? The night of the handover.'

He knows. 'There's nothing to tell, George. I picked 'em up and drove 'em to the meadow. Then the Yanks flew 'em off. And you should've seen the aircraft they used. Never seen anything—'

'So, it all went as planned,' George butted in.

'Of course.'

George wiped his fingers with a napkin, folded his thick arms, and leaned across the table. 'So why am I hearing that it was *you* who begged the Yanks for a ride out of here?'

Bertie swallowed. *Time for Plan B.* He held his hands up in surrender.

'Cards on the table? Yes, it's true, I tried to make a run for it. Do you know why? It was a double-cross, George. I caught Al-Kaabi talking on a phone. You said no phones, right? When I confronted them, Al-Kaabi pulled a gun. It all kicked off after that, and I only just fought 'em off. They were going to kill me, George.' He thought about Gates then, his bizarre and troubling death. It still haunted him.

'You're lying.'

'It's the truth.'

'Al-Kaabi was risking everything to get out.'

'No, George. He had us fooled, him and the poof. The whole thing was a set-up to expose the resistance. And yes, I tried to blag my way on board that transport because I panicked. That's the God's honest truth.'

'So, Gates was in on it too?'

'Defo. I told you, they were whispering in the car.'

George stared across the table. 'So, let me get this straight; Al-Kaabi and Gates faked a gay relationship to suck you into a conspiracy, the aim of which was to expose your involvement in the resistance. A conspiracy that also involved The Witch and Judge Hardy.'

'I know it sounds mad, but what else could it be?'

George leaned back in his seat and ordered a coffee. He said nothing, not until the waiter set the cup down in front of him. George sugared it and sipped it carefully. Then he glared at Bertie.

'Let me ask you a question; do you think I'm some sort of mug?'

Bertie shook his head. 'Of course not. What d'you mean?'

'If any of that lot thought you had something to do with the resistance, you'd be in a cell somewhere with your balls wired up to the mains.'

'Are you calling me a liar, George?'

George leaned across the table until his nose was almost touching Bertie's. 'Yes, I am. Because your story is a crock of shit. I think you killed them in cold blood, then you tried to buy your way out with Al-Kaabi's intel. After the Yanks fucked you off, you made up that ridiculous fairy tale to cover your tracks.'

'No, I—'

'Yes, you did. See, if you'd stuck to the plan, the love-birds would've flown the nest and nobody would've been any the wiser. Now the cops have got two bodies, one of them a military intelligence spy, and the other a homosexual who'll lead them right to The Witch's door. *Your* door, Bertie. And after they've lifted you, after they've shaved your Jaffas and run a couple of hundred volts through them, it'll be my name bouncing off the walls of that cell, won't it?'

Bertie's voice was a desperate whisper. 'I'd never grass you up, George, you know that.'

'I can't take that risk, Bertie. But don't worry,' he said, patting a large paw on Bertie's sleeve, 'I'm going to find somewhere safe for you to go. Where no one will ever find you.'

Bertie swallowed. 'Where?'

'Somewhere safe,' George repeated. He wiped his mouth with a napkin and stood. He pulled on a dark windbreaker and slipped on a pair of sunglasses, then he rapped a knuckle on the table. 'I'll be in touch.'

Bertie watched him go, realising that George had no intention of seeing Bertie to safety. None at all. He knew the man too well, knew his tells, like the knuckle on the table. George used that one back in the old days, a deliberate gesture, to signal his boys to get ready before the tables went over and the beer glasses started flying. Like a whistle, or a flare gun. Which meant someone was watching, listening. Which meant Bertie was finished.

You stupid idiot...

Bertie scrambled out of his seat and left the café. He hurried into a quiet residential street towards Holborn where the Toyota was parked. He'd barely gone 50 metres when he heard footsteps running behind him. Two men had followed him into the side street, slowing their pace when they saw him. One of them had a phone clamped to his ear. The other one, a sizeable lump with ginger hair, was trying his best to look casual and failing miserably. Bertie didn't recognise either of them, but he knew one thing for certain; George had sent them.

He kept his pace brisk but casual. There was another street a few metres ahead, and when he reached it, Bertie strolled around the corner. Then he sprinted along the pavement, arms and legs pumping, eyes searching for a hiding place. The third house along had an impressive, unkempt hedge outside and Bertie ducked into the gate and crawled behind it.

A few moments later, the runners pounded past his hiding place. After they'd faded, Bertie got to his feet. He took a careful peek along the pavement and saw his would-be assassins some distance away, looking around, heads swivelling left and right. Bertie crouched low and headed back the way he'd come. At the end of the road he turned right towards Holborn, and then he ran again, as fast as he could.

By the time he got to his car, he was sweating heavily and wheezing like an asthmatic. He started the Toyota, pulled out into the traffic and headed west, then north towards Bloomsbury Square. He saw a cop car passing in the opposite direction, and for the first time since the invasion, Bertie was glad to see them.

Fucking George, he simmered as he drove past St Pancras station and through the checkpoint. All those years they'd known each other, none of it counted for shit. Now Bertie was just another slag, another wrong 'un, a potential grass. That label hurt Bertie the most.

He parked the car in Belsize Park and bought some groceries from the supermarket on Haverstock Hill. Twenty minutes later, safely ensconced back behind The Witch's high Hampstead walls, Bertie washed the car again. He'd already washed it twice since he'd got back from Buckinghamshire, in a paranoid quest to remove every speck of mud, every blade of grass, every smear of blood that could implicate him in the murders. So, he scrubbed it again, inside and out, washing the seats with a mild detergent, hoovering them until he thought he might suck out the stitching. His journey that night couldn't be traced electronically, so he was in the clear on that front, but physically, he had to be sure. Just in case someone came knocking.

When he was done, he sat in the kitchen and chatted with Chef as he prepared dinner. Every other word was a curse or an expletive, but the man knew how to cook, and Bertie was happy to be his tasting guinea pig. He was just starting to relax when a bell chimed.

'No rest for the wicked,' Bertie said, getting to his feet. Chef laughed and called him a *lazy shitbag*.

He trudged upstairs, passing through the dark-panelled hallway to The Witch's study, passing the oils and water-colours on loan from the National Gallery. Now that Gates was gone, Bertie wondered if they'd ever be handed back. He knew nothing about fine art; all he saw were a lot of fat, naked birds and chubby cherubs, a lot of hazy sunsets and vases of flowers. All except one. It had never bothered Bertie before, but lately, it seemed to taunt him every time he walked past it, like one of those laughing cavalier paintings where the eyes followed you around the room.

It was a mediaeval representation of the crucifixion, Jesus and the thieves on either side of him, all dying under a dreary sky, a distraught, ashen-faced crowd at their impaled feet. It was stark and unnerving, and a shiver ran down Bertie's spine as he knocked on the study door.

Perhaps he'd give the car another wash, just in case.

HENRI PLATT AND JEAN MICHEL BROUGHT THEIR diesel locomotive to a screeching, clattering halt at the red light, a mere ten kilometres short of the Eurotunnel in northern France. Henri opened the window and looked down the length of the train. They'd stopped in a forest, which was good, Henri decided. At least they were out of sight. He picked up the radio-telephone and spoke to the line controller for less than a minute before hanging up.

Jean-Michel raised an expectant eyebrow.

'Trouble ahead,' Henri told him. 'We've been ordered to wait.'

'For how long?'

'A troop train has broken down at the tunnel entrance. Shut everything down. Residual power only.'

Henri heard whistles and stuck his head out of the window again. Soldiers were jumping down from the train and deploying into the surrounding woods. Above them, the overcast sky threatened rain. Henri hoped that was all it threatened.

'We're exposed here.'

Jean-Michel chuckled. 'Still worried about those American satellites?'

Henri grimaced but said nothing. He had a bad feeling, and this was the third incident that had forced them to interrupt their journey across France. Outside of Lyon, a soldier had fallen ill with appendicitis, forcing an unscheduled stop. Later, the train had hit a herd of deer as they'd motored through the Avesnois National Park. *And now this,* Henri fretted.

The broken-down train was ferrying a combat division to England. Those troops would have to detrain and the locomotive towed out of the way, a process that would take hours.

'Of all the places to break down,' Jean-Michel complained.

'Just our luck,' Henri agreed. 'They'll keep us here until sunset.'

'You think?'

'That's what I would do. No sense in crowding the terminal.'

'We'd make a nice fat target for the American cruise missiles, no?'

Henri gave him a withering look. 'Don't say such things.'

'I'm kidding.' Jean-Michel winked. He unwrapped a

cheese baguette and took a bite. 'A long time since I've been to England. Me and a few pals went to see France play England at Wembley once. It was a good time, a lot of fun. Doubt there's much to laugh about anymore.'

But Henri wasn't listening. Instead he leaned out of the window and looked down the length of the train. It curved out of sight, the last third lost behind the trees. Soldiers wandered beside the tracks, weapons held loosely, chatting, smoking. No one was expecting any trouble. He glanced back up at the sky.

No one except Henri.

[18]
THE FUSE

As soon as the MSS-2 had taken off from that Buckinghamshire meadow, the data that Al-Kaabi had killed and died for was sent via encrypted micro-burst to the NSA's dedicated communications hub at the Keflavik Naval Air Station in Iceland.

From there it was bounced to Fort Meade, Maryland, and within two hours of Bertie being forcibly ejected from the top-secret aircraft, military planners at *Site R*, the secret defence facility known as Raven Rock Mountain Complex in Adams County, Pennsylvania, were sifting through it. They knew that the military intelligence officer who'd stolen the data would already be compromised, so they had to move fast, trawling through the thousands of files, cherry-picking, debating, discarding. In time, intel specialists would pore over it byte by byte and extract anything useful that could be factored into future strategic planning. What they needed now, however, was a quick win.

It came in the form of the transcribed notes, previously hand-written by the now-dead Al-Kaabi, digitised at the naval station in Iceland, and almost overlooked by the planners. It was a record of a recent planning meeting held by senior intelligence staff at Northwood, a gathering that included one of the caliphate's top generals, Faris Mousa. In his notes, Al-Kaabi had described the atmosphere as tense, and the orders issued of the highest priority. It was just the opportunity the planners were looking for.

The conference table was swept clear. Digitised maps were projected onto the data wall, overlaid with weather charts, road and rail routes, and theatre-wide strategic assets maps, forming a digital tapestry of 21st-century military planning. A strategy was agreed upon, and a telephone call quickly followed. The president arrived from Camp David shortly thereafter, a six-mile journey made through the tunnel system that connected both facilities. The planners presented their commander-in-chief with a rapid, detailed brief. The president listened for several minutes, asked a dozen pertinent questions, then ordered Prime Minister Harry Beecham to be dialled into the briefing.

From his own secure facility outside of Boston, Harry and his military team watched the video presentation. The window of opportunity would only be open for so long, he learned. Ultimately, the decision was his, the president told him. *Your backyard, your people.*

Harry Beecham didn't blink.

Do it.

THE ORDER WAS RECEIVED 2,500 MILES AWAY IN Iceland at the US Air Force DABS, located in a dark, icy valley near the rugged north-east coast of the island. The Deployable Air Base System comprised a collection of transportable pods, shipping containers, and vehicles that could be deployed anywhere on the planet and stand up as a fully operational airbase without the need to plug into local utilities. *Airbase-in-a-box,* they called it, and the site located deep inside the narrow Hallestrom Valley was self-sufficient and about as covert as they could make it. Hidden beneath a vast roof of emission-reflecting camouflage netting and panels, the DABS was invisible to prying electronic eyes. And it needed to be, because it was a temporary home to two of the US air force's most secretive and expensive aircraft ever built.

The Northrop-Grumman B-21 Raiders rolled out of their hardened shelters and on to the two-mile stretch of arrow-straight civilian tarmac road widened and strengthened to accommodate a range of military aircraft. The Raiders were state-of-the-art stealth bombers, but unlike the MSS-2, these aircraft were powered by twin F-140 jet engines, albeit quiet, fuel-efficient, and hugely powerful. Like the MSS-2, however, the Raiders used a level of stealth technology unrivalled on planet Earth. Built with composite materials and incorporating an entire range of radiation, acoustic, and thermal absorbing technologies, the Raiders could fly low and slow, high and subsonic, yet never emit a signature bigger than a small flock of tiny birds. An anti-aircraft system had yet to be developed that could detect a Raider, and that included most of the American ones.

Looking similar to their predecessor, the B-2 Spirit bomber, the Raiders were matte black, had no tail fins, and resembled a large sweeping wing that bulged slightly in the centre of the airframe. Inside that bulge, the pilots manoeuvred their aircraft until they lined up one behind the other down the centre line of the empty Icelandic road.

The lead aircraft was nicknamed *Doolittle* after the famous World War Two raid on Tokyo. Inside the cockpit, the pilots sat quietly, their eyes scanning the high-tech instrumentation panels and touch screens, the Raider's engines whistling on low power as the pilots waited for the order. Two hundred metres behind *Doolittle*, the crew in the other Raider, *Hornet,* did the same. Across the snow-capped valley, they received the order from Raven Rock inside the communication pod and passed it on to the mobile ATC trailer. Moments later, *Doolittle* and *Hornet* received the launch order.

Ahead of them, runway lights blazed into life. Throttles were pushed to their stops, and *Doolittle's* engine exhaust ports glowed blue as it cleared the artificial roof and acceler-ated towards the mouth of the valley. Ten seconds behind it, *Hornet* did the same, rocketing along the tarmac. A few moments later, the Raiders were airborne, wheels up, and climbing into the freezing night sky.

Within seconds, they were lost to the naked eye.

A moment after that, they were lost to the world.

The Hilton Newcastle Gateshead Hotel was located on the southern bank of the Tyne River, between the Tyne Bridge to the east and the high-level railway crossing immediately to the west. Before the invasion, it was an establishment popular with shoppers, wedding parties, and professional footballers on a night out, and one of the few hotels to have escaped the violence and destruction as caliphate forces had descended on the city prior to the border war. As they'd returned defeated, still the hotel had remained untouched, commandeered instead as an upmarket accommodation venue for the caliphate's more senior army officers. Throughout the occupation, it had maintained its status, although now most of its guests were traitors and quislings from the Regional Assembly, including senior local cops who policed the city by consent of the caliphate.

'A den of vipers,' Roz muttered as she shut off the van's engine. None of the seven armed and masked men sat behind her said anything. There was no need, because Roz was merely stating the obvious. Newcastle was a divided city, split between those who had embraced the opportunities the fall of Europe had presented, and those who had no choice but to deal with it. The former group comprised local politicians, business people, and civil servants, most of whom had asked *how high* when told to jump by their new masters. But not all.

In the weeks after the border war, some had rebelled against the invaders. To the horror of most decent Geordies, those rebels were executed on the pitch inside St. James' Park football stadium, along with several dozen captured British soldiers. The authorities had removed the goalposts in front of the Gallowgate stand and replaced them with a row of thick wooden stakes. That day, 123 men and women were shot, and those few hundred local citizens forced to watch had never forgotten. Roz had been one of those witnesses and had seen her husband's torso ripped apart by the firing squad's bullets. Jed's mum and dad had been murdered too, a tragedy that had brought them together. Only death would part them now.

Roz leaned over the wheel of the van, her eyes roaming the night outside. She'd parked beneath an arch of the Tyne railway bridge, unseen in its black shadows. Between the arch and the hotel, a wintry wind drove silver sheets of rain across the service area. The security lights were few, and staff smokers were nowhere to be seen, which didn't surprise Roz. They were probably too busy servicing the meeting that was being held in the *Windows on the Tyne* restaurant on the top floor of the hotel.

The governor of the North-East Territories had gathered his assembly of traitors together, no doubt to address their concerns. Ireland had been liberated and Alliance troops were landing in Scotland. The frontier was only eight kilometres away, just beyond the former Newcastle International Airport, now a sprawling military camp. North of that installation lay the oceans of razor wire, the fields of land mines, the surveillance towers, and the hunter drones. In the dark hill beyond that, the forces of freedom were gathering. The traitors knew it too. And they would be worried.

'They'll be well pissed by now,' Roz muttered, looking up at the top floor of the hotel. Rain fell through the roof lights.

'Alright for some,' grumbled a man behind her. 'I haven't had a drink in three years.'

'That's about to change,' one of the others told him.

Roz checked the clock on the instrument panel. Almost 11 pm. It was time to move. She turned in her seat. The seven men in black assault vests, ski masks, and armed with M4 carbines, waited for the resistance leader to give them the nod.

'You know what to do,' she told them. 'Jed will give you the signal.'

She pulled up the collar of her dark raincoat and slipped out of the van. The passenger door opened and Jed climbed out too. Roz held an umbrella aloft, took the ten-year-old's hand and headed out of the shadows and across the rain-swept service area. Ahead of them were the security doors, handle-less and sealed against the elements. Roz peeled away and Jed ran towards them. She got down on the soaking tarmac, her legs and arms sprawled. Jed's small fist pounded against the security doors.

'Help!' he yelled, his voice almost drowned by the rain.

He kept thumping. After a moment, light flooded the service area. Roz heard a gruff voice. 'What's the matter?'

'It's me mam, she fell over! Please help her!'

She heard the security guard swear, heard his shoes splashing through the puddles towards her, and then he was kneeling by her side. 'Are you all right, luv?'

He turned her over. Roz jammed a pistol under the man's chin. 'If you want to live, keep your mouth shut and do exactly as I say.' She got to her feet and forced the guard towards the doors. Jed was flashing a torch towards the bridge, and seconds later, the van pulled up sharply by the service entrance, the armed men piling out and streaming into the hotel. Roz jabbed the gun in the guard's spine. 'Move.'

Her people moved fast, breaking up the security guards' poker game and disabling the fire alarm and telephone systems. Inside the security suite, the terrified night shift were relieved of their phones and shoved at gunpoint into a store cupboard. A can of petrol was poured across the floor around their feet, soaking their shoes and trousers. Roz warned them to say and do nothing or they'd burn to death inside the locked room. Roz could tell by their faces they believed her.

With their escape route secured and young Jed watching the CCTV with a radio at the ready, she led the others out into the corridor. They waited silently as she checked her phone. *This is it,* she realised, *the moment we've all been waiting for.* Her heart thumped as her eyes flicked between the signal bars of her mobile phone and the clock on the wall. The second hand flicked up towards the hour. Roz waited, her chest rising and falling fast.

The clock struck 11 pm. She looked at her phone.

No Signal.

She held it up for the others to see. 'And so it begins.'

Roz tugged down her ski mask and moved quickly towards the service lift. They crammed inside, and one man stabbed the button for the *Windows on the Tyne* restaurant. They cocked their weapons and flipped off their safeties as the lift hissed upwards. Hearts beat fast, including Roz's. She thought of her husband then, her beloved Brian, his face ashen beneath his blindfold, her name the last word screamed from his lips before he died. She'd loved him dearly and missed him every day. She gripped the pistol in her hand as the lift slowed, the spike of raw emotion now smothered by a cold, vengeful fury.

Because tonight there would be a reckoning.

Tonight, the uprising would begin.

HENRI STABBED THE STARTER BUTTON AND BROUGHT the powerful diesel locomotive into life. His crew had spent most of the day checking the train, the air lines, the couplings, then chatting, smoking, and pissing against trees in the surrounding woods where the guards patrolled, watching for dog walkers and ramblers.

Finally the call had come. The broken-down engine had been cleared from the tunnel, and now that the sun had set, Henri's train had been given priority by military command. Ahead, through the driver's window, the distant signal light glowed green.

'About time,' Jean-Michel said, releasing the brake.

Henri felt the diesel engine shudder as the forward

motion rippled along the 700-metre-long train behind him. Wheels spun on well-worn tracks, then bit. Black smoke belched, and the train started to move. Henri slid open the window and watched as the distant munitions cars rumbled through the darkening forest. All its lights were extinguished, and as the driver's engine cleared the trees, empty fields stretched away on either side of the track. On the horizon, a thin band of blood-red sky was all that remained of the day. Nightfall was upon them, and the darkness was their friend. That's what Henri told himself, though he knew it to be a lie. Instead, he focussed on the task ahead.

'Eight kilometres to the tunnel entrance,' Jean-Michel reported.

Henri checked the routing screen. 'They've reduced our transit speed. It'll take us around 50 minutes to get through.'

Jean-Michel nodded, then said, 'You think if this lot blew it would bring down the tunnel roof?'

Henri felt his stomach lurch. The thought had crossed his own mind, but he was no engineer. Besides, they were safe beneath the sea bed, at least until they cleared the tunnel. 'Let's just worry about getting to our destination.'

'Have you ever been to Banbury?'

'I've never heard of it.'

'A guard told me it's the biggest munitions dump in Europe. If you ask me, there's going to be trouble. I heard a rumour that—'

'I don't want to hear about rumours,' Henri snapped. The co-driver gave his boss a Gallic shrug and studied the track ahead. Henri softened his tone. 'Let's just deliver our cargo and get back home, okay?'

'You're the boss, boss.'

The train clattered toward the unseen tunnel complex somewhere in the distance. Before the invasion, the Eurotunnel terminal could be seen for miles at night, its giant cluster of arc lights visible from space. Now it was a world of shadows and bristled with mobile anti-aircraft guns and SAM batteries. Henri watched one such unit sliding past his window, some sort of tracked vehicle parked behind a nearby farmhouse, its pepper-pot launch pod pointed at the night sky. It wasn't the only one Henri noticed as the train made slow but steady progress towards the terminal.

'You okay, boss?'

'We're approaching one of the biggest strategic targets in Europe,' Henri told him. 'You should be worried too.'

'It's not been hit in three years. I guess the English don't want to cut the cord either.'

'That doesn't make me feel any better,' he said, searching the night sky through his window. Then he saw the hillside looming out of the darkness ahead, the gaping circular entrance to the westbound tunnel marked by green lights. Henri slid the window open and leaned out. Maintenance engineers stood in ghostly groups by the tracks, watching them. They wore hard hats and overalls, their faces barely visible. They reminded Henri of mourners, gathered by the graveside as the train descended beneath the earth.

Another omen. Henri swallowed. He slammed the window shut.

'You worry too much,' Jean-Michel told him. 'Besides, you can't exactly refuse to do the job, right? Not unless you want to be sent east.'

'Don't talk like that!' Henri snapped again, but he knew his co-driver was right. Refusal to serve the caliphate often resulted in deportation. Where those people ended up, God alone knew.

The track ahead sloped towards the tunnel, and then

the engine was inside, the roar thundering off the smooth concrete walls. Two hundred metres ahead he saw the tunnel all lit up, and Henri finally relaxed. He knew the tension would build again once they reached Folkestone, but at least there was some respite from the danger. They were on the last leg of the journey, and as far as Henri was concerned, the most dangerous. The British were arrogant and rebellious, and the only force in the whole of Europe who'd stopped the caliphate army cold. Maybe word had reached them that a huge shipment was coming their way. Maybe they planned to attack his train somewhere between Folkestone and Oxfordshire. So many unknowns.

The track ahead continued its downward angle, and Henri looked out of the window again as the tunnel swallowed the train. He caught a final glimpse of the French night sky.

He couldn't shake the feeling that he'd never see it again.

[19]
ADVANCE TO CONTACT

THE NIGHT SKY WAS CLEAR OF ENEMY EYES. INSTEAD, the troops on the ground were being monitored by their own satellites and orbiting drones, watching over them like the ancient gods of Olympus as they swarmed through the broken streets of Morpeth.

Mac led Three Section through unlit alleyways and abandoned housing estates, where walls and fences had been dismantled to speed their passage. At crossroads, intersections, and other choke points, military policemen waved glow wands, demanding their silence, urging them forward, wishing them luck. They moved swiftly across the railway tracks and onto the industrial estate at the edge of town, the frigid night air alive with the drum of booted feet, the rustle of clothing, the rattle of equipment and weapons.

As he jogged behind Steve, Eddie noticed more destruction here, more burned out vans and warehouses, and then the night sky disappeared beneath a ceiling of thermal panel netting suspended between the buildings. Eddie saw it then, the dark entrance ahead, the shadows of Charlie

Company vanishing inside its gaping mouth like plankton sucked into a giant whale. Moments later, he was crossing the threshold.

The interior of the warehouse was unlit, and a road of rubber matting marked with green luminous discs absorbed the rumble of their boots. The air reeked of mud and metal, and Eddie glimpsed giant machinery looming in the shadows of the warehouse, industrial monsters covered in rust and dirt. There were more MPs ahead, waving more glow-wands and guiding them down a wide tunnel that dipped beneath the earth. Harsh whispers ordered them to *keep moving, stay in your groups, no talking!*

All Eddie could see were helmets bobbing in the darkness, from wall to curved wall. He could feel himself sinking lower beneath the earth, but the sensation didn't bother him. In fact, since the mission brief, he'd felt elated. *No, wrong word,* he cautioned himself. *Relieved.* That was it. And he wasn't the only one. That feeling wouldn't last though, he knew that.

They kept moving, ever downward, hundreds of soldiers in front and behind, the whole of the Second Mass. After a couple of minutes, he saw a bright white light ahead, and then the ground beneath their feet levelled out. As it did, the rail terminal came into view, a huge cathedral of light and concrete that arched over their heads.

The pace slowed as the Second Mass filed up onto a wide platform flanked by monorail lines that stretched for 200 metres towards the distant tunnel. They'd been told to expect a marvel of engineering. Those expectations were duly fulfilled.

They moved along the platform, staying between the bright yellow safety lines. Logistics Corps NCOs wearing orange vests directed the troops towards the far end of the terminal. Eddie saw a huddle of senior battalion officers, decked out in full combat gear and helmets, talking in hushed tones as they consulted data tablets. Colonel Butler was among them, arms folded, head nodding, his eye-patch barely visible beneath the grey and black streaks smeared across his face. On the walls, huge blue arrows pointed towards the far end of the platform, and stencilled words encouraged the soldiers to *Keep Moving! Observe Noise Discipline!*

Halfway along the platform they slowed, finally rippling to a halt, and Eddie found himself standing just behind the yellow line. He looked down and saw the raised steel line, the concrete floor beneath spotted with oil and pools of dirty water. Along the crowded platform, he saw Alpha Company to his right, HQ Company to his left, everyone else crammed in between. Beyond the HQ lads, hundreds more soldiers were streaming out of the darkness of the down-ramp and crowding onto the platform. That would be the 216th Pennsylvania British Volunteers, Eddie knew. Somewhere behind them would be three regiments of the US Army's 2nd Infantry Division, all of whom would roll through this tunnel during the night.

'How far down d'you think we are?' he heard Digger whisper.

'Couple of hundred metres at least,' Mac said from the corner of his mouth. 'This place is something else, ain't it?'

'It's a get-out-of-jail card,' Steve agreed.

'Keep the chatter down,' a voice said somewhere behind them.

Eddie looked to his right. There wasn't much to see other than the string of faint blue tunnel lights that seemed to stretch into infinity. After a moment, he felt a gust of warm air on his face, and digital wall displays began flashing: *Caution! Train Approaching.*

'Here it comes.' Steve pointed, and Eddie saw the blue lights being swallowed by something dark that filled the tunnel. The breeze picked up then, swirling around the 800 men of the Second Mass, and then the driverless train was whistling into the terminal, towing dozens of open flat-bed cars behind it. The train slowed, then stopped. A low hum filled the station.

'It's a Maglev,' Eddie told them, watching the train ripple as it bounced on the magnetised air of the rail beneath it.

'Fast and quiet,' Mac said. 'Just what the doctor ordered.'

The orange vests directed everyone aboard the flat-beds. Eddie scrambled over the side and moved across to the far side of the open carriage before sitting on the thick rubber matting. Digger dropped in front of him, his assault pack between Eddie's legs, then Steve and Mac, until they were squeezed in tight. The carriages filled quickly, and Eddie saw Butler again, joined by the RSM, walking along the carriages, chatting quietly, slapping a few shoulders, exchanging a few brave smiles. He'd be there, with them, once they were back on the surface.

On the wall, departing signs flashed.

'Here we go,' Digger said.

The orange vests stepped back behind the yellow line. Then the train was moving, almost silently, leaving the station behind as the tunnel crowded in around them. Eddie's ears popped, and he felt himself sinking as the train accelerated and the tunnel dipped further beneath the earth. The walls flashed by, blue lights flicking past at speed. *Twenty-one kilometres long*, Eddie recalled the OC telling them, a journey of roughly 25 minutes. It was the sweetest train ride Eddie had ever experienced.

The wind whipped past them as the train hummed almost silently through the tunnel. The blue wash of light that filled the tunnel suddenly changed to bright yellow, and they all knew what that meant:

Frontier approaching.

Helmets tilted towards the ceiling. A minute later, the yellow was replaced by a hellish red...

Above them, the frontier itself.

The train kept moving, banking left and right, the air rushing through the tunnel. The red lights stayed with them, a reminder they were now in a combat zone. The train slowed, the tunnel roof fell away, and Eddie found himself inside another vast terminal bathed in the glow of red overheads. More orange vests helped them out of the carriages, and Eddie stepped onto the platform, working the blood back into his legs. They formed back up into companies, and then they were moving again, towards a huge concrete wall 200 metres distant.

At this end, the terminal roof was lower, and the concrete walls had a rough, unfinished look, Eddie noticed. Beneath his boots, mud squelched between the holes of the rubber matting. He passed medics gathered outside the inflatable tents of a mobile hospital unit, and orange vests swarming over mountains of supplies and equipment. He passed a long row of tracked M5 Ripsaws, Unmanned Fighting Vehicles armed with a mixture of 30-millimetre auto-cannons and Avenger hydraulic Gatling guns. He passed other specialist units too; drones and their operators, combat signals teams with their radio masts and satellite dishes, quartermasters loading dozens of six-wheeled Unmanned Ground Vehicles with ammunition and supplies.

The tide of the Second Mass swept him along, then it slowed as the end of the tunnel loomed. The wall was made of the same rough concrete, the rectangular opening at least fifty metres wide and ten metres high. Beyond it, Eddie saw the glow of green chem lights and nothing else. Above the opening, a massive sign edged in black-and-yellow warning stripes read:

YOU ARE NOW ENTERING A COMBAT ZONE!

EDDIE CRANED HIS NECK AND WATCHED ALPHA Company disappear inside. Bravo Company shuffled up towards the opening, and Charlie Company followed. A Logistics Corps sergeant walked past them, talking low, his Brummie accent strong.

'Last chance, lads. You need anything, more ammo, grenades, first-aid gear, chem-sticks, batteries, speak now or forever hold your peace.'

He kept moving. Mac turned to Three Section and said, 'Radio and equipment check. Buddy up and get it done.'

Steve grabbed Eddie and began a visual check of his gear and equipment. He spun him around, checked his assault pack, tac-vest, his exoskeleton mounts. He slapped him on the shoulder.

'You're good.'

Eddie returned the favour and then there was nothing

more to say, nothing to do but wait their turn. Eddie flexed his fingers to stop his hands from shaking. Some of it was fear, yes, but mostly it was adrenaline. *Focus on the mission,* he urged himself.

Equipment-wise, he was in the best shape possible. His Advanced Combat Helmet was virtually indestructible, ballistic glasses shielded his eyes, and Kevlar plates protected his chest, back, and groin. He wore shoulder, elbow, knee, and shin pads, and he carried NVGs and a respirator. He wore combat gloves and waterproof boots, and his uniform was water-resistant and flame retardant. He was carrying 180-rounds of 5.56mm for his M27, plus flares and four frag grenades. He carried his SIG Sauer P226 pistol on his war belt, and the exoskeleton would make it all feel like nothing much at all. He wore his IR Velcro patches with his blood group and the coiled snake logo of the Second Mass, and he wore his Union Jack right there on his chest. He was good to go, as ready as he'd ever be.

His chest rose and fell. He felt the adrenaline pumping, energising him, filling him with an unbridled urge to explode into action.

'Charlie Company, move up!'

The dark opening beckoned. Separated by two-minute intervals, the platoons disappeared inside. Finally, it was Nine Platoon's turn. An orange vest staff-sergeant held them at the entrance.

'Check your safeties, make sure they're on. When I give the word, follow the green chem-lights. Green path only, understood?' He checked his watch, then pointed into the opening. 'Go.'

Eddie followed Mac into the darkness. They were in single file now, and suddenly the tunnel walls were no longer smooth concrete but shored up with metal plates and huge timber braces. The ceiling was lower now, and the rubber flooring squelched beneath their feet as they snaked through the damp tunnel, following the trail of luminous green discs fixed along the rough walls. The air was stale and thick, and Eddie felt like he was in a mine shaft. Orange vests waited at intersections, guiding them onwards. Eddie slowed behind Mac as they entered a large, square concrete chamber. Tunnels headed off in several directions, round concrete tubes marked by yellow, green, red, blue, and purple chem lights. Rainwater fell from a rusted grate in the ceiling and ran beneath their feet. The warning signs here were smaller but no less urgent:

NO TALKING! NO RUNNING! SAFETIES ON!

WAITING SOLDIERS CHECKED THEIR UNIT designations, then directed them onwards. The tunnel twisted to the left, and Eddie saw a red torchlight waving ahead. A wide ladder descended from the darkness above and Eddie followed Mac as he pulled himself up it. At the top, waiting soldiers manhandled them to one side. Eddie found himself in a sizeable basement room, with pipes running across the ceiling. The hole he'd just climbed out of was a jagged gash in the concrete floor, and he watched the rest of the section clambering out of the storm drains below.

'Keep moving.'

Eddie followed Mac out into the corridor and up a narrow flight of stairs. Then they were crossing a large, high-ceilinged corporate office space that looked like it had been mothballed since the invasion. The windows were boarded up, and the furniture piled against one wall was covered with dust sheets. Stacked in the centre of the room were hundreds of boxes of ammunition and crates of supplies. The OC held them until Nine Platoon had assembled, and then he sent them down another corridor towards a large, heavy door. They lined up along the wall and took a knee.

'This is it,' Steve whispered. 'We stick together, okay?'

'Zip it,' Mac said over his shoulder.

Eddie looked behind him, saw Digger wink beneath his helmet. He turned back, held his M27 a little tighter.

The dark knot of soldiers gathered at the door were watching a small TV feed. After a few seconds, one of them broke away and waved Mac forward. Eddie was on his feet and moving right behind him.

The door to the outside world was thrown open, and a cold, damp wind barrelled along the corridor. Eddie glimpsed a narrow alleyway, the rain falling between the dark, damp buildings. Mac ducked left into the rain. Eddie gave him a count of three and then he was moving too.

The alleyway was long and dark, but there was enough ambient light from the street ahead to operate safely. He hurried to the end where Mac knelt in the shadows. Eddie saw shops across the street, the light poles shining brightly, the rain gusting through them, falling on a row of parked cars. *Normality* was his first impression of the scene. That was about to change.

He heard more boots behind him, then Digger's hand slapped his shoulder. Three Section were ready and waiting.

Mac turned around, the rain dripping off his helmet, his painted face grinning.

'Time to go to work,' he whispered, and then he was up and running.

Eddie followed, his heart beating fast, his eyes watching the road, the pavements, the windows above, praying that the thousands of British troops now moving quietly into position across the deserted streets of Newcastle city centre would pass unnoticed.

[20]

KNOCK ON WOOD

HER PRIVATE STUDY WAS ONE OF EDITH'S FAVOURITE rooms in the Hampstead house. She loved her floor-to-ceiling bookshelves, the brass lamps that threw warm pools of light across her antique desk and across the vivid water-colours that lined the wood-panelled walls, and she loved the tall windows, framed by heavy, wine-coloured drapes that overlooked the distant city. It was a quiet space, intimate, a room where one could reflect, a room where she'd made many important decisions throughout her career. And today was no exception.

Edith had thought long and hard about her next move. She'd balanced the potential loss of a valuable asset against the vicious stab of betrayal and concluded that the sensible option would be to maintain the status quo, to keep the good ship Spencer on an even keel. But the waters ahead were troubled, and one had to navigate a careful course if she was to make port safely. It was why she'd asked Victor to join her, because, for one of the few occasions in her life, she'd sought counsel from a friend. And besides, Victor was a co-

conspirator and just as keen to draw a line under the whole sordid affair.

'He'll be here in a moment,' she told him.

Across the desk, Victor occupied a chair positioned at a slight angle to the empty one directly facing her own.

'I think you're making the right decision,' he told her. 'Best to tie up loose ends. Especially now, considering the caliphate's recent troubles.'

'You seem remarkably unconcerned, Victor.'

The white-haired judge advocate smiled. 'France beckons, my dear.'

'You're retiring?'

'Margaret and I have spoken at length. We feel it's time.'

Edith sat back, winded. Victor had always been a powerful ally, and like her, had embraced the Great Liberation while making the most of the opportunities that had presented themselves. A survivor, also like her.

'Provence has never looked lovelier. Come and join us, Edith. I can talk to the local *agent immobilier* if you'd like.'

'France,' Edith echoed, her mind conjuring up visions of lavender fields, of rolling hills and endless summers. Perhaps Victor was right, perhaps the time was approaching. And she'd be safe there. The caliphate has always considered France to be a colony of itself. Wazir would never consider pulling out of that country. 'It's tempting,' she had to agree, 'but there's work to be done here first.'

'Yes, those loose ends.' He turned towards the respectful tap on the door. 'Ah, perfect timing.'

Edith adjusted the brooch on the lapel of her black suit, a small crystal spider, and sat a little straighter in her leather chair. 'Come.'

Bertie entered the room and paused by the door. 'You rang, Lady Edith?'

She gestured towards the empty seat next to Victor. 'Sit, please Bertie.' She kept her voice even, her face neutral. She saw Bertie hesitate for just a moment, then he crossed the room and sat down. Victor smiled and nodded.

'How are you, Bertie?'

'I'm fine, Judge Hardy.'

Edith folded her arms on her desk and studied her manservant before she spoke. 'Do you like living here, Bertie?'

'Of course, Lady Edith. It's an honour.'

'I've been good to you, no? Provided food and lodging, a decent wage. You've enjoyed the privileges and freedoms that have come with your employment, yes?' Bertie nodded, and Edith's eyes narrowed. 'So why do you continue to deceive me?'

'I don't know what—'

'Liar!' she screeched, and Bertie flinched as if someone had slapped him. 'You told me Timmy had passed away peacefully at home, but that's not the truth, is it?'

Victor wore a wicked smile on his face. 'Think carefully before you answer, Mister Payne. The next words out of your mouth might well decide your fate.'

She watched Bertie deflate. He hung his head and twisted his hands. Edith slapped her desk. 'Speak!'

Her manservant flinched again, then the words tumbled from his mouth. 'I'd only been in the flat two minutes when Al-Kaabi showed up. I tried to make my excuses and leave but Al-Kaabi pulled a gun. He forced me to tell him every-thing. Mr Gates was very upset.'

Edith felt a flush of shame. Timmy had gone to his grave

knowing that she'd betrayed him. 'How did you end up in Buckinghamshire?'

'Al-Kaabi made me drive him there. He said he had friends up that way. When we got there, he forced me out of the car. I thought he was going to kill me, so I lunged at him. We struggled...'

He looked at Edith with pleading eyes, and he reminded her of the criminals who'd stood in her dock and expressed that same emotion. *Desperation.*

'So, you killed them both.'

'I didn't have a choice, ma'am. It was them or me.'

'An unnerving ordeal, I'm sure. Who else knows of these adventures? Chef, perhaps?'

Bertie shook his head. 'No, ma'am, I've told no one. I swear.'

She caught Victor's eye across the table and saw the man was quietly fuming.

'And what you've told me is the absolute truth, Bertie? You've left nothing out?'

'No ma'am. That's how it happened. There was no one else involved.'

'I see.' Edith took a breath and sighed. 'Well, in that case, there's no harm done. You can go, Bertie.'

'Thank you, ma'am. Sir,' he said, half bowing to both of them before scuttling from the room. Edith let him get to the door before she called him.

'Make yourself available for the next few days, would you, Bertie? No trips into town, no leaving the house in fact.'

She saw his face cloud. 'Ma'am?'

'Others may wish to talk to you. The authorities. Do you understand?'

He stared at her for a moment, the blood draining from his face. 'Yes, Lady Edith. I understand.'

'Good. Tell Chef there'll be two for dinner this evening, 8 pm sharp.'

'Yes, ma'am.'

Bertie closed the door, and Edith leaned back in her chair. 'Well, what d'you think?'

'Guilty,' Victor decided, snipping the end off a large cigar.

'As sin,' Edith agreed. 'Come, let's adjourn to the reception room. I think a large whiskey is in order.'

'Excellent.' Victor smiled, getting to his feet. 'A shame, though. Good help is often hard to come by.'

'Chef has recommended a replacement, a chap called Tucker. The driver-bodyguard type.'

'Sounds like a solid chap.'

'But you're right, Victor, loyalty is a precious commodity, and I'm afraid Bertie has shown very little, despite everything I've done for him.'

Victor held the door open. 'Ungrateful bugger.'

Edith smiled. 'Indeed. And he shall rue the day he betrayed me.'

Bertie closed his door and leaned against it. His heart hammered in his chest, and a ring of sweat stained the collar of his white shirt. *She knows*, he realised. Her anger had been visible, her parting words as cold as ice. Bertie was done, finished, just like Gates. It was just a matter of time before they came for him.

But not tonight. He still had time. He had something else, too.

A plan.

Hope for the best and plan for the worst, that's what his mum had often told him. Bertie had remembered that advice shortly after he'd moved into The Witch's Hampstead residence, when he'd discovered how cruel she'd become. The invasion had brought out the worst in some people, and The Witch was no exception, embracing the opportunity for unbridled barbarity. The power of life and death had gone to the vicious old hag's head. She was enjoying herself, Bertie had realised a long time ago. He'd also realised that eventually, it would all come on top.

He crossed the room and removed a large sandwich of clothes from the cupboard. These were the clothes he never wore, the stack of underwear, vests, t-shirts, hiking trousers, and fleeces that were clean and sealed in a clear plastic bag. He yanked a black rucksack from beneath the bed and packed the clothes inside, adding two towels and a bag of toiletries. The pockets of the rucksack were already stuffed with camping essentials, and Bertie zipped it all up and stashed it back inside the wardrobe.

Having a plan and taking physical action helped to calm his jangling nerves. The sound of clattering pans echoed along the corridor outside. Bertie checked his watch; Chef was starting preparations for dinner, which Bertie would serve at eight, as ordered. Afterwards, he'd wait for the vile old bitch to retire for the evening, and when the house was quiet, he would fill a bag full of food and drink, take it to the garage, and put it in the Toyota, along with his tent and sleeping bag.

Then he would return to the house one last time. He would don an apron and a pair of rubber gloves and tread quietly up to The Witch's chamber. Once inside, and with Chef's favourite boning knife in his gloved hand, he would slice Edith Spencer's shrivelled neck wide open.

Afterwards, he would drive to Hertfordshire, where Bertie used to do a fair bit of fishing back in the day. He knew of two quiet spots, where the water was dark and deep, and that's where the Toyota would go. Then he would make his way north on foot, up through Cambridgeshire, camping as he went, lying low, sticking to the woods and fields. And when he crossed the border into Lincolnshire, when he finally made it to his uncle's farm – and if the old bugger was still alive – he would get his head down and wait. He would work the land, tend the animals, mend the fences, *anything* – until the sound of guns rumbled on the horizon and the Alliance forces finally liberated them. Then, and only then, would Bertie be free.

That was the plan, all mapped out in his head a long time ago, a plan he never thought he'd have to put into play, and yet here he was, his bags packed, and living on borrowed time. The police would come for him, tomorrow probably. In Bertie's experience, The Witch rarely put things off, so tonight would be a farewell dinner of sorts. Tomorrow was another story. Tomorrow, the vicious old cunt would be all business. Except she wouldn't be, because she'd be lying dead in a pool of her own blood.

And for the first time that afternoon, Bertie smiled.

[21]
UPRISING

THE ELEVATOR DOORS RUMBLED OPEN AND ROZ stepped out into the lobby, her head twisting left and right, her pistol raised, her ice-blue eyes behind the slit of her ski mask bright and alert.

She led her team of black-clad fighters along the service corridor towards the growing buzz of laughter and conversation from the nearby restaurant. Her heart beat fast, her breath, rapid. She was pumped, juiced to the max. She was on a mission; the biggest one she'd undertaken so far. But this time it was different. This time she knew she was not alone.

She held the pistol out in front of her, arm stiff, as they approached the swing doors of the restaurant kitchen. Behind the big circular windows, staff hurried back and forth. Suddenly, one door swung open and a young waitress backed out into the corridor carrying a tray full of dessert dishes. When she saw the masks and guns running towards her, she dropped the tray, her feet frozen, her hands clasped over her mouth to stifle the scream she thought might get her killed.

Crockery shattered. Chocolate brownies and ice cream were stamped into the carpet. Roz held a finger to her lips as she shoved the girl back into the kitchen. Behind her, the team spread out, filing past the catering tables, guns up. White-coated chefs and terrified waiting staff were herded into a corner, their hands held high.

'Go home,' Roz told them, 'right now. Take the stairs and leave by the staff entrance. Don't speak to anyone, don't call anyone, move quickly and quietly, and don't stop 'til your home. Be with your families tonight, got it?' They nodded silently. 'Go!'

They hurried out into the service corridor, shepherded by two of her team. With the kitchen staff gone, Roz went to the double doors and stared out into the restaurant where sixty members of the National Assembly (North-East), and their families and friends, were rounding off an evening of fine dining.

As her eyes roamed across the faces of Newcastle's grandees, she didn't see doubt, worried frowns, or troubled conversations. Instead she saw happy, smiling faces around those busy tables. She saw smart suits and cocktail dresses, and jewellery that shimmered beneath the intimate lighting. She heard laughter and soft music, and her blood boiled. She saw her beloved, blindfolded Brian, lashed to a wooden post, heard him calling her name, his voice echoing around the stands of St James' Park before the gunfire severed his last words. She watched them with hostile eyes, the traitors who occupied the *Windows on the Tyne* restaurant, the quislings who'd sold their country out for personal safety and a comfortable life, who'd turned a blind eye to the suffering and death of their countryfolk. When the caliphate had seized power, those same people had made a choice.

They were about to discover they'd chosen badly.

Roz pushed open the door and stepped into the restaurant. The others fanned out left and right, hurrying to cut off the exits. For a moment, no one reacted, the soft cones of light above the tables throwing the periphery into shadow. Roz watched them, surprised that no one had yet seen them. She looked beyond the enormous glass windows to the Tyne Bridge, arching across the nearby river, its superstructure slick with rain. Roz loved her city, loved its people. Except for the ones seated before her.

It took almost 20 seconds for their presence to register and the first scream to shatter the ambience. Diners scrambled to their feet. Glasses toppled and smashed. Roz raised her gun.

'No one move!' she yelled. She swept the pistol across their ashen faces, forcing them back into their seats. 'Be quiet, all of you!'

The room faded into silence. Women and men kept their heads down, frightened to meet the vengeful eyes behind the ski masks that watched them. Roz weaved her way through the diners until she reached the governor's table, larger than the others, loaded with bottles of alcohol. She looked at the faces around that table. She saw concern there, but no genuine fear. They'd become accustomed to power and enjoyed wielding it. She stood over the table, glared at the governor, Gerrard Cox, his bald head and rotund face flushed with alcohol. Next to him was the former chief constable of Northumbria Police, Robert Keenan, now Newcastle's chief of internal security. He wore his uniform, the police insignia replaced with the crossed swords of the caliphate, and he watched Roz with sharp, unblinking eyes, noting her description for his report. Flanking Cox was his chief advisor, Debbie Bacon, the city council's former head of human resources, a woman who'd become a ruthless zealot, drunk on power. Roz smiled behind her mask. She barked an order over her shoulder.

'Weed them out!'

She never took her eye off the traitors as three of her people yanked several pre-selected individuals to their feet and herded them across the room.

'Stop it! Leave them alone!'

Roz turned. One of the female guests, a middle-aged woman wearing too much makeup, was on her high-heeled feet, shouting across the room as a man from her table was forced away at gunpoint.

'How dare you barge in here!' she spluttered drunkenly, spittle flying from a vicious slash of red lipstick. 'Do you know who we are? What we can do to you?'

The man sitting next to her tugged her arm. 'Sit down, Marjorie, for God's sake!'

The woman turned on him. 'Don't touch me!' She looked around the room. 'Well? Isn't anyone going to do something? Or are we going to let these resistance scum just march in here and point guns at us?'

Roz walked towards her. Marjorie saw her coming and cocked her chin aggressively. 'Don't get in my face, bitch. If you didn't have that gun, I'd tear your fucking eyes out.'

'Majorie!' someone bellowed.

Roz raised her pistol and held it against the woman's temple. Marjorie's eyes narrowed. 'You don't have the balls.'

Roz pulled the trigger, the gunshot deafening, the bullet exiting the back of Marjorie's head and shattering one of the floor-to-ceiling glass panes across the room. Blood, hair, and grey matter splattered across the table behind her. Marjorie's legs buckled, her coiffure cracking off the table's edge. She collapsed in a heap of lifeless meat at Roz's feet. Blood oozed from the hole at the back of her head.

'Anyone else want to gob off?' Roz looked around the room, but there were no takers. 'When I say move, you'll get up and leave the hotel by the back stairs. Go home, while you've got the chance, and trust me, it's the only one you'll get. Move!'

And they did, all of them, stampeding for the door, knocking into tables, falling to the ground, trampling over broken glass, over each other. As the door swung shut behind the stragglers, Roz heard heavy clanging coming from the kitchen; that would be her boys opening up the gas pipes, positioning the IEDs, setting the traps. She checked her watch. They didn't have long, five minutes max. She turned to the nine traitors, pre-selected for retribution. She saw the defiance on their faces and wished she had longer.

'Against the wall, all of you.'

The governor and his people strolled across the room. They stood against the wall facing Roz and her line of guns, staring each other down like a Mexican stand-off. Roz tugged the ski mask from her face. She saw the governor drop his chin and stare at his shoes.

'Look at me,' she told him. Cox looked up, the red flush of alcohol now a chalky grimace.

'Don't do anything stupid. Just tell us what you want.'

Keenan sneered. 'They're going to murder us in cold blood, Gerry, can't you see that?'

Cox sobbed. Roz stared at the security chief, who stared right back.

'I've seen you twice in person—'

'Congratulations.' Keenan's face was a mask of contempt.

'The first time was at the Pride march a few years ago.

You were waving from the police float, with your little rainbow lanyard around your neck, surrounded by all your friends in the LGBT community.' Her face darkened. 'How many of them did you have arrested? How many were hanged on your orders?'

'I don't make the rules.'

'No, you just enforce them, right?' She took a step closer, the gun hanging by her side. 'The second time I saw you was at St James' Park, standing on the pitch, sucking up to your new masters while their soldiers shot my husband and a hundred others right in front of you.' Roz shook her head. 'You didn't bat an eyelid.'

Keenan held her gaze. There was no remorse there, no empathy, just a troubling conviction that Roz only now understood. He'd become a fanatic, a tyrant. Unbridled power did that to people.

'They'd broken the law, defied the regime.'

'You've had thousands deported. Men, women, children, babies, all gone to God knows where.'

'Bigots and troublemakers,' Keenan said. 'And nothing compared to the reprisals that will decimate this city if you pull that trigger.'

A cold, damp wind gusted through the missing window. Roz looked out across the river to the north of the city. 'There'll be no more executions, Keenan. No more deportations. You're no longer in charge, see?'

'What are you talking about?'

It was Bacon who spoke, the dumpy former human resources manager who'd shown not a shred of humanity in the last three brutal years. Roz pointed towards the shattered window.

'I'm talking about the British troops across the river, thousands of them already in the city, waiting for the signal.'

'That's impossible,' Cox blustered. 'They'll never get across the frontier.'

'They're watching this hotel as we speak,' she told them. The traitors wavered, their icy defiance melting fast. 'They're waiting for the signal. Your deaths will be that signal. Remember that as you die.'

'Rot in hell,' Keenan cursed.

Cox shook his head. 'Please, don't do this. We'll hand ourselves in, surrender.'

Her radio crackled. 'Go for Roz,' she said.

'We're set,' came the response.

Roz took a step backwards. The other ski masks raised their weapons.

'Wait!' Cox stammered, holding up his hands. 'We had to do what they told us. What else could we have done?'

Roz regarded the fat slob with utter contempt. 'Better to die on your feet than live on your knees, Gerry.'

And that's where she shot him, first in the right knee, and then, as he dropped to the floor, through his left knee. There was a sudden, desperate chorus of panic and screaming, and then her boys opened fire, chopping the rest of them down to the carpet, their legs shattered by bullets.

Roz watched them as they moaned in agony, their bloodied hands clutching their wounds. 'Get the juice, quickly!'

The ski masks returned with jerry cans of petrol. Roz snatched one and stood over Keenan. His right knee was shattered, and another bullet had broken his shin. He looked up at Roz with genuine fear in his eyes, the arrogance finally extinguished. *Good.* He thrashed and spluttered as she poured petrol over his face and uniform. She did the same to Bacon, Cox, and the others, soaking the surrounding carpet. She tossed the empty can to one side.

Their painful cries, the coughing, and their wails of desperation and terror filled the restaurant. She knelt over Keenan, took the small orange tube out of her pocket and waved it in his face. His eyes widened.

'Please...'

She unscrewed the cap, pulled out the tab inside, then jammed it under Keenan's backside. She smiled and patted his cheek. 'Whatever you do, don't move.'

Roz led her people back out into the service corridor and down to the ground floor. The phone system was reconnected, and she made the breathless call from the security office.

'Please, send someone quickly! There's been a shooting at the Hilton, in the top-floor restaurant. Terrorists with guns have taken over! People are dying! Help us!'

She left the phone on the table, the line open. Outside, they piled inside the van and Roz yanked the ski mask off her head. Seconds later they were pulling away from the hotel and heading back across the Tyne. She looked in the rear-view mirror and saw everyone had their masks up, grins across their faces. Sitting next to her, even Jed was smiling. She reached over and ruffled his hair.

'You did good, Jed. You're a proper little soldier. Your mum and dad would be proud of you.'

The boy shrugged. 'I didn't really do anything, Aunt Roz.'

She smiled. 'There'll be plenty more chances, son. The night is just beginning.'

'Here they come!'

From the third-floor window of a deserted office building, Eddie saw blue lights flickering through the streets of

Newcastle as security forces converged on the hotel across the river. Mac stood next to him, a spotter scope pressed to his eye.

'Air is inbound,' he reported, then they all heard it, the unmistakable *whop-whop-whop* of a large helicopter.

Eddie pointed to the west. 'There, three o'clock.'

Collision lights winked in the distance, approaching from the south-west. Moments later the Merlin roared over the arch of the Tyne Bridge before banking hard and flaring above the hotel roof.

'Assault team,' Mac observed through his scope.

Steve was looking through the sight of his rifle. 'That was quick.'

'This close to the frontier, the Hajis are jumpy.' Mac glanced at his watch. 'Let's go. The fireworks are about to start.'

They made their way down to the lobby where the rest of Nine Platoon assembled. They stood quietly in the darkness, and Eddie knew they were only moments away from the commencement of hostilities. He was ready. More than that, he just wanted it to start.

He heard Sarge's voice echo around the lobby. 'Remember lads, the second they find out we're here, they'll throw the kitchen sink at us.'

It was Digger's familiar snarl that answered him. 'I fucking hope so.'

[22]
LIGHT 'EM UP

HENRI SAW THE DARKNESS AHEAD AND FELT THE pressure rising once more.

Another 24 hours and you'll be back in France, he told himself. Summer was coming, and he hoped their next assignment would be something far less stressful, like ripping the TGV down to the Côte d'Azur for caliphate VIPs and their families. He was getting too old for such nerve-wracking work.

They left the safety of the lights behind them as the engine rolled up the final 200 metres of tunnel and resurfaced at the Folkestone terminal. Like its sister across the channel, the transport hub was blanketed in darkness, and as the train rumbled out in the night air, Henri's mouth was suddenly dry.

'Welcome to England,' Jean-Michel quipped.

Henri said nothing as he drank from a bottle of water. He opened his side window and leaned outside. The air was fresh and salty, and Henri took several deep lungfuls to calm his growing anxiety.

There wasn't much to see, aside from the usual crews

loitering trackside, although the British faces that watched the huge train rumbling past them were far more sullen than their French counterparts.

Henri cursed them for their stubbornness. The French had accepted the slow and inevitable conquest of their country with a Gallic shrug and a *c'est la vie*. They had their own troublemakers, men and women who clung to an outdated vision of the old Republic, but their numbers were few and their ranks riddled with caliphate spies. They had beheaded a dozen of them in the Place Vendôme last month, an event attended by several thousand people. Such a crowd had shocked Henri. It was beyond his comprehension why anyone would care to witness such mediaeval barbarism, but he'd kept his mouth shut and his thoughts to himself. As long as he did his job, he'd get by. One day, things might change again.

The train clanked across a set of points, and Henri looked out of the window. Roughly 500 metres of the train had cleared the tunnel so far. 'Keep her at ten kilometres, Jean-Michel, until we—'

CRACK!

Henri felt the detonation beneath his feet, and then the locomotive rattled violently and lurched to the left. The screech of grinding metal was almost deafening.

'Brake!' he yelled, but Jean-Michel was already there, yanking the levers as Henri disengaged the engine's motor. The train's momentum continued to drive it forward, its wheels biting into gravel beds as it rolled off the broken track. Both drivers held on tight as the 30,000-tonne train shuddered and several cars behind them rolled off the tracks, twisting their couplings. The screeching, deafening ring of buckling metal finally stopped as the train twisted to a halt.

'What the hell was that?'

'Shut it all down,' Henri ordered, flicking switches and twisting dials. Jean-Michel knocked off the power, and the cab was plunged into darkness. It took a moment for their eyes to adjust. The engine had tilted to the left, not dangerously so, but enough to force both men to climb out on the other side.

Henri dropped to the track and made his way around the front of the engine...

'*Mon Dieu,*' he whispered.

Several of the freight cars had left the tracks and were twisted at dangerous angles. All of them were closed cars, and Henri knew they contained munitions.

'Shit! This is no longer a delivery,' Jean-Michel said. 'It's a recovery operation.'

They walked back down the track. Henri crouched down and shone his torch beneath one of the tilting munitions cars, unwilling to get any closer. The rail beneath was blackened and buckled.

'What could've caused that?'

Henri shrugged. 'An electrical surge, perhaps. Blew the rail off its sleeper. I've seen it happen before.'

'And we still haven't cleared the tunnel.'

Jean-Michel was right. There were several cars still inside the distant, dark cavern, and his heart sank. A recovery like this was a complex operation involving specialist equipment. It would mean an additional 24 hours at the very least.

Further down the train, he saw the shadows of soldiers jumping to the ground and stamping their way towards the wreck. But that's all he saw. What he didn't see were the track and maintenance crews rushing to the scene with torches and equipment. Where were those sullen-faced gangs he'd seen only a few minutes ago? They should be swarming all over this by now.

Beside him, Jean-Michel crudely verbalised Henri's troubled observations.

'Where the fuck is everyone?'

After lifting off from their temporary airbase in Iceland, the B-21 Raiders climbed to a cruising altitude of 40,000 feet and headed south towards a rendezvous point 63 miles off the west coast of Ireland. There, in the roiled air above the restless Atlantic Ocean, *Doolittle* and *Hornet* took turns to drink from the extended refuelling boom of an orbiting KC-46 Pegasus.

After topping off their tanks, the Raiders banked away and readopted their loose, one-mile separation formation. They flew east over the dark landmass of Ireland, climbing to an altitude of 54,000 feet before levelling out above the Irish Sea.

Inside each aircraft, the array of high-definition touch-screen displays gave their two-man crews a complete tactical overview of the surrounding environment. They could see 3-D maps of enemy airspace, the radar cones of anti-air ground units, and they could predict the patrolling patterns of caliphate fighters. They saw drones and heli-copters, missile units and rocket batteries, the overlapping sweeps of a wide variety of airborne detection systems, and the heat blooms of military convoys on roads far below them. None of it posed any significant threat.

As they crossed the coastline of North Devon, each aircraft dialled back the power and dipped their noses into a gentle glide angle, their sophisticated auto-navigation systems making corrections based on the tactical information they were receiving from their on-board systems. Now the Raiders were practically noiseless and invisible in the night sky, so invisible that they passed within a mile of a flight of enemy fighters without being detected.

The aircraft sliced through the bitter night air, heading due east now, passing Salisbury and Winchester before banking to the south and looping around Crawley to avoid the congestion of Gatwick airport, once a busy hub for British holidaymakers, now a major military airbase.

After resuming their due east heading, the Raiders continued their downward glide, finally levelling out at 3,000 feet. Then they increased power, hurtling above the dark English countryside. With the autopilot engaged and the terrain-guidance software keeping them out of danger, the crews turned their attentions to the weapons systems, scrolling through their limited onboard inventory and selecting their weapons of choice: AGM–178's, the US Air Force's Joint Air-to-Surface Stand-off Missile. *Doolittle* and *Hornet* both carried two of the advanced cruise missiles inside their weapon bays, each one capable of delivering its 2,000-pound penetrator warhead to its target from a range of up to 250 nautical miles. The planners didn't want to take the chance of such a long shot over a highly-defended swathe of British real estate, so they set the launch point to approximately 50 nautical miles.

In the cockpit of *Doolittle,* the on-board infrared targeting systems were activated, and the software responded with an immediate IR acquisition signal, one they'd been expecting. With the weapons programmed, the bomb bay doors were opened. *Doolittle* launched both its missiles first, then banked hard to the south. *Hornet* released its own weapons ten seconds later and followed *Doolittle*

towards their next waypoint, the town of Haywards Heath.
Once clear of the area they would head west, undetected.

Leaving chaos in their wake.

As Henri Platt considered his dilemma, he had
no idea that one of the sullen faces he'd glimpsed earlier was
a former member of the Special Boat Squadron, a man who,
in a past life, had had considerable experience with many
types of explosives. He was also a current member of the
British resistance and had recently taken covert delivery of
an Active Infrared Beacon. For the past two days, he'd
hidden in the ranks of the track maintenance team, the
purpose of his presence known only to three other trusted
personnel. He knew the train was coming, and knew of its
cargo, so when word had reached his ears, the former SBS
operator was waiting.

The explosive charge was big enough to rupture the
running rail's expansion joint but small enough not to
warrant any immediate suspicion. As the French drivers
clambered down to the track and disappeared out of sight,
the resistance fighter had climbed up the locomotive ladder
and attached the magnetic transmitter directly above the
driver's window. After giving a quiet nod to the other workers, they moved away, slowly and casually, melting into the
surrounding darkness and heading for the distant maintenance sheds with their deep, concrete inspection pits.

The cruise missiles were not stealthy, nor were
they particularly fast, but they flew very low and were very
hard to hit. All four weapons were now rumbling across the
undulating Kent countryside, jinking left and right, up and

down, their terrain-avoidance systems mapping the ground ahead, making corrections, homing in on the sweet music being played by the IR transmitter clamped to the cab of the distant locomotive.

A lucky sweep from a military ground radar briefly painted the missiles, and a dated yet still-lethal Chinese-made PGZ-95 self-propelled gun opened up with its 25-millimetre cannon, but the rounds fell away behind the near-invisible missiles that were now flying at over 500 miles per hour towards their target. Obeying their internal programming, *Hornet's* trailing weapons banked to the south and towards the nearby coast.

On the ground an emergency call went out, and other caliphate SAM crews began bombarding the air with their search and targeting radars, desperate to stop the missiles that they could neither see nor engage effectively. Yet someone on the ground had interrogated the brief radar track. They crunched the data, the speed and course of the missiles, then sent out a general alert.

Enemy aircraft inbound towards Eurotunnel Terminal.

HENRI SCRATCHED HIS HEAD AS HE LOOKED ACROSS THE vast terminal. Way in the distance he could see the lights of the control tower, and around the periphery he saw a few more along the access roads. He saw people too, his crew, the soldiers, but no locals. It was as if everyone had just walked away.

'Where d'you think they've gone?' Jean-Michel asked.

'I've no idea,' he told his co-driver.

'Lazy bastards.'

'I'll get on the radio, try to find out what's going on.'

Henri had taken less than ten steps when a mobile gun

opened up on the hill behind him. He yelped with fear as the strobe-like gun barrels lit up the rail yard, the ripping sound of the outgoing rounds deafening. Henri cowered on the tracks, his hands clamped over his ears. The noise and light intensified as other guns surrounding the terminal opened up, and from beyond a nearby hill, he saw several missiles screeching into the air, their rocket motors glowing like Roman candles and leaving trails of thick white smoke. The noise was tremendous, and sirens wailed menacingly, compounding Henri's terror. He felt a firm hand grab his arm and drag him to his feet.

'Run, Henri!'

He struggled up and followed Jean-Michel, the rail yard lit by the flickering strobes of the surrounding guns. His co-driver was leaping like a Springbok as he ran towards the vehicle embarkation platforms and Henri followed, arms and legs pumping, his breath ragged, watching the tracks, the gravel, the sleepers, a myriad of trip hazards that might mean the difference between life or death. The roar of gunfire was deafening now, the night lit up like a macabre firework display as outgoing rounds and missiles lanced through the sky. He knew he didn't have long, seconds maybe, and he was still a hundred metres short of the closest platform.

He saw Jean-Michel standing on it, his arm waving, his mouth screaming, his words drowned by the roar of guns, sirens, and missiles. And then Henri was there, scrambling onto the platform, being shoved across it and down onto the tracks on the other side. He fell to the gravel, cutting his hands, but he didn't feel it. Jean-Michel dropped beside him and dragged him beneath the concrete lip of the platform. They pressed themselves against the wall, and Henri curled up tightly, his eyes squeezed shut.

The gunfire intensified.

Then the world exploded.

DOOLITTLE'S AGM-178 CRUISE MISSILES ROCKETED across the M20 motorway at an altitude of 60 feet and a speed of 492 miles per hour, unscathed and unstoppable. They were too low and too fast to be hit by anything the ring of anti-air defences scattered across the terminal could throw at them. The missiles roared across the perimeter fence and thundered past the windows of the Eurotunnel control tower, heading directly for the IR transmitter still pulsing its signal from Henri's train—

The weapons nosed into the target and exploded, a combined detonation of 4,000 pounds of high explosives that obliterated the train in a furious blast of heat and pressure that instantly engulfed the hundreds of missiles and bombs inside the train's boxcars. The additional pulse of destructive energy annihilated what remained of the train into a billion shards of metal and wooden splinters that flew across the terminal in a lethal wave of death for hundreds of metres.

Still inbound from the south, *Hornet's* cruise missiles thundered across the coastline and the rooftops of Folkestone before nosediving towards the GPS coordinates that put their aiming point directly at the mouth of the Eurotunnel. The missiles dived into the fireball below and pulverised the tracks and marshalling yards, bringing down thousands of tons of earth and concrete and sealing one of the cross-channel tunnels.

The explosions sent shock waves rolling across the countryside, causing vehicles to swerve and crash on the M20 motorway, and shattering half the windows in Folkestone. The flash of the explosion lit up the night sky for miles, and the tremor rippled across the channel to the coast of France.

Those that saw it, trembled.

Jean-Michel helped Henri climb up onto the shattered platform, and the older man stared open-mouthed at the giant crater gouged out of the ground for hundreds of metres. Thick smoke drifted on the air and the entire world looked like it was on fire. Of his train, there was nothing left.

A short distance away, smoking on the platform, was a twisted shard of metal taller than Henri, and he realised then how lucky they'd been to survive. The tunnel they'd almost cleared was now blocked by a mountain of earth, and every signalling tower and gantry was scorched, buckled, or missing.

'Look.' Jean-Michel pointed, and Henri saw the terminal control tower in the distance, its upper floors ablaze. As for people, he couldn't see another single living person, and given the tremendous force of the explosion, Henri wasn't surprised.

'You saved my life,' he told Jean-Michel.

They looked at each other, their faces blackened and bloodied, their clothes ripped. Jean-Michel didn't answer, he just tapped his ear with a finger.

'Can't hear you, boss. I think my eardrums have burst.'

Now it was Henri's turn to act. He grabbed his saviour by the arm and steered him towards the other side of the platform. They jumped down, and Henri led the way towards the mouth of the surviving tunnel, stumbling and weaving through twisted metal and smoking craters. When they got there, he could see debris had partially blocked it, but not enough to stop two guys on foot.

Jean-Michel tugged his sleeve. 'Henri! Where are we going?'

He leaned close to Jean-Michel's ear and pointed to the gaping black cavern. 'We take the service tunnel and get the hell out of here. We're going home, Jean-Michel.'

His co-driver nodded, relieved, thankful. 'Sounds like a plan, boss.'

They clambered over the rubble and into the tunnel, leaving the desolation behind them.

They'd just survived the first shot of a new war, one about to erupt far to the north.

[23]
BATTLE CRY

Twenty-seven miles off the rocky coast of Northern Ireland, the *U.S.S. John F. Kennedy* was turning back into the wind to recommence flight operations. Earlier, six E/A18 Growlers had taken off from its pitching, rain-lashed deck and were now orbiting over Scotland, ten miles behind the frontier. The Growlers were the navy's Airborne Electronic Attack aircraft, and they flew fuel-efficient circles as they waited for the order to begin their assault, although theirs wouldn't involve any ordinance. The Growlers' job was to suppress enemy radar and disrupt communications, and their onboard scanned-array radars were already tracking targets to the south, both in the air and on the ground.

Two hundred miles to the east of the Growlers, cruising at 46,000 feet above the stormy Atlantic Ocean, sixteen B-52 strategic heavy bombers were inbound to the battle zone. The venerable B-52, with over 60 years of operational service, remained a key strategic asset in the US Air Force's weapons delivery inventory, and tonight they carried a formidable payload. The aircraft had lifted off from Barksdale Air Force Base in Louisiana and flown north, crossing the Newfoundland coastline before heading out into the bleak expanse of the Atlantic Ocean. Their target was the frontier itself, and their mission was to obliterate the defences and carve a path between Alliance and enemy territory at two specific points on the map. To accomplish their objectives, each aircraft carried a 70,000-pound payload of precision-guided bombs. Their operation was called *Rolling Thunder,* and the unsuspecting enemy troops along the frontier were about to find out exactly what that meant.

Fifteen miles to the north of the frontier, US Army and British artillery units were racing from their jump-off points to their pre-planned firing positions. Small convoys of self-propelled guns and high-mobility artillery rocket systems rumbled at speed through deserted towns and villages, determined to stay one step ahead of the enemy surveillance drones and aircraft that might get a lucky break and pinpoint a target.

The Alliance also possessed another invaluable surveillance platform in their inventory; the Mark One Eyeball. On the ground, members of the local resistance were observing military installations and their movements and sending that intelligence to Alliance forces via satellite transmitters. That same intelligence went out to the guided-missile cruisers nosing south into the Irish Sea, and coordinates were programmed into the ships' targeting systems for their onboard Tomahawk Land Attack Missiles.

Closer to shore, rolling through the dark waters of that same sea, two *America*-class amphibious assault ships stood ready to start their own operation. Their target was the flat, rural coastland just south of Whitehaven in enemy-held territory, and their aim was to seize the town and create a beachhead for the rest of a Marine Expeditionary Brigade. To accomplish that mission, the assault ships each carried twelve Osprey MV-22 transports, six F-35 Lightning fighters, four CH-53 heavy transport helicopters, eight Viper attack helicopters and six Seahawk utility choppers. Below decks, 3,000 US Marines waited impatiently to be ferried ashore. A smaller force would head for the nuclear power station of Sellafield, a few miles further south along the coast where the SEALs of DEVGRU were already ashore and waiting for the green light to engage.

While hostile satellites were looking elsewhere, thousands of troops moved into the tunnels at Morpeth and Gretna. Like the soldiers of the Second Mass, and the other battalions of the King's Continental Army, the spearhead battle groups were all British. Behind them, the Americans were sending two combat brigades through the tunnels in support, because the brutal fact was, the British didn't have the numbers to win the fight. Over 1,700 English, Scottish, Welsh, and Irish troops had been killed during the campaign to retake Ireland, and if the After-Action Reports were anything to go by, the liberation of England and Wales would be very costly. It was the Brits who would bleed first, and rightly so.

As the clock wound down towards midnight, the Maglev shuttles hummed back and forth between Morpeth and Newcastle, Gretna and Carlisle, passing unseen and unheard deep beneath the vast frontier that stretched across the country. The troops they ferried made their way into the storm drains and tunnels that intersected with covert egress points above, moving quickly and quietly through the streets to their pre-planned RV points.

In Newcastle, 15,000 troops had entered the city, many of them using the tunnels of the Tyne and Wear Metro to seize and hold strategic locations north of the river where the rooftops bristled with soldiers armed with Stinger and Starstreak man-portable anti-aircraft weapons, while other high-vantage points suddenly sprouted communications masts and satellite dishes.

Below the rooftops, but still enjoying good visibility across the city, drone operators already had their birds in the air, flying high and quiet, watching the streets to the south of the river. Down on the ground, mobile network infrastructure was disrupted, and the city's telephone exchange was quietly infiltrated. Its trunking networks were rerouted through to a specialist team whose job it was to monitor the calls, to listen for curious, panicked, or traitorous voices, and silence them. From a communications perspective, the north of the city had been cut off from the outside world.

To the east of the city, a team of operators from the Special Reconnaissance Regiment killed the bored soldiers guarding the entrance to the Siemens power station on Shields Road and took control of the city's power supply. One by one, the streets across the river were plunged into darkness, allowing the troops to move faster to their rally points.

As for the people of Newcastle, the nine o'clock curfew saw most of them at home. For those working into the night, the blustery rainstorm sweeping across the city kept them inside too, and the few vehicles that navigated the slick streets were distracted by the deteriorating driving conditions, unaware of the troops watching them from darkened buildings, alleyways, and car parks.

Those that came into direct contact with allied troops, by luck or design, were both elated and terrified. They were told to go home, barricade their windows, and stay there. As for the others, who'd gratefully accepted the invaders' 30 pieces of silver – like the police car that picked out a fast-moving squad of troops with its headlights – the outcome was very different. Instead of surrendering, the police officers had lit up the scene with their blues and twos while attempting to call it in over the radio. Both police officers had died in a hail of suppressed small-arms fire. Bodywork punctured, its windows shattered, the car was left in the street, doors open, the hissing engine leaking precious fluids, the bullet-riddled cops leaking the same. There was no time to hide the car and no longer any point.

The clock had run down.

All across the city they watched and waited. The airspace to the south was covered by surface-to-air weapons, and all major land routes, bridges, and intersections were being watched by anti-armour teams with enough munitions to stop a motorised brigade. The King's Continental Army was tooled up to the max, primed and ready.

As for motivation, none needed any. Many had lived through the initial invasion, and most had lost count of the people who'd died or vanished in the chaos of war. Husbands, wives, fathers, mothers, sons and daughters, friends and comrades, all gone. They were angry. And they were ashamed.

They'd taken for granted the freedoms that had been hard-fought and won by previous generations. They'd become blind to the determined dismantling of those same freedoms, psychologically manipulated by an enemy who'd recognised tolerance and compassion as weaknesses to be exploited. They'd stood idly by as Britain's institutions were subverted, its history rewritten, its statues torn down. A mirror had been held before the face of the nation, and it had looked away in shame. Britannia had been defeated, long before the truck bomb had detonated outside Downing Street.

It was almost three years since that fateful, terrible summer's evening. Three long, bitter years in which those troops lying in wait on the rain-swept streets of Newcastle had had time to mourn, to lick their wounds, and to reflect. They knew now that they'd been taken for fools, blinded by enemies both foreign and domestic, but now those eyes were wide open. Now they were back on home soil, and when it began, the roar of battle would be carried on the wind to every corner of their green and pleasant land. The call to arms, so desperately anticipated, would finally be heard.

And the fight back would begin.

GENERAL FARIS MOUSA LEANED BACK IN HIS CHAIR and swung his boots up on the desk. He folded his arms and stared at the wall, his face blank, his tired eyes vacant. The room was stuffy, and he knew he should climb the eight flights of stairs and get out of the command bunker for a while, but frankly, he was exhausted.

The last few days had been a desperate exercise in damage limitation, and Mousa's thoughts once again turned to the traitor Al-Kaabi. He wondered again how much damage the man had inflicted. Right now, it was hard to tell because he was still waiting for the report from the Information Management team. Mousa knew there was a reluctance to submit their findings because he'd had their senior officer summarily executed in a fit of rage, which is why he couldn't blame them. He would visit their office tomorrow morning and offer his personal guarantee that there would be no more punishments, no more bloodshed. It was counter-productive. What he needed were answers.

He saw a shadow lurking beyond the frosted glass of his office door, heard the respectful knuckle-tap.

'Enter.'

The duty sergeant appeared with a steaming mug. 'Sorry to disturb, sir, but I thought you might like a coffee.'

Mousa nodded at the desk, and the soldier put it down. 'How's it looking out there?'

The sergeant shrugged. 'The same, general. The usual spikes of radio chatter and radar emissions. The last satellite pass revealed an increase in enemy traffic across the frontier, but nothing significant. There's been a surge in seaborne transmissions from the Irish Sea, but the Ops Team believe it's minesweepers, clearing sea lanes to the south. A drone reconnaissance operation is being organised.'

'Thank you, sergeant.'

With the loss of Ireland, the Welsh coast was dangerously exposed, Mousa knew. He needed those Chinese anti-ship missiles fast. He'd get an update on their progress after he'd had his coffee.

Mousa frowned as the faint tapping grew into the sound of running feet. He swung his legs off the desk and yanked the door open. A young orderly was racing along the subterranean corridor towards him. His boots squeaked on the linoleum floor as he pulled up short and threw up a hasty salute.

'Tried to call you, sir,' he said, puffing.

'I said I didn't want to be disturbed. What is it?'

'There's been an attack on the Eurotunnel terminal in Folkestone, sir.'

Mousa felt the blood drain from his face. 'What?'

'They hit the missile shipment coming out of the tunnel. The damage is...'

The orderly hesitated. Mousa screamed. 'Speak!'

'The damage is total, sir. The train has been completely destroyed. The eastbound tunnel has caved in too, and there's not a single working track left across the terminal.'

The sergeant was wide-eyed. 'My God, all that ordinance.'

Mousa turned and stared at him. That's when he realised...

'They're going to invade.'

The sergeant shook his head. 'But that's impossible, general. The frontier is impenetrable.'

'They've found a way. Broadcast an emergency alert immediately.'

The sergeant snatched at the phone on Mousa's desk. The general was already out of the door, running towards the operations room, the orderly puffing behind him.

Mousa had no idea what would happen next, but he knew one thing for sure.

The mystery of Al-Kaabi's betrayal was finally solved.

[24]
WITCHING HOUR

BERTIE SAT AT THE KITCHEN TABLE, NURSING A BLACK coffee as he watched the minute hand of the clock creep towards midnight. Only 20 minutes had passed since Judge Hardy had left and The Witch had retired for the evening, and Bertie was feeling anxious.

He ran over the plan in his head, confident that all he needed was a good start, the chance to put as much distance between himself and Hampstead in the shortest space of time. The other crucial point was the Toyota. It had to disappear without a trace, and he wondered if those deep pools he'd fished all those years ago were still there. The one he had in mind was a former quarry close to the Cambridgeshire border, its waters black and deep, and he would feel a lot better once the Toyota was sleeping with the fishes. From that point on, the rest of his journey would be on foot.

He would make his way north through the countryside, sticking to empty lanes and footpaths, avoiding human contact, camping in quiet woods and meadows. He had enough food to last him a month, by which time he would be at the farm where he'd start again. *New beginnings.*

He finished his coffee and placed the mug in the sink. He thought about George and wondered if there was someone watching the house, waiting for him. Bertie was still struggling, knowing that his former friend had tried to kill him, but he didn't blame him. He'd rolled the dice and lost. George was just trying to clean up the mess, protect himself. Bertie would probably do the same in his shoes.

He refocussed, checked the time. It was five-to-midnight, and the house was sleeping. Bertie slipped Chef's boning knife from its block and held it in his hand. It had a soft red handle and a six-inch blade that Bertie knew would be razor-sharp. He'd seen Chef use it many times, slicing joints of meat with a speed and dexterity used only by the highly skilled. All he needed to do was run it hard and deep across The Witch's neck and that would be it. No noise, no screaming, just a rapid bleed out. He glanced at the ceiling. She'd be up there now, sleeping soundly, a belly full of good food and alcohol. All he had to do was climb the stairs, enter her room and play Zorro. Easy-peasy, Japanesey.

Except it wasn't.

Despite everything, Bertie knew he wasn't a stone-cold killer. He'd done Al-Kaabi and Gates in, sure he had, but they'd stood between him and freedom, and Bertie had every right to try to save his own skin. Besides, neither man was an angel. The Witch was in a different league, however. Her murder would send the National Assembly into a vengeful rage and that would be a stupid move. They would hunt him like an animal, and they'd never let up. No, better to just slip away and disappear.

He pushed the knife back into the block and stepped

out into the basement corridor. He took a moment to listen, but the only sound he heard was a faint snoring leaking from under Chef's door. He crept to his own room and retrieved his rucksack and coat, then made his way out into the rear gardens. The night was crisp, and the air was clear and dry. And no moon, which was even better.

Beyond a neat row of manicured hedges stood the large double garage. Bertie swung the doors open on their recently oiled hinges and dropped his rucksack into the boot of the Toyota. He stabbed at the starter button and the hybrid engine hummed into life. He rolled the car out of the garage, closed the doors, and got back in. Ahead, the drive curved towards a high wall and the electric gate. He kept the lights off and eased the car slowly towards it. The front wheels tripped the pressure plate, and the gate rolled open—

Bertie stamped on the brake.

A police van was blocking the road. *What the hell was—*

Then they were running towards him, a scrum of armed black-clad police officers. They surrounded the Toyota, their lights blinding him, their hateful mouths screaming a jumbled cacophony of noise. His window exploded, and it showered Bertie with glass. Powerful hands wrenched the door open and dragged him out. They bent him over the front of the car and secured his hands behind his back with plastic cuffs.

'For fuck's sake, what are you doing?' He felt hands searching his pockets, then someone grabbed his collar and yanked him upright. Torches blinded him. The voice behind them was unmistakable.

'Oh, Bertie. How could you?'

He blinked as The Witch stepped into the light. 'Lady

Edith, w-w-what's going on?' he stammered. This time it wasn't an act.

She looked up at him, her hands thrust into the pockets of a long overcoat, her chin raised, revealing the scrawny throat that Bertie could've deboned before he left. Should've.

'You're a liar, a thief, and a murderer, Bertie.'

'I don't know what you're talking about, ma'am.'

'You murdered poor Timmy and stole his precious things. How could you?'

'What?'

'Deny it if you must, but the truth will out.'

Bertie's stomach lurched. The scenario he'd feared had come to pass. Her word against his. Who'd believe him?

'But you ordered me to kill him!'

The Witch shook her head. 'That's not true, is it Bertie? Still, the point is moot now.' She glanced at the police officers. 'Take him away.'

Bertie struggled as they dragged him down the path. He twisted his head around, and he yelled over his shoulder. 'There's a target on your back, you fucking old slag! They're coming for you, for everything you've done!'

'Wait!' The Witch shrilled.

Bertie swallowed as she marched down the driveway towards him. She drew her hand back and slapped his face. It stung, but Bertie was more in shock than pain. Her eyes, like dead black coals, bored into his, and then he realised the magnitude of being on the wrong end of that ruthless glare.

'You've just made a terrible mistake, Bertie. One you'll live to regret. Of that, I'll make certain.'

She turned on her heel and marched back towards the

house. They bundled Bertie into the back of the police van, and as the door slammed shut, the brief flame of defiance sputtered and died.

He was doomed, he knew that now. The best outcome he could hope for was a long sentence in a small cell, but it wouldn't be like the old days. There would be no TV, no ping pong, no jazz mags or puff to make the time pass a little easier. Now the regime was brutal. Now it was all work parties and punishment beatings and religious brainwashing.

You've just made a terrible mistake, Bertie. One you'll live to regret. Of that, I'll make certain.

No, The Witch's promise meant something else, something far worse. Deportation perhaps. George had heard a rumour of some far-off desert hell-hole where thousands of slaves were put to work and life expectancy was measured in weeks. He wasn't sure if it was true or not, but George said that no one had ever come back to refute it.

Bertie held his head in his hands and cursed his stupidity. He'd made the worst enemy possible, and the rest of Bertie's life would be a living hell.

Then he lifted his head, the bleak visions suddenly banished from his mind. The sound he could hear was a familiar one, and the last time he'd heard it was almost three years ago before the stricken airliner had roared across the London skyline trailing smoke. A sound that had marked the passing of the Old World. A sound that heralded fear, death, and destruction.

Bertie pressed his face up against the reinforced window and saw the pigs standing outside, their black helmets tilted towards the night sky. He saw fear on their faces, and for maybe the last time, Bertie smiled.

Across London, sirens wailed.

FROM ALL POINTS OF THE COMPASS, SWARMS OF
military vehicles descended on the Hilton Hotel in
Newcastle.

As rain lashed across the city, a hundred caliphate
troops threw a security ring around the area. Humvees and
police cars blocked every approach road and sealed both
ends of the Tyne Bridge with M2 Bradley Armoured
Fighting Vehicles. A Black Hawk helicopter appeared overhead, turning circles above the Hilton's roof at 500 feet, its
navigation lights winking in the darkness. On the ground,
assault teams were assembled and ordered to breach the
building at every access point.

The 14 soldiers who made their way into the Hilton's
service corridor were running on high octane. After months
of barrack boredom, they were finally being called upon to
do the job they'd trained for. None of them was a counter-
terror specialist, but they were proud soldiers of the 17th
Light Motorised Brigade of the Islamic State Armed Forces
and they were keen to make their mark.

Their leader, a staff-sergeant from the town of Ramallah
in Palestine, was the first to hear the furtive whispers
coming from the security office storeroom. Creeping closer,
the whispers became more urgent before gasping into
silence. The staff-sergeant, along with two other soldiers,
opened fire with their HK33 assault rifles, shredding the
door and silencing the whispers. As blood ran across the
floor tiles, it soon became clear that the bullet-riddled
bodies piled inside the narrow closet were hotel workers
and not terrorists.

Ordered to the top-floor restaurant, the staff-sergeant

and his eager team pounded up the stairs as other units cleared the floors below. Reaching another service corridor, they heard more voices, only this time they were desperate cries of pain. He led his team into the *Windows on the Tyne* restaurant, and they fanned out across the room, weaving their way through the tables. He saw toppled chairs and broken glass that spoke of a recent mass stampede, and he wrinkled his nose disapprovingly at the sight and smell of so much alcohol.

Someone cried out across the far side of the restaurant, and they moved quickly, discovering the bodies scattered across the carpet. Some were dead, but others were still alive, groaning in agony. All were members of the Regional Assembly, and the staff-sergeant's orders were explicit; protect them at all costs and hunt down the terrorists.

'Medic!' he yelled, and two of his men ran forward. It surprised him to see that they had shot the victims in the legs, and he figured it was probably more of a punishment attack than anything else. *The infidels have a lot to learn about terror,* he realised. 'Help them, quickly!'

He took a step closer and looked down at one of the wounded lying on the carpet, an infidel who wore the black uniform of the security police. He was also close to death, but his lips moved and his bloodshot eyes pleaded. As he knelt down, the staff-sergeant's nose wrinkled again, only this time it wasn't alcohol that offended his nostrils.

It was petrol.

The man was trying to speak. The staff-sergeant leaned in closer. 'What?'

'Trap...' the man whispered. '...don't move.'

That's when the staff-sergeant saw it, a bright orange tube tucked beneath the man's left buttock. He pulled it free—

The signalling flare erupted in a cloud of smoke and flame, igniting the infidel with a solid *whump,* and engulfing the staff-sergeant and surrounding bodies in a sheet of flame. Screams shrilled through the restaurant as the surviving Regional Assembly members burned alive, but the staff-sergeant couldn't see or hear them because his own eyes were burning and his ears filled with his own screams as he staggered between the tables like a human torch...

At that precise moment, four of the staff-sergeant's team were about to breach the kitchen, unaware that the air inside was thick with escaping gas. They were also unaware of the tripwire stretched across the doorway. As the screams of their comrades reached them, they charged into the kitchen, overextending the tripwire and detonating the 50-pound HMX charge waiting for them.

The blast was instantaneous, and the resulting shock wave, travelling at 26,000 feet per second, punched its way through concrete, glass, and flesh, and obliterated everything in its path. It turned supporting columns to dust, bringing down the roof above as the entire floor of the hotel erupted in a thundering wall of flame, smoke, and dust.

At street-level, soldiers ducked as debris rained down around them, and a bright orange fireball roiled up and over the collapsed roof of the hotel. The building rocked as the fractured gas main triggered secondary explosions down through the building, killing a dozen more soldiers and hurtling glass and masonry for hundreds of metres.

Watching from their hidden positions, thousands of British troops heard and felt the rippling detonations that thundered across the city. Weapons were gripped a little tighter, selector switches flipped, and hearts beat a little faster. Adrenaline pumped and blood flowed as limbs prepared to explode into action. All they needed now was the signal.

As the second hand reached midnight, the order crackled over the encrypted airwaves...

'All units this is Sunray, engage, engage, engage!'

[25]

TEAR UP

EDITH STOOD IN THE DARKNESS OF HER UNLIT STUDY and stared out of the window. There was nothing much to see other than the shadowy expanse of the gardens below and the sharp outline of nearby rooftops. But the sound, that terrible wailing, filled the wood-panelled room.

She heard police sirens too, rising and falling across the city. The sky above was clear and moonless, but there was nothing in the heavens to alarm her. She crossed the room to her desk and scooped up her mobile phone, speed dialling a number. It was answered after two rings.

'Edith, I was just about to call you.'

'What's happening?'

She heard Governor Davies' muffled voice barking orders as he covered the mouthpiece of his phone. Then he was back, crystal clear.

'Sorry, Edith. It's bedlam here.'

'Just tell me what's happening.'

'We know nothing yet, but I'm hearing rumours of an explosion in Folkestone. Some kind of air attack. There's something happening up north too. The army has issued a general alert, and Congress has ordered me to impose martial law. I'm calling an emergency meeting of the Assembly.'

Now it was Edith's turn to clamp her hand over the mouthpiece. The situation was kinetic, but there was nothing to concern her, not until the picture became clearer. Instead, she turned her mind to potential opportunities.

'Excellent idea,' she told Davies. 'It's important we get ahead of this and lend support to our stakeholders.'

She heard Davies scoff on the other end of the line. 'This isn't a bloody procurement meeting, Edith. This could be it, a full-scale invasion.'

'All you're hearing are rumours, Hugh. You must try to calm yourself.'

Davies lowered his voice. 'Have you started cleaning house yet? There's still a way out of this, you know.'

'A way out?'

'Yes, for God's sake. I'm talking about the Gulf. I've told Molly and the kids. They're packed and ready to go, just in case.'

'In case Wazir orders a withdrawal from Britain, you mean?'

'Jesus Christ, it's like pulling teeth,' he muttered. 'Yes, that's exactly what I mean.'

'Please, Hugh. I'm seeking clarity, nothing more. Now, to be clear, you're preparing to leave the country, yes? Abandon your post?'

Davies' voice was barely more than a whisper. 'If things fall apart, yes.'

'Don't you think you should show leadership at this time?'

'I'm not going to be left behind, Edith. You know what'll happen to us both if that happens.'

Edith heard raised voices in the background. She imagined the panic, fed by Davies himself.

'I'm sending a car for you,' he told her. 'We convene in an hour.'

The call ended, and she checked her phone. The recording was short, but it would be enough.

She plucked the business card from her handbag and dialled the number printed on it.

In one of the large tributary spurs dug beneath Newcastle, a shaped charge blew out a large section of wall close to the metro station at Haymarket, and the first of thirty-six M5 Ripsaw Unmanned Fighting Vehicles bounced over the rubble, spinning left on its tracks before accelerating up the tunnel. The others followed, humming through the tunnel before breaking the surface just beyond the Jesmond Metro station. Engineers had demolished the dividing wall between the tracks and the street minutes earlier, and one by one the M5s breached the shattered wall and entered the battlefield.

Ten Ripsaws turned right and headed north to support the anti-armour teams that were watching and waiting for the enemy troops to deploy from their bases at Newcastle Freeman Hospital and the disused International Airport, close to the frontier. The rest headed south, racing through the streets towards the Tyne River, their operators watching the screens carefully from the deep basement beneath the Newcastle City Assembly building, where the roof now sprouted dozens of communications masts, satellite dishes, and whip antennae. The building and its former occupants had overseen the tyranny that had oppressed the city for the last three years. Now it was the command-and-control centre for the King's Continental Army, and the flood of information flowing in from its multitude of communications and information system nodes was rapidly building a digital, multi-layered graphical representation of the battlefield above.

And information was power.

THE BRADLEY ARMOURED VEHICLES BLOCKING BOTH ends of the Tyne Bridge were the first targets to be hit.

From out of the darkness, eight Javelin anti-tank missiles screamed towards them and destroyed all four vehicles in a blinding crack of orange flame and showers of sparks. The blackened hulks left behind belched thick black smoke into the air.

Above the hotel, the circling Black Hawk had no time and no chance against the incoming Stinger missiles that blew its engines out and severed its rotor blades. The aircraft nosedived 500 feet into the hotel's courtyard entrance where it exploded, killing the caliphate soldiers taking cover in the reception area.

From hundreds of rooftops, windows, and vantage points overlooking the southern bank of the Tyne, a thousand weapon systems opened up on pre-selected targets, chewing up men and machinery in a wave of devastating fire. Tracer rounds lit up the streets like lasers, and when the firestorm ended 60 seconds later, any enemy troops still standing – and there were very few – scattered for their lives.

At the power station on Shields Road, electricity was cut to the rest of the city, plunging the battlefield into darkness. For the waiting British troops, it was all about speed now.

'MOVE! Go!'

Eddie ran hard and fast across the Swing Bridge towards the southern bank. He glanced to his left, saw the burning Bradleys up on the Tyne Bridge, glimpsed soldiers streaming past them, racing to the other side.

Eyes front.

Focus...

Looming ahead, the Hilton hotel burned brightly in the darkness, its windows blown out, fires raging on almost every floor, throwing flickering orange light across their path.

Bravo Company veered right towards the west side of the hotel. Charlie Company turned left, spreading out across Bridge Street as they hard-targeted towards the up-ramp of the Tyne Bridge and the road junction beyond. As platoons started peeling away towards their objectives, Eddie realised he was point man, with Digger and the others just behind him. Ahead, dark figures broke cover, and Eddie slowed, bringing his M27 up and opening fire. The others joined in, and the volley of outgoing rounds cut down three of the runners. As they reached the bodies, Digger shot them all again for good measure.

Eddie kept going, eyes moving left and right, watching the doorways, the windows, the side streets. The burning hotel threw long, suspect shadows. His headset was alive with company-level chatter, and he caught snatches of intel from around the city and beyond. Enemy forces were mobilising, and now it was a race to see who could dominate the battleground first.

They had the element of surprise on their side, Eddie knew that, and the Hajis couldn't know the scale of what they were facing, not yet. Right now, they probably thought they were reacting to a significant and coordinated terrorist attack. They had no idea that thousands of troops were pouring into both Carlisle and Newcastle city centres, that thousands more were making the 20-minute journey through the tunnels. The Hajis would be unaware of the hundreds of SAMs waiting for the expected aerial counter-attack, but soon they would realise the battle wasn't localised. And when they did, they would throw everything they had at the Allies.

So, Newcastle had to be taken, all the way out to Gateshead where *The Angel of the North* metal sculpture once stood, before she'd been cut down and left to rust. Then they would dig in, because one thing was for sure; Wazir would not give up easily.

Eddie led the section into the black shadows of the railway bridge at the junction of Askew Road and the Gateshead Highway. He took a knee in the darkness. He'd been running for half-a-click, had survived their first contact, and was barely out of breath. The exoskeleton was an amazing piece of kit, he realised. He was carrying almost 30 kilos of gear, but he barely felt it. As if to prove his point, a dozen guys from Fire Support Company leap-frogged them, carrying anti-tank weapons, long guns, and belt-fed Sig Sauer M68s like they were nothing. They disappeared into cover across the junction, and Eddie felt a little better knowing they had some decent firepower protecting the Tyne Bridge behind them.

'Hold your ground,' Mac said over the radio. 'Friendly armour approaching from the north.'

Eddie turned and saw two black vehicles racing down

the bridge's off-ramp. They were about the size of a compact car but that's where the similarity ended. The recent arrivals were running on tracks, and the 30-millimetre cannon that swivelled left and right packed a serious punch.

'Ripsaws,' Digger said next to him. They slowed and stopped beneath the bridge, their hybrid engines emitting a quiet whine, and then they lurched forward again, out into the rain, their tracks kicking up rooster tails of spray as they headed south along the Gateshead Highway. Eddie stared through the holographic site of his M27 and watched them disappear into the darkness. The OC's voice hissed in his earpiece.

'We're pushing south, 200 metres, to the north end of the high street. You know your RVs, so get to them fast. Prepare to move...'

Eddie straightened up, tensed—

'Move!'

Then he was running, following Digger out into the rain, leapfrogging their way uphill, cover, move, cover, move, eyes watching the terrain. Unseen drones buzzed above them, scanning the ground ahead, but they couldn't see inside buildings, where a team might be tracking them, frantically loading their belt-fed heavy guns, racking the cocking handles, zeroing in on Eddie through their optics...

Move fast! Stay low!

Eddie did both, heading for the big Tesco superstore on the corner ahead. Digger got there first and brought his rifle up, eye pressed to his hi-powered scope. Eddie bundled in next to him, then Steve, Mac, and the rest of the section. Across the road, the other sections had regrouped and were taking cover. Eddie leaned over Digger and took a quick look at the route ahead. The road sloped gently uphill between lofty buildings, and apart from the line of parked cars, there was hardly any cover.

Digger winked in the dark. 'So far, so good, eh?'

'So far,' Eddie echoed, wondering how and when the enemy would push back.

Mac squeezed in next to them. 'All right, lads?'

'We should keep moving,' Steve said, his eyes fixed on the road ahead.

'And run head-first into a Haji QRF? Yeah, good plan, Steve.'

'Every step south gets me closer to my girls.'

Mac grabbed him by the strap of his tac-vest and yanked him close. 'Forget about home, for fuck's sake! I need you to focus on the here and now, got it? Switch the fuck on!'

Steve stared right back at Mac. 'Take your hand off me.'

Mac pulled him closer, and their helmets banged together. 'Say the word and I'll CASE-VAC you back across the frontier on a psych ticket. Is that what you want?' Steve grimaced, shook his head. 'Good, because I need you. All of you.'

Distant gunfire rattled somewhere behind them. As the shots faded to nothing, Eddie realised that the city had fallen quiet. *The calm before the storm.*

Mac dropped his chin as he listened to an incoming message. He acknowledged it, then said, 'Listen in, we've got hostile traffic inbound from the south. Four soft-skinned Humvees, two with top cover, no armour support. Probably a recce unit. Get into position, watch your front, and wait until I give the word. Move!'

Eddie scuttled over to a low wall nearby and picked a spot behind it. He looked up the road, now dark and deserted, the surrounding buildings lifeless. As the minutes ticked by, all Eddie could hear was the sound of his own breathing and the steady hiss of rain as it swept across the empty road. Then he heard something else.

The whine of approaching Humvees.

FIVE HUNDRED METRES BEHIND THEM, TROOPS WERE still swarming across the Redheugh, the Swing, and the Tyne bridges. Six thousand soldiers had now secured a foothold on an eight-kilometre front south of the river. Ahead of them, spearhead units were pushing further south, securing major road junctions and the rooftops of prominent buildings, establishing communication relay stations and sending drones further south, watching the streets, mapping the battle zone, sniffing the air for the scent of prey. Unmanned ground vehicles raced through the streets, their six-wheeled platforms delivering additional ammunition and supplies to the soldiers guarding the expected routes of enemy counter-attack. So far, those routes were empty, except for the occasional civilian vehicle, and those drivers were quickly appraised of the situation in no uncertain terms:

Go home!

Warn your neighbours!

Stay inside and away from the windows!

Wait for the all-clear...

At the Shields Road control room, power was restored to Newcastle Central train station, to the electrified tracks and signalling equipment. On darkened platforms, 2,000 heavily armed troops from the First, Second, and Third battalions of the New York Volunteers Infantry (British) crammed aboard the waiting carriages. When the train was full, the signal was given, and it clanked and clattered out of the station, its lights extinguished, its wheels spitting bright-white sparks. It curved south, rattling past the former Northumbria Police station, where the night shift was now reflecting on their misplaced loyalties in the questionable comforts of their own cells, guarded by a small team of military policemen.

The train continued on, escorted by a surveillance drone circling beneath the low cloud above, heading for the town of Birtley six miles to the south, close to where the Angel had fallen, and where one day soon she would rise again.

[26]

WATCH AND SHOOT

FROM A WEED-CHOKED DRAINAGE DITCH CLOSE TO
Newcastle International Airport, two ghillie-suited troopers
from the Special Reconnaissance Regiment recorded the
size, strength, and composition of the reaction force that was
surging out from the sprawling installation. They filmed the
Humvees mounted with heavy machine guns and grenade
launchers, the Bradley fighting vehicles, the Oshkosh M-
ATVs, the Chinese Type 96 battle tanks, and the dozen
troop trucks stuffed with caliphate soldiers that followed on
behind. Thirty vehicles, roaring and clattering onto the
southbound A696 and heading for Newcastle. The troopers
filmed it all, including the two Apache attack helicopters
that flew low and fast over the airport's perimeter fence and
disappeared into the darkness beyond.

The footage was broadcast in real-time to the battle
group's HQ and the subsequent encrypted message was
flashed to the troops lying in wait three kilometres to the
south.

Incoming. Standby...

· · ·

IN THE OPERATIONS ROOM AT NORTHWOOD, GENERAL Mousa stood immobile, his arms folded, his eyes glued to the wall of display screens, his ears filtering the nervous chatter around the room. Inside, his stomach churned and his pulse raced. Something was happening, something big, he could feel it in his bones. His gut told him the invasion was beginning, and his soldier's nose smelled trouble of the worst kind, but right now, the situation was confused, and in the absence of clarity he had to rely on the facts.

Fact one; his precious consignment of Chinese missiles had been intercepted and destroyed in a planned attack based on the intelligence stolen by the traitor Al-Kaabi. Seventy per cent of those missiles had been the YJ-78 anti-ship variant, and that was a serious blow to his coastal defence plan. Present stocks were severely limited, crippling his ability to defend the western coast and the Irish Sea beyond, a stormy channel that was even now slowly succumbing to the US Navy.

Fact two; Newcastle and Carlisle had both suffered major terrorist attacks in that last half hour. Both cities were located close to the caliphate's northern frontier and at opposite sides of the country. In Newcastle, anti-tank and surface-to-air weapons had been employed against the reaction force, a sophisticated level of technical planning and execution that the resistance had never used before now, mainly because of the threat of reprisals against local civilians. But not this time.

Fact three; in those same cities, all landline and mobile communications had been lost, and power outages had blacked out the streets. And then there were the reports of enemy troops on the ground, a detail that confused and concerned Mousa the most. So, raiding forces had infiltrated both cities in numbers, but how, and to what end?

Those locations were behind an impenetrable border and surrounded by thousands of caliphate frontier troops, an army that was even now undergoing further reinforcement. Mousa didn't disbelieve the reports – his frontier commanders were not fools – but what he needed now was visual confirmation, especially with his own eyes.

'Where are those QRF fighters?' he asked the room.

One of his intelligence officers, hunched over his terminal, turned and straightened. 'There was a problem with the tanker truck, general. A replacement had to be found. All planes are now fuelled and are preparing for take-off.'

'Once they're airborne, split the formation and vector them to Carlisle and Newcastle. And where are my Seeker drones?'

The officer hesitated. 'Still on the ground, general. ETA to target, three-zero minutes.'

Mousa's black eyebrows knitted together. 'That's the best we can do? Thirty fucking minutes?'

'They were down for a routine maintenance check,' the intelligence officer explained.

'Both of them? At the same time? Whose bright idea was that?'

Everyone in the packed operations room was suddenly deaf and dumb. *It's your fault*, Mousa scolded himself. He'd been away for over two years, and in that time, the battle to conquer Europe had been won, and a formidable barrier built between caliphate territory and Scotland. As a result, the forces of occupation had become complacent. When the infidel task force had set sail across the Atlantic, that complacency had lingered. Now Ireland was lost and the military build-up in Scotland was gathering pace.

It's not your fault, his other voice consoled. Yes, he'd been away for two years and more, but he'd spent much of that time in Baghdad restructuring the armed forces, over-seeing the redeployment of new formations, redrawing the maps of Europe, and carving up the continent into its new protectorates.

There were also additional threats to be anticipated, not just from local resistance groups but from the global players – China, Japan, and the United States among others. Mousa had always suspected the Chinese, despite the pacts made with Beijing. The Chinese trusted no one but themselves, and there was still lingering resentment from some quarters in Baghdad regarding Beijing's historical mistreatment of the Uyghurs. Many of them had moved to the caliphate, but many had stayed in China. After the nuke and the massacres that followed, there was no going back to the era of détente. Diplomacy was failing. War loomed in the east, one that might end them all.

A vile curse brought his attention back to the room. Major General Kalil Zaki, Commander of the North-West Territories, was berating a junior officer while the rest of the room pretended not to notice. Mousa walked over, and Zaki saw him coming. He grabbed the junior officer by the arm and spun him around.

'Tell General Mousa what you just told me!'

Mousa could see the boy was terrified. There was a time and a place for verbal assaults, but now was not one of them. Mousa raised an eyebrow. 'What is it?'

'Enemy troops have landed south of Whitehaven, General Mousa. Size and composition are unknown, and the report is still unconfirmed. I've been trying to re-establish contact—'

'Try harder, idiot!'

Mousa glanced at Zaki. 'Let's hear the boy out, shall we?'

The young officer's hands and voice shook. 'I've been trying to confirm that message but the local transmitters are being jammed, sir.'

Mousa leaned closer. 'You're sure?'

'No, he's not,' Zaki said.

'I've tried the coastal battery too, but they're not responding at all.'

'Get that confirmed,' he told the young officer, and the boy scuttled away. Mousa turned his back on Zaki and walked to the large digital map display. Sure enough, an area of the north-western coast now glowed red. They had lost communications.

'Divert a reinforcement battalion to Whitehaven,' he told the comms officers lined up behind their laptops. 'I want to know when they're close. Do it now.'

'A prudent move, General Mousa.'

Mousa saw that Zaki had sidled up next to him. He was shorter than Mousa, with thin shoulders and thinner grey hair that was slick with pomade. He sported a thick grey moustache, and his dark green uniform was tailored to his slight frame and bedecked with medals and ribbons for achievements and campaigns that Mousa knew he'd neither earned nor deserved. He was the kind of career officer that Mousa despised, and for good reason.

It was Zaki who'd seriously overestimated his ability to prepare for the Alliance assault on Ireland while underestimating the motivation and determination of the invading troops. When that grim reality had finally dawned, Zaki had abandoned the battlefield and decamped to a military bunker in Wales, from where he hoped to direct the defence of Ireland. The resulting string of costly defeats, and the disorganised escape across the Irish Sea, had been an embarrassment. More than that, Mousa had learned of the death of his former 2IC, Colonel Allawi, a loss that still stung. Allawi's death, and those of his men, had been avoidable. They'd died after being ordered to hold an untenable defensive position outside of Belfast, and Mousa discovered later that it was Zaki's crippling indecision that had got his protégé killed. For his crimes, the incompetent blowhard should've dangled kicking and choking at the end of a hangman's noose. Instead, Zaki had ordered the execution of several of his own staff officers to mask his failings.

Mousa despised the man, but he had to swallow that frustration because Kalil Zaki was the only male nephew of the caliph himself, Mohammed Wazir. The man was untouchable, and he knew it. So did everyone else. And now the spineless toad was standing next to him, and the proximity made Mousa's flesh crawl. He took a subtle step away as Zaki's pungent cologne assaulted his sinuses like a blast of tear gas.

'I was just about to order that diversion myself,' the Major-General told him, smoothing his moustache. 'We have two mobile missile launchers armed with ship-killers on that headland. If we lose them, we also lose significant sea defensive coverage.'

Mousa tried and failed to keep the edge from his voice. 'We *have* lost them, Kalil, otherwise they would've reported enemy activity and launched their weapons. Their silence speaks volumes.' He pointed to the map. 'We must also assume that the enemy has landed a considerable mobile force in this area. From Whitehaven they can link up with their troops in Carlisle, or they can push east to Penrith and cut off the M6 motorway from the south. If they can achieve that, our western flank could be compromised.'

'I agree,' Zaki said, puffing his chest. 'The situation is troublesome. What are your orders, general?'

'Get those fighters and drones in the air. Send a reinforcement division to Kendal, here, in the Lake District, then rush another one north to Penrith. The 77th Airborne Battalion is standing by at Manchester Airport. I want them on the ground, at Penrith, to seize and hold the town before Alliance forces can get there. Every other military unit north of Nottingham is to deploy to their defensive positions as per standing orders.'

'Understood. Anything else, general?'

'Yes. I want all of our fighter-bomber squadrons in the Dutch and Belgian protectorates to be fuelled, armed, and ready to deploy.'

'I'll send the orders immediately.'

Mousa found a spare chair and sat down, his eyes studying the digital maps and TV screens. There were skirmishes erupting here and there, and a probable landing force south of Whitehaven, but there was no powerful gesture of intent, no artillery or rocket attacks, no mass movement of troops. *What the hell is happening?*

Whatever this thing was, Mousa's gut was telling him that things were about to get a lot worse. It was also telling him something else, something he'd suspected for a long time, a suspicion that had recently been confirmed.

And one that would change the course of a war that was about to engulf the country.

QRF

'*INCOMING.*'

The platoon commander's transmission was unnecessary. The whole of Nine Platoon saw the convoy of Humvees racing down the hill towards them. Eddie looked left and right along the wall. Digger was on one side, Steve on the other, both with their eyes glued to their gun sights. The Humvees slowed for the junction, and Eddie saw that the earlier intel was correct. Only two of the vehicles had heavy weapons mounted in the top turret, and the vehicles, though stuffed with troops, were soft-skinned, their open windows bristling with gun barrels.

The platoon commander again...

'*All sections stand by. Watch your rounds. Wheels and engines intact.*'

The Humvees were dark shapes against a darker background, but Eddie's holographic sights made them jump out. The vehicles stopped. Three Section's target was the second vehicle, and Eddie was going for the driver. He saw the guy's face in his sight, settled his red dot just beneath the man's eye. He was looking straight ahead, unaware of the gun barrel pointed at him. Eddie heard voices talking in rapid-fire Arabic.

'*Engage*—'

Eddie squeezed the trigger and the M27 kicked in his shoulder. He saw the driver's head snap backwards, and he fired again. Eddie switched targets and pumped rounds into the passenger seat, saw the guy there jerk and slump over. He switched again, firing several more rounds at the guys in the back before he clicked on empty and swapped his magazine out. That's when he saw the rear vehicle attempt to escape. It made a wide, desperate turn, wheels screeching, engine screaming, and then the windscreen blew out and the doors were peppered with dozens of five-five-six millimetres. The Humvee stalled, jerking across the road before coming to a stop.

By the time Eddie had his rifle back in his shoulder, the order went out.

'*Cease fire, cease fire!*'

Thirty-six guns were trained on six immobile, bullet-riddled vehicles. Smoke hung in the air as the rain fell across the intersection.

'*Movement, rear vehicle!*'

Suppressed weapons opened up around him. Eddie didn't engage. He had a full mag on, and besides, his rounds were unnecessary. The firing stuttered away. Whoever had moved in that vehicle, it was the last one they'd ever make.

'*Three and Four Sections, advance. Watch your step, lads.*'

They got to their feet, and Eddie was moving fast through the rain towards the front of the convoy. He headed for the lead vehicle, watching over his sights, Digger moving up on his right. The engine was still running. Eddie scanned the bodies for any signs of movement. Digger didn't bother. He rested the barrel of his M38 on the door and pumped rounds into the corpses. They jerked lifelessly, heads lolling, mouths bloodied and gaping.

'For fuck's sake, Digger!'

The young soldier ignored him. He was already moving on to the second Humvee. Eddie double-checked the corpses, and he swallowed when he saw the deadly green orbs clipped to their webbing. *Grenades.*

Boots crunched on broken glass as doors were thrown open and the bodies dragged to the side of the road. All six vehicles were serviceable, and Nine Platoon was ordered aboard. Mac and the rest of Three Section piled into the second Humvee. There was blood all over the seats, but none of them had time to worry about that now. Steve got behind the wheel and Digger rode shotgun, smashing out the rest of the shattered windscreen with the barrel of his rifle. Eddie sat behind Steve and trained his weapon out of the side window. Next to him, Mac covered their left flank.

'That was lucky,' Eddie grumbled.

Mac gave him a look. 'They didn't get a single round off.'

'I'm talking about Digger, emptying rounds into dead bodies with grenades hanging all over them. Fucking idiot.'

'Stop whining, Novak. You're still here, ain't ya?'

'No thanks to you, you sloppy little prick.'

Digger swivelled around, his camouflaged face twisted in anger. 'Go fuck yourself—'

'Shut the fuck up!' Mac said, punching the back of Digger's seat.

'Problem, Corporal Mac?'

The platoon commander leaned in Eddie's window. Mac shook his head.

'All good, boss. The girls were moaning about the weather, that's all.'

The commander's face said he wasn't buying it. 'Whatever it is, keep a lid on it, got it?'

'Aye, sir.'

'Right, we're heading south,' he told them. 'Mission is to recce the route ahead, then hold the road junction at the A1. GPS has been linked.'

Eddie flipped his wrist, thumbed the button on his Garmin watch, saw the new grid reference. Mac checked his too.

'All received, boss.'

'HQ is reporting an enemy convoy mobilising out of Durham, about 15 klicks to the south, so we need to beat them to that junction. We're waiting on the signal to move, so stand by.'

'Roger that.'

The commander lingered. 'Are we good?'

'As gold, boss.'

He walked away. Mac waited until he was out of earshot. 'You fuckers are making me look bad,' he fumed. 'Whatever beefs you've got – grenades, stranded family – I don't want to hear about it, understood? We've got a job to do.' He punched the back of Digger's seat again. 'And you, use your fucking head or you'll get us all killed. I won't tell you again.'

There was silence in the Humvee. When Mac spoke again, his voice snarled dangerously. 'You'd better fucking acknowledge me or—'

'Sorry, Mac.'

'Sure.'

'Won't happen again.'

Outside, the OC spun his finger in the air and Steve

gunned the engine, swinging the Humvee around until it lined up behind the others. Now they were facing south, engines idling, rain drumming on the roof and falling through the missing windscreen. The minutes ticked by.

Steve clipped his NVGs on his helmet and flipped them down. He drummed his fingers on the wheel. 'Any idea what we're waiting for?'

All eyes were on Mac. He was listening to the battalion chatter, his head down, a finger pressed to his ear. 'That,' he said, jerking a thumb over his shoulder.

Eddie twisted around in his seat and looked back towards the Tyne Bridge.

'What?'

The northern horizon lit up in a storm of light and thunder.

THE QRF CONVOY WAS TRAVELLING SOUTH AT SPEED along the A696, using both lanes of the southbound carriageway in two tightly-packed cavalcades. A hundred metres short of the Newbiggin Lane exit, controlled explosions brought the concrete overpass crashing down onto the road in a mountain of rubble, steel, and dust, completely blocking both sides of the four-lane highway. The lead Humvees slammed on their brakes, skidding on the wet surface and disappearing into the rolling dust cloud. One turned hard left, careering up the grassy bank and crunching into the trees by the side of the road. The other hit what was left of the bridge at 40 kilometres an hour, its back end flipping over and slamming down on to the rubble, crushing everyone inside.

Right behind the Humvees, AFVs swerved, skidded, and ploughed into each other, swiftly followed by the tanks.

Collisions rippled along the convoy as panicked drivers stamped on brake pedals and wrenched their steering wheels and stick controls, resulting in a deadly, chaotic pileup.

From the trees above the now-blocked highway, British troops launched round after round of smoke, CS gas, and fragmentation grenades amongst the pile-up. Within seconds, half the convoy was wrapped in a thick, choking fog of blinding smoke, and grenades detonated amongst the tightly packed traffic jam of tanks and armoured vehicles.

Two hundred metres behind the convoy, more British troops scrambled down the banks and onto the road. A dozen of them held Javelin fire-and-forget anti-tank missiles, their Command Launch Units pre-selected for the *Top-Attack* flight profile. Within seconds of their boots hitting the tarmac, the gunners had acquired their targets and fired their weapons. The missiles launched in blasts of white smoke and flew up into the air, screaming skyward before arcing over and slamming down into the thinner top metal of the tanks and AFVs. The targeted vehicles blew spectacularly, and one tank turret spiralled into the air in a ball of fire before crashing to earth. Burning fuel spilt across the highway, flooding the scene in orange light and engulfing undamaged vehicles desperately trying to escape the conflagration. As crews abandoned their burning rides, ammunition began cooking off as blackened and crippled armour began to 'brew up'.

But the British gunners weren't finished yet. Assisted by their ammo-bearers, they loaded new missile tubes onto their CLUs and selected *Direct-Fire* mode. They launched again, and 12 more HEAT rounds roared down the road, slamming into several more vehicles. Explosions rippled through the convoy, sending more fireballs rolling into the night sky. Two of the HEAT rounds were fired at the packed troop transports, blasting men and machinery to bits and blocking any escape to the north.

Breaking cover once more, the troops above the destroyed bridge rained down more smoke and gas before making their escape across the surrounding fields to their commandeered vehicles. The Javelin teams had already fled, leaving their discarded missile tubes scattered across the road behind them. The ambush had lasted less than 60 seconds.

The driver of the lead troop truck had cringed in fear as missiles destroyed everything in front and behind him. As the world around him burned, he glimpsed the nearby off-ramp through the thick black smoke and gunned his truck towards it. As a handful of other trucks followed, the driver failed to see the Ripsaw that straddled the road ahead, nor did he see – or feel – the 30-millimetre subsonic round that punched through his cab and blew his torso apart. The truck lurched to the right, careering down the grass bank before flipping over onto its side. The Ripsaw advanced down the off-ramp, firing its auto-cannon into the other troop trucks, stopping them in their tracks, chopping men and machinery to bloody pieces and cutting down the runners who'd scrambled from their disabled, shredded transports.

The Ripsaw accelerated past the fleeing figures and down onto the road, spinning around on its tracks and heading for what was left of the convoy. It manoeuvred through the swirling smoke, seeking out still-serviceable tanks and fighting vehicles, its explosive shells blowing out tracks and wheels, punching rounds through engine blocks and turning terrified clusters of cowering troops into wet pulp.

As the wind picked up and the fog of war dispersed, the Ripsaw started to take incoming rounds, but it fought back valiantly, expending its ammunition in an auto-storm of kinetic violence until its magazines were empty. Only then did it succumb to the RPGs and the grenades thrown its way, but by then the deadly UFV had done its job. As its electrics fried and its CPUs failed, its smoking cannon barrel dipped for the last time...

Overhead, a Predator UAV broke through the low cloud and circled the ambush site below, sending live footage back to the Battle Group HQ, where it was analysed by damage assessment teams and a group of senior officers. The conclusion was unanimous; the enemy convoy had been successfully neutralised.

The battalion commander of the Second Mass, Colonel Butler, put it a little more succinctly as he smiled beneath his eye patch.

'Those boys just got their arses well and truly kicked.'

Several hours after leaving Barksdale Air Force Base in Louisiana, the flight of B-52s, now split into two formations of eight planes, lined up on their targets and began their bombing runs. *Rolling Thunder* was about to begin.

Thirty-two thousand feet below the aircraft, and separated by a distance of twenty-one kilometres, two stretches of no-man's-land had been pre-selected for the next phase of the ground operation. The target areas were located between the cities of Carlisle and Newcastle, sites that were also home to the dense clusters of surface-to-air missile batteries that populated that barren region of the frontier.

Fifteen nautical miles apart, the two groups of B-52s

made their final course corrections and armed their weapons. Bomb bay doors opened, and one by one, each aircraft dumped its 70,000-pound payload of explosive ordinance into the choppy night air before banking away to the north.

Far below them, huddled in their bunkers and inside their launch vehicles, frontier troops and SAM crews were desperately trying to make sense of the electrical interference that had disrupted their targeting radars. They knew they were being jammed, but they were unaware that the culprits were the Growlers who had given the escaping B-52s the electronic cover they'd needed to do their job. Those troops were also unaware of the storm of death falling towards them from the night sky above.

The precision bombs and proximity-fuse munitions continued to fall unseen from the heavens, whistling through the frigid air, rushing towards the ground that was rushing up to meet them...

The detonations rippled along the heavily-defended hilltops in strobe-like pulses of white light, throwing fountains of damp earth hundreds of meters into the air. The first salvo of bombs took out 90 per cent of the target's mobile SAM launchers, even as their oblivious crews continued to recycle their targeting software. In the bunkers beneath the hills, penetrator munitions burrowed deep before detonating, destroying sub-surface command centres, heavy-weapons emplacements, and strategic overwatch positions, killing everyone and destroying everything both above and below ground.

For the other B-52s, their targets were the areas of no-man's-land beyond those bunkers and hilltop fortifications, the dark, deadly ground that symbolised the gulf between freedom and oppression. Over 15 tons of explosive ordnance stamped across the earth in the wake of the aircrafts' passage, obliterating thousands of mines and shredding every trap and obstacle that had been dug, planted, and buried in that shadowy valley between the worlds.

The bombardment lasted for 12 minutes and lit up the sky for 30 miles in all directions, the God-like thunder still rumbling long after the B-52 pilots had jammed their throttles to the stops and escaped towards northern Scotland. Behind them, thick smoke hung heavily over the devastation, blanketing the hills and valleys, but that wouldn't last long.

Watching from across the frontier, British and American engineers steered their multi-wheeled UGVs down into the shattered valleys and ran them over the broken ground, just in case. The word came back soon enough. The route was clear, the door now open.

The engineers exploded into action.

[28]
REGIME CHANGE

Edith made her last call just as the Mercedes glided to a halt outside the Regency building on Pall Mall. Waiting flunkies hurried forward, opening her door and shielding her with umbrellas from the damp, squally wind barrelling along the pavement.

Crossing the carpeted lobby, she ignored the fawning salutations from the liveried staff who took her raincoat and escorted her to the large, white-pillared meeting hall. As her low heels clicked across the parquet flooring, she noted that every member of the National Assembly was in attendance, including Governor Davies.

Every *living* member, she reminded herself.

Davies was clearly peeved by Edith's late entrance, but she ignored his irritation as she took her seat at the large circular meeting table. She put her bag by her feet and nodded to Victor a few chairs away. There were other figures gathered in the shadows around the walls of the impressive room – Assembly deputies, assorted bag carriers – and Edith suspected that her guests were there somewhere amongst them, watching expectantly. It behoved her not to keep them waiting.

'Chief Justice, thank you for joining us,' Davies began, his cold attempt at sarcasm not lost on the other attendees. She said nothing in reply, folding her arms on the table, the lighting above picking out the crystal dragonfly pinned to her austere navy suit jacket that was buttoned to the neck.

Davies shuffled the reams of official papers in front of him and cleared his throat. 'Thank you all for making the journey here this evening. I've convened this meeting to discuss a matter of the utmost gravity.' He paused dramatically, then said, 'For those of you who don't yet know, several major terrorist attacks have been carried out against targets in our frontier cities, and there are reports – as yet unconfirmed – of British and American troops on our soil, constituting an illegal invasion.'

Gasps of shock circled the gathering. Assembly members traded worried looks, their tired faces stretched with sudden anxiety. Edith ignored it all, her lips firmly closed, her eyes focused on Davies. The governor held up a hand for silence.

'Yes, the news is troubling; however, the situation has been contained, and Caliph Wazir, *peace be upon him,* has publicly condemned the actions as acts of terror. A robust response has been promised.'

'Is this war?' someone asked.

Others gave voice to their anxiety, and a nervous jabbering filled the hall. Once again, Davies raised his hand, and his voice. 'We must remain calm,' he cautioned. 'I'm liaising closely with Congress and will keep the Assembly updated as necessary.'

Edith had heard enough. She got to her feet and waited

until all eyes in the hall were watching her. Davies glowered.

'I'm not finished, Edith, so please sit. You can have the floor in due course.'

She ignored him, pointing to the single empty chair. 'You may all be wondering why Director Cox hasn't joined us this evening—'

'Edith, take your seat,' Davies interrupted.

'Quiet!' she bellowed, turning on him, her eyes bulging behind her glasses. The hall fell silent. Davies' face was frozen in shock. 'Gerrard isn't here because he's dead,' she told her stunned audience. 'He was assassinated earlier this evening, along with several of his Regional Assembly. The hotel where they were meeting has also been destroyed, and all contact has been lost with the city of Newcastle.'

She could see genuine fear on the faces around her now. Only Victor remained composed, because only Victor knew what was coming.

'Governor Davies has failed us,' she told them, pointing an accusing finger at the pale-faced politician. 'He has failed us as a leader, and as a founding member of this Assembly. He has betrayed us all.'

Davies snapped to his feet. 'Enough, Edith—'

'Traitor!' she barked at him, then looked at each of the Assembly members. 'Hugh Davies has already decided to abandon his post in the event of a major escalation of hostilities. Not only his post, but us, his comrades, and his friends in the Islamic Congress. He has shredded official documents and deleted important and sensitive emails to cover his tracks. In a time of crisis, these actions are unforgivable.'

Davies thumped his fist on the table. 'Those are lies! It is you who...'

His voice trailed away as several suited figures stepped out of the shadows. Edith watched Davies' eyes widen as he recognised Colonel Al-Huda of the CID.

'What's happening here?' he stammered.

'A change of leadership,' Edith explained. 'Colonel Al-Huda has evidence of your betrayal. It is him you must answer to now.'

'What are you talking abo—'

Al-Huda cracked Davies around the mouth with his knuckles. The governor staggered into the arms of two large, suited men behind him. Al-Huda approached the table as a suddenly terrified Davies stood in silent shock, blood streaming from his lip.

'Chief Justice Spencer has shown unswerving loyalty to the caliphate,' Al-Huda told them. 'You would do well to thank her. And take heed of her wise counsel.' Then he turned and walked away, a limp, frightened Davies in tow.

No one said a word as the footsteps receded, and Davies was frogmarched from the hall. The last thing they heard was his desperate pleas before the distant door slammed closed.

Victor got to his feet. 'We need to put this business behind us, and quickly. In light of the current crisis, and in the absence of an official ballot, I propose Chief Justice Spencer for the post of interim governor, effective immediately. All those in favour say *aye.*' A chorus of single-syllable affirmations echoed around the table. Victor smiled and gestured to Davies' empty chair.

'Governor Spencer, if you please.'

Edith picked up her handbag and circled the table. She sat down in the governor's high-backed leather seat with its embossed gold seal and wheeled it into the table.

'Thank you.' She nodded, looking at each of them. 'You should know I have asked for, and expect to receive, an endorsement of my governorship from Chief Judge of the Supreme Judicial Assembly of Europe, Abdul bin Abdelaziz himself. In the meantime, as interim governor, my first appointment will be Victor Hardy to the position of chief justice, and Andrea Clarke to assume Victor's former role as judge advocate general. If anyone has any objections, voice them now.' Her cold eyes scanned the faces for dissenters, but there were none. 'Good, now to business.'

Edith kept the discussion rooted in local issues to restore calm and order. She opened up the floor to questions, most of which concerned the conflict along the frontier. The discussion continued until Edith brought a halt to the proceedings.

'It's almost four am,' she told the drawn faces around the table. 'Tomorrow I shall meet with Congress and seek further updates regarding the unfolding crisis. In the meantime, I want you all to return to your districts and to prepare for difficult times ahead. This country is now on a war footing, and martial law is in force. I urge you to control your people. Punish dissenters and punish them severely. This is not a time for squeamishness. Remember, our erstwhile colleagues in Newcastle were savagely murdered. You might be next. Good night.'

The table rose as one, and the delegates filed from the hall, followed by the audience in the wings. Edith leafed through the official papers abandoned by her predecessor.

Across the table, Victor lingered behind his chair, and after the last person had left the room, he retook his seat, a broad smile on his ruddy face.

'Bravo, Edith, well played.'

Edith said nothing as she made notes on a pad.

'You had them eating out of your hand,' he continued. 'Very impressive.'

Edith finally looked up. 'It's important to assert the authority of office,' she told him, glasses balanced on the end of her nose.

'Even if it's only temporary.'

Edith put down her pen. 'Meaning?'

Victor leaned closer. 'France, Edith. Have you thought about it?'

The governor frowned. 'France? My dear Victor, that's out of the question.'

Victor winked. 'I understand. You've taken on a considerable responsibility. But bear it in mind, in case things really *do* go tits up.'

Edith swept the glasses from her face. 'Let me clarify. France is out of the question for *you,* Victor. Were you not listening? You're now Chief Justice of the British Territories, a hugely important and symbolic position. You have a duty to this administration and to the people of this protectorate. There'll be no swanning off to France with Margaret, no early retirement, do you understand?'

Victor's brow furrowed, his eyes narrowing with uncertainty. Then the moment passed. He got to his feet and buttoned his jacket. 'Yes, of course, Edith. It's been a long day, and the old brain's a little foggy. I should go.'

Edith slipped her glasses on and settled into her reading. As he walked away, she called to him.

'Yes, Edith?'

'You will address me as *governor* from now on,' she told him without looking up. There were a few moments of silence before the new chief justice answered.

'Yes, Governor Spencer.'

'Here.' She scratched her signature on a sheet of headed paper and pushed it across the polished surface with a finger. Victor picked it up.

'What's this?'

'Orders for the crucifixion of Gordon Tyndall and his co-conspirators. To serve as a lesson to those who would take up arms against us, and to remind others who might consider such actions that my administration will not tolerate rebellion.'

Victor stared at the paper, then at her. 'Governor, if I may—'

'Somewhere public, Victor. So that lesson is fully understood.'

The chief justice gave her a curt nod. 'I'll see to it.'

She watched him disappear into the shadows. After the closing door had echoed behind him, Edith put down her pen and replayed recent events in her mind. Victor was right, she'd outmanoeuvred Davies, but then Victor himself had learned that he'd also been compromised. Right now he would wonder if his own conversations about fleeing to France had been recorded, how those words might be misconstrued, his loyalty to the caliphate questioned. Victor was squeaky clean and had served his time well as judge advocate, but he was only human, and he'd seen enough to know that under a totalitarian regime, one was never far away from denouncement and ruination. As Hugh Davies and his family were about to find out.

No, under such regimes it was far more prudent to acquire power than to avoid it, far better to stand on that pedestal than hide beneath it, hoping the cold eye of authority would look elsewhere. Like the weakling he'd proven himself to be, Davies had folded at the first hint of trouble, desperate to save his own skin. Edith had no intention of doing the same. Quite the contrary, in fact.

To secure her future with the caliphate and its rulers, the newly appointed governor of the British Territories had every intention of showing just how ruthless she could be.

[29]
WILLIE GUNN

SOMEWHERE ABOVE THEM, A DRONE WATCHED THE road ahead, its live feed monitored by battalion HQ. If there was significant trouble ahead, they'd know about it beforehand. If there were tripwires strung across the road, or landmines strapped to street lights, they'd find out about that too. The hard way.

Eddie swiped the rain from his ballistic glasses. His rifle was resting on the window frame, barrel out, but if there was a target out there, he'd never see it in time. They were passing through a dark, dead world. Shops, houses, yards, car lots, all flashed by. They were travelling fast, to get to the junction before the enemy organised themselves. Steve drove with his NVGs. Digger was next to him, the stock of his M38 jammed into his shoulder, the bipod resting on the hood of the Humvees. Both of them were soaked by the rain lashing through the shattered windows, but neither man seemed to notice. As they rounded a curve in the road, bright lights washed over them.

'Watch it!' Mac warned, as the lead Humvee suddenly slowed. They were running tactically, which meant no brake lights. Eddie was thrown into the back of the driver's seat as Steve stamped hard on the anchors. They all heard the boss' voice in their ears.

'Mac, get those civvies turned around!'

Mac kicked open his door. 'Eddie, Digger, let's go!'

Eddie did the same and ran through the rain towards the lead Humvee. Fifty metres beyond it, a row of civilian vehicles had double-parked in the road, a group of shadowy figures having a discussion. The top gunner looked down at Eddie and cocked his helmet.

'Go, Novak. We got you covered.'

He moved forward, watching the vehicles, watching the ten or so pale faces gathered in the rain. Some of them raised their hands. Mac held his rifle low, but Eddie knew he could open that baby up in a blink of an eye. He moved closer, watching the cars. There were women and children in a couple of them, and he heard a baby crying too. Mac raised his voice over the rain, over the screaming kid.

'I'm Corporal McAllister, Second Massachusetts Battalion, King's Continental Army. We're taking control of the city. You need to go home, right now. All of you.'

Eddie watched a big guy in a black coat and baseball cap step towards Mac. He seemed unafraid, and Eddie tensed. When he spoke it was with a local accent.

'You're British?'

'Yep.'

'And you're here to stay?'

Mac nodded. 'Abso-fucking-lutely.'

The man pointed to the idling Humvees. 'You'll need more than that, pal. There're thousands of 'em down in Durham. That's only ten miles from here.'

'And they're on their way,' Mac told him, 'so go home

and stay away from the windows. Tell your neighbours too. Take care of your families until you get the all-clear.'

The man stepped closer, snatching a quick look towards the car Eddie was standing behind. Inside, a woman had a toddler on her lap, and she looked terrified. *The guy's wife and kid,* Eddie assumed.

'How bad's it going to get?' the big Geordie asked in a gloomy voice.

'Bad enough,' Mac told him, grim-faced. He pointed south. 'Anything we should be worried about down there?'

'I've just driven up from Crowther,' a young woman in a damp hoodie told him. 'That's about three kilometres away. The roads are quiet. I didn't see any of their soldiers. It's the police and security people you have to watch out for.'

'Bastard traitors,' cursed the big man.

Mac jerked his thumb. 'Go home, quick as you can.'

The civvies scattered back into their cars and headed off into the night. Eddie and the others re-boarded their own vehicles, and the convoy headed south again. The girl in the hoodie was right, the road was empty almost all the way. The only other traffic they saw was the odd civvy car, but there was no time to stop and warn them.

As the buildings fell away and the dark countryside opened up around them, Eddie saw a familiar silhouette by the side of the road and realised what it was; *The Angel of the North,* cut down from her mount yet partly raised by a rusted wing. Then she was behind them, and suddenly the Humvee was slowing.

'Hang on,' Steve warned, as he wrenched the wheel hard left and followed the lead vehicle into a dark, tree-lined side road a hundred metres short of the junction of the A1. Eddie caught a sign as they drove along the narrow lane, and he thought it said *Care Home.* That was confirmed when they stopped outside a flint-walled building. Gathered by the main door, a group of worried nurses huddled beneath their umbrellas.

Orders were issued, and Nine Platoon started spreading out through the hamlet of grey stone houses, evacuating the buildings, sending the civvies back towards Newcastle and out of harm's way. Some didn't want to leave and slammed their doors shut. Eddie didn't blame them, and besides, the settlement was well hidden from the nearby roundabout behind a thick screen of leafless trees and a boundary wall. Three Section gathered in the dark.

'We're the first ones here,' Mac told them, 'so we're gonna deploy across the southern flank of this hamlet and watch the roads until the rest of the company gets here. Spread yourselves along that boundary wall and keep your eyes front. The boss is setting up back at the care home. You see anything, call it in.'

'We've got no fire support,' Digger observed. 'If there's armour on its way, we're fucked.'

'The boss is on it, so stop your bitching and get into position.'

They moved out into the open ground beyond the hamlet. The flint wall loomed out of the dark, wet and shiny in the rain. It was thick too, Eddie noted, resting his rifle on top. He squinted through his battle sight. There was another 50 metres of dead ground to their front, before the trees thinned out at the roundabout. Their fields of fire were restricted but they'd be hard to spot from the roundabout and the A1 overpass which was good news. Mac came over and gave them some more.

'The rest of the company is inbound, ETA, 15 minutes. First, Second, and Third New Yorkers are taking the train south to the town of Birtley, about five klicks that way,' he told them, pointing into the darkness. Their mission is to secure the big road junction to the south of the town, block the major routes to the north and west, but they might not get there in time to intercept the Haji convoy. Things are fluid, boys, so stay sharp, watch your front and keep your ears open.'

Then he was gone, melting into the dark. Eddie stared through his battle sight again. He caught a movement to his right, and two Ripsaws hummed past the roundabout and disappeared to the south.

He heard Steve mutter something. Eddie leaned closer. 'What was that?'

'I said, I'm only 18 miles from home now. Getting closer all the time.'

'Put it out of your head,' Eddie warned. 'And for chrissakes, don't let Mac hear you.'

'That's what, a 20-minute drive?' Digger said.

Eddie flashed him a look. 'Let's stay focussed, yeah?'

'Nipper's right. Twenty minutes in a car, half-hour tops.'

'Steve, please...'

All of them heard the whistle that rose to a scream—

'Incoming!'

BOOM! BOOM! BOOM!

Eddie curled up tight against the wall as the earth shook and a sky full of rock and mud rained down on them.

EIGHTY-SIX MILES TO THE WEST, THE 26TH MARINE Expeditionary Unit had begun their assault on the Cumbrian coast. First to make dry land were the MV-22 Osprey transports, skimming low across the sea, then rising over the bluffs at St. Bees Head before tilting their rotors and setting down in the flat fields surrounding the village of Sandwith. Within minutes the aircraft had disgorged over 600 US Marines before heading back to their respective assault ships to reload with more troops.

As the Marines advanced towards the unsuspecting harbour town of Whitehaven, landing craft appeared out of the darkness of the sea and nosed their way into St. Bees beachfront, a mile-long stretch of sand and shingle already secured by US Navy SEALs. The landing craft pilots lined up their vessels and took it in turns to run them up onto the concrete slip road used by the local RNLI. The first vehicles ashore were four M1 Abrams battle tanks, and they roared into the abandoned hamlet of St. Bees itself, past the burning wreckage of the Haji missile launchers and the scattered corpses, men who'd had the serious misfortune of engaging in a gunfight with a SEAL Team Task Unit.

At the southern end of the beach, more landing craft powered inland, their forward ramps slamming down into wet shingle and disgorging ten ARVs and the same number of Ripsaws. The ARVs roared up the beach and into the visitor car park, quickly linking up with the tanks and forming two distinct elements. One headed south to secure the nuclear power station at Sellafield, currently being held by another SEAL Task Force. The other element headed towards the outskirts of Whitehaven, providing cover on the approach roads leading to the town.

As the first hour passed, the Marines encountered little resistance. There were several sporadic small-arms fire engagements, and an ARV was taken out by an anti-tank weapon on the road into Whitehaven. As the harbour there was seized, the ships of a Marine Expeditionary Brigade had already cleared the rocky coast of the Isle of Man and were steaming towards the Cumbrian shoreline. The brigade comprised another 12,000 combat Marines and their support elements, and their mission was to reinforce the bridgehead and push inland towards the Lake District National Park, sealing off every route to the north-west coast.

To achieve its mission, the Atlantic Alliance needed to dominate the airspace over the frontier.

Over a hundred Global Hawk surveillance drones took to the night sky from the runways of Belfast, Glasgow, and Edinburgh airports. They climbed to a cruising altitude of 6,000 feet, where they grouped into loose formations that stretched along a front of over 50 kilometres.

The drones were not the sophisticated and hugely expensive Global Hawks, however. These aircraft were a new variant constructed especially for this mission, stripped-down of all essential parts, with unpainted fuse-lages, shorter wings, and reconditioned engines. They had no sensors or aerial surveillance equipment of any kind. These were 'dumb' drones, equipped only with IFF transponders, a guidance package, and a swarm-management software program that enabled a single ground operations team to control dozens of Global Hawks at any one time.

Turning in fuel-efficient circles behind the frontier, the ground controllers programmed the UAVs into intelligent swarms. As the software took over their guidance, they moved into combat formations, making flight corrections in absolute synchronicity. On a command from their operators, the swarms turned to the south and increased power.

As they approached the frontier, their transponders began announcing their presence to the world.

The blind, defenceless aircraft were about to play a hugely critical role in the unfolding campaign.

As bait.

[30]
COUP DE GRACE

THE WARNING BUZZER SCREECHED AROUND THE WALLS
of the operations room, startling Major-General Zaki out of
his dream-like wanderings.

'We're getting something, general! Multiple inbound
bogeys approaching our airspace from multiple vectors.'

Zaki hurried across to the seated operator. 'Show me.'

'I've put it up on the primary screen, sir.'

Zaki glanced up at the wall display and saw clusters of
red icons heading towards caliphate territory from the Scottish border and the Irish Sea. As they approached, the red
icons faded, disappeared, then glowed again.

'What's happening?'

'Intermittent jamming, sir. It's difficult to get a fix.'

'What are they?'

'Hard to say.'

Zaki glared at the young hijab still tapping at her laptop.
'Take a wild guess.'

She turned her veiled head and looked up at him with
cautious eyes. 'Judging by speed, altitude, and vector, I

suspect they are fighter-bombers or similar ground-attack aircraft, sir.'

Zaki watched the screen, the angry red bees swarming towards caliphate territory.

'We're burning through the jamming,' reported another seated technician. 'Target acquisition is imminent.'

'How many SAM units can we engage?'

'Because of the recent bombing, we've lost significant coverage,' the hijab told him, 'however, our tactical envelope along the frontier remains intact. All SAM units are currently running in passive mode to avoid enemy counter-batteries.'

'I know that,' snapped Zaki. 'And someone turn that fucking buzzer off!'

He watched the screen, the swarm that was approaching caliphate airspace along a 60-kilometre front. He glanced to his left, to the gaggle of Ops Team officers who stood watching, waiting. He knew they hated him, knew he was tolerated only because of his lineage, and yet he felt an irrational desire to impress them.

What would Mousa do? he wondered. He'd be decisive, that was for certain, but Mousa wasn't here. He'd stepped out, and now Zaki could feel the tension in the room, the furtive looks, the doubt. The expectancy...

'Enemy aircraft have entered caliphate airspace,' the hijab announced.

This is no time for uncertainty, the voice whispered in his ear. It was the same voice he'd heard these last few nights, a low, gravelly whisper from the shadows of his private quarters. Last night, that voice had taken form and emerged from the shadows. Last night it had sat on his bed.

They treat you as a child, it had told him, and it was

right. He *was* a leader of men, a decision-maker, confident and forthright.

Zaki took a deep breath and squared his shoulders. 'Order all SAM units to go active. Stop those bombers now!'

'At once, general!'

FAR TO THE NORTH, STATIC, MOBILE, AND MAN-portable surface-to-air launchers went to active-seeker mode and found their targeting radars cluttered with fast-approaching bogeys. All along the frontier, missiles launched in a spectacular display of firepower, the weapons streaking into the pre-dawn sky, the explosions rippling through the massed ranks of Global Hawks, shredding fuse-lages, igniting fuel tanks, and sending flaming wreckage tumbling to earth and sea.

MOUSA RETURNED TO THE OPERATIONS ROOM AND SAW a smiling Zaki clapping a hand on the shoulder of one of his techs. He hurried across the floor. 'What have I missed?'

Zaki beamed. 'Success, General Mousa. I have stopped a major assault by enemy aircraft in its tracks.'

'An assault? When?'

'Moments ago.'

Mousa stared at the screen. 'Play back the recording.' He watched the enemy aircraft approach, then cross the frontier. He studied their vectors, their IFFs, their altitude and speed. Then he studied their reaction to the incoming missiles. He checked the live screen again; there were two survivors, flying together, still heading south, now deep over caliphate territory. The red icons made no abrupt changes in height, speed, or course. Nothing at all. Mousa closed his eyes.

'Are you feeling all right?'

They snapped open, and he glared at Zaki. 'Follow me.' When they were out of earshot, Mousa rounded on him. 'Kalil, you just engaged multiple decoy drones.'

Zaki looked faintly amused. 'Impossible. Their transponders identified them as fighter-bombers.'

Mousa shook his head. 'They were drones. How many SAM units engaged?'

'All of them.'

Mousa fought to control his temper. 'They did it to deplete our missile stocks. Now we're exposed.'

Zaki faltered. 'But we have hundreds of missiles and our SAM units—'

'Have been compromised. By the time we finish this conversation, half of them will be lost.'

Zaki took a step back, his face twisted in confusion. 'A trap?'

'Undoubtedly.'

'Excuse me for a moment.'

Mousa watched him walk back across the room. Before he could react, Zaki pulled his pistol and shot the female operator through the back of the head. Blood and brain matter sprayed across her terminal, and her body slipped out of its chair and onto the floor in a lifeless heap. Zaki puffed out his chest and scanned the shocked faces around the room.

'She failed in her duty to the Caliph. See that you do not fail in yours.' Zaki returned to Mousa's side, holstering his pistol. 'So, what now, Faris?'

Mousa was momentarily speechless. He watched the woman's body being carried out of the room, her veiled head lolling lifelessly. He pulled himself together, now knowing with certainty what had to be done. 'I've been summoned to Baghdad,' he lied.

'Then do not keep my uncle waiting. I will take charge here.'

Mousa took a step closer and spoke quietly, 'Kalil, the Ops Team officers are at your disposal. I would urge you to make use of their knowledge and experience before you make any tactical decisions. Please.'

Zaki frowned. 'Do you doubt me, Faris? This is hardly my first operation.'

InshAllah, it will be your last, Mousa didn't say. 'This is a team effort, that's all I'm saying.' He threw up a salute and Zaki returned it. 'I'll be back in 12 hours. Twenty-four at most. Good luck, General Zaki.'

Mousa headed for the door. Above ground a waiting helicopter flew him to London City Airport, where a Gulfstream executive jet idled on the runway. As it lifted off and headed south-east, Mousa saw the blinking collision lights of his escort, a single Typhoon Eurofighter, off the starboard wing. It was a discreet escort, and all that Mousa needed. He also needed time to think, because once he was in Baghdad, in Wazir's presence, there would be no turning back. He would need to choose his words carefully to make his case. If he was successful, it might avert disaster.

If he was not, then it would be General Faris Mousa's head on a spike outside the heavily-defended walls of Caliph Wazir's marble palace.

[31]
TANK ACTION!

A SCREAMING, PIERCING TONE FILLED HIS HEAD. HIS vision swam and his legs felt like jelly, but he could still feel the rifle in his hands and that was something. He felt pain too, shooting up his arms and legs, and he realised he was crawling over a shattered section of jagged flint wall. He didn't know where he was going because he wasn't sure where he was, but he knew he had to get away. The ground thumped and shook beneath his body, and a sharp detonation split the air close by. He heard muffled gunfire and screams, but it all sounded far away. He kept moving, dragging himself across sharp stones and wet grass. A figure crawled out of the darkness and blocked his path. Their headgear collided. He squinted through his ballistic eyewear.

'Eddie! It's me, Mac. Are you hit? Can you move?'

Eddie recognised the camouflaged face, the voice, and nodded. 'I'm okay.'

Mac pointed to the stone cottage nearby. 'They're dropping mortars all over! Get yourself behind cover! Go!'

As Eddie crawled away, he saw others around him, stumbling to their feet and heading for the hamlet. Eddie stayed on his belly, crawling fast, the painful tone fading, the fog of confusion clearing. He knew where he was, who he was, why he was there. That was a start.

He felt the adrenaline surging. He pushed himself up and ran towards the house, dodging left and right, his boots crunching and slipping on the shingle border that surrounded the property. He made it around the back and crouched against the wall, breathing hard.

Lucky they were only mortar rounds. He remembered being on the wrong end of a big artillery barrage back in Ireland, one that had shaken the earth and blown 30 Bravo Company soldiers to pieces. They were the lucky ones, Eddie remembered. The unlucky ones had survived but were horribly injured; limbs blown off, guts spilt, clothes and skin burned to a crisp. Worst of all, he remembered the screams. Eddie didn't want to go out like that. A bullet through the brain, instantaneous, that was the hope. Unless he lived, survived the entire thing, came out the other end unscathed. *What are the odds of that happening?* he wondered, then pushed it from his mind. The next five minutes, that's all that mattered. Then the five after that. Anything else was hopeless optimism.

He checked his gear, weapons, and equipment. Nothing broken, nothing missing. He swapped out his mag, then felt for his knife because something told him he'd need it.

Boots crunched on the gravel, and more guys from Nine Platoon bundled to safety behind the cottage. Steve and Digger were among them, dragging a couple of wounded. Mac was the last to appear.

'Where's Sarge?' a voice asked.

'All over that garden. Took a direct hit. OC's down too.'

Troops scrambled out of the darkness, guys from Three and Four Platoons. 'Where's the rest of the company?' Mac asked. 'We're getting battered here.'

A breathless corporal jerked a thumb over his shoulder, his black face streaked with green camo stripes. 'Lead element got chopped up by a gunship a couple of klicks back. The road's blocked, and they're still taking fire. Right now, it's just us.'

'Minus the casualties, that's what, 50 guns? There's a Haji armoured convoy heading our way.'

'I know. Four Platoon have got a couple of Javelins.'

Mac raised an eyebrow. '*Two* Javelins? We'll be fine then.'

'Our boss is KIA, so the Four Platoon OC will call the shots. Keep your ear to the net, yeah?'

'Got it.'

The corporal pulled up a map on his tac-tablet and pointed. 'My guys will set up over there, in the trees between these houses, and Four Platoon will cover the overpass with the Javelins, in case the Hajis try to bypass us and head straight for the city centre. You've got the eastern flank all the way out to these fields here, got it?'

'Understood.' Mac nodded, then said, 'this is turning out to be a shit day.'

The corporal's black face split into a wide grin. 'Ain't that the truth.' And then he was gone, into the darkness.

'You heard the man,' Mac told the rest of Nine Platoon. 'Spread out, find cover, and watch your front. Last man in the line, get a bug in the air, monitor our eastern flank. You see anything, call it in, pronto. Fallback RV is the care home, but don't even think about it unless I say so. If I see anyone retreating, I'll shoot you myself, ya ken?' Helmets bobbed in the darkness. 'Go!'

Mac turned around and booted the door of the house open. 'Inside,' he ordered Eddie and the others.

They piled in and cleared the ground floor. Eddie followed Mac up the narrow stairs, keeping low as they entered the main bedroom. It was neat, but the windows had been shattered by gunfire and rain had soaked the glass-strewn carpet. The occupants were an elderly couple, Eddie reckoned, clocking the frames of beaming kids on the sideboard.

A volley of incoming rounds cracked off the flint wall outside, but they were wild. Mac took one window, Eddie the other. He peered over the sill and checked the open ground they'd just vacated. The wall he'd taken cover behind had been blown apart in several places. Dead bodies lay sprawled in the grass.

'Fuck me, that was close,' Eddie whispered. Somewhere to the south, gunfire rattled. There was no mistaking the repetitive thump of the Ripsaw's auto-cannon.

Mac grinned. 'Give 'em hell, ya wee bastard.' His smile slipped as he pressed his scope against his eye. 'Here they come.'

Eddie did the same and saw a sizeable group of armed men crossing the distant roundabout and heading through the trees towards the hamlet. 'I count 30, maybe more.'

Mac keyed his radio. 'Digger, bring your gun up here.'

Boots thumped up the narrow stairs and Digger appeared a moment later. 'Where d'you want me?'

Mac pointed. 'Window. Arc of fire is everywhere in front of you. Take out the HVTs, signallers, and any heavy weapons.'

'Roger.'

'Where's Steve?'

'Getting a brew on.' He saw Mac's face and winked. 'He's covering the downstairs with two other guys.'

Digger set up next to Eddie and squinted through his more-powerful scope. 'I've got movement, trees on the other side of the roundabout, one-five-zero metres.'

Mac swung his rifle around. 'Sneaky fuckers,' he whispered. 'Possible command element. When it starts, thin 'em out.'

'Rog.'

Eddie rested his gun barrel on the sill, and the world jumped a little brighter through his holographic scope. 'Another 20-plus targets moving towards our location. That's what, 80 now? Maybe a hundred.'

Next to him, Digger grinned. 'Try not to shit your pants, Novak.'

'Piss off.' Eddie kept his eye pressed to his scope. There was shouting from the darkness below, voices down in the trees, in a tongue Eddie didn't understand. The intention, however, was clear enough.

'Here we go,' Mac warned, jamming his M27 into his shoulder. 'Make your rounds count, boys.'

No one moved. Eddie breathed slow and easy, a gloved finger resting on his trigger, his heart pounding.

The shadowy world outside sparkled like Christmas lights—

A storm of noise and gunfire slammed into the house, chewing flint and timber, and punching dusty holes through the walls. Digger was already firing, the semi-automatic DMR kicking in his shoulder while he jabbered away to himself.

'Hit! Down you go, fucker. Next one...stay still...good boy.' *Boom.* 'Hit. Stupid twat. Who's next?'

Eddie was firing too, trying to focus on his targets, his eyes distracted by the hundreds of red and orange tracer rounds crisscrossing his line of fire. Grenades cracked in the garden below, smoke and fragmentation, and the first screams shrilled on the night air. Eddie couldn't tell if they were friend or foe, but he saw Hajis running from tree to tree, charging towards the house. Rounds poured in through the window, then something hit the wall outside with an almighty bang. Eddie hit the deck. Dust filled the air.

'RPG!' he yelled.

Mac was on the carpet too, coughing violently. Digger was still firing. Mac yanked him to the floor.

'Downstairs, now!'

Digger went first, oblivious to the rounds that were chewing the walls to pieces and filling the air with dust. Mac shoved Eddie forward. 'Move! Next one is coming straight through that window!'

Eddie rumbled down the stairs on his belly. He got to his feet and ran into the kitchen, scrambling behind the marble-topped centre island with the others. The windows that overlooked the garden were all smashed, the frames splintered. Steve crouched beneath the sink, changing out his magazine.

'They're closing in, Mac.'

'Then get some fucking rounds downrange! You see anyone with a heavy weapon, drop 'em first!'

Mac stood up and fired in short, controlled bursts. Eddie did the same, and Digger was rocking his DMR from the shoulder. Steve racked and pumped a couple of grenade rounds out towards the shadows that were dodging towards them, firing, screaming.

Despite the noise, the yelling and the gunfire, the thump and crack of grenades, Eddie felt an unusual calm envelop him, and he wondered if his own death was imminent. He wasn't scared now. He was simply fighting for his life, for the lives of his friends, for the terrified families he knew would be cowering in their homes.

Fire, switch target, fire, switch target...

He swept his rifle barrel left and right, squeezing the trigger, controlling his rounds, his breathing. He saw targets dropping, and for a moment he thought they might hold their position. Then a fresh sound reached his ears and suddenly the spell was broken. The distant rumble was building into a loud, terrifying clanking.

'Tanks, 12 o'clock!'

Everyone saw them, two French *Leclerc* battle tanks rolling up the A1 slip road towards the hamlet, belching white diesel smoke. Fifty-tonne monsters bearing down at 50 miles an hour. Eddie flinched as their 120-millimetre guns roared in unison. The ground shook as a house nearby exploded in a furious blast and a shower of flint shrapnel.

'Jesus!'

He saw the other two guys from Three Section scramble out of the door and knew they should be right behind them because the tanks would go for the buildings first.

Mac knew it too. 'Get the fuck out!' he screamed. 'Move—'

The house exploded in a giant fireball. Eddie felt a wall of pressure before the building came down in a thunderous roar. He fell to the floor, and grey dust swirled and billowed, blinding and choking him. He coughed and spat, then tried to get up, but something immovable was pushing down on his assault pack. The ground shook again as another shell detonated close by. More debris crashed down on top of him. But he didn't feel it crushing the life from him. He was on all fours, blind and breathless, but he could move. Gunfire rattled, rising and fading, and urgent voices whispered in the dark. Eddie stayed motionless, knees and hands on the ground, trapped in a smoke-filled hole. A Kalashnikov chattered right outside the kitchen window. Something metallic bounced and rattled across the room.

Grenade—

Eddie lay flat as the blast rocked the kitchen, and more dust filled the darkness of his tomb. He felt no pain, and he could still move. Then he felt a hand squeezing his arm. He fingered grit from his eyes and Steve's face loomed out of the dark. Mac squeezed next to him, a pistol in his hand. As the dust cleared he saw Digger, lying face down next to Mac, unconscious and covered in dust and blood. Mac held a finger to his lips and pointed.

Eddie turned his head slowly, then realised two things at once. The ceiling above had caved in, but they'd been caught in the narrow gap between the sink and the centre island. It had saved them, bearing the brunt of the collapse and trapping them in a dark, dust-filled pocket.

Then he realised the other thing; they were not alone.

He heard rapid jabbering in a language he didn't understand. Through the mesh of collapsed timbers, he saw torches sweeping the wreckage. There was a shout from outside, and the lights disappeared. Close by – too close – a tank engine roared and the walls of the house shuddered. Eddie felt a surge of panic as he imagined the beast rolling over what was left of the house.

'We have to get out of here,' he whispered.

Mac shook his head. 'Don't move. Don't talk.'

Eddie swallowed his fear. They heard more gunfire,

some of it their own, but most of it was AK. What remained of Charlie Company was getting pushed back hard.

Tank guns roared again. The ear-splitting bangs dislodged more debris, filling the shattered room with choking dust. Explosions shook the ground, and then the firing all but stopped.

Steve was the first to hear it, a terrible wailing that drifted on the surrounding air, a sound so harrowing that Eddie wanted to clamp his hands over his ears. He knew what it was. So did the others.

'That bastard tank took out the care home,' Mac said.

AKs chattered, and the wailing stopped. No one said anything, not until Digger stirred.

'What the fuck?' he drawled sleepily.

Mac whispered in his ear. 'They've overrun the hamlet. Get yourself together. We're moving.' And then Mac was easing the timbers and broken slabs of plaster aside, making a hole, crawling out. Eddie was the last man; he stayed low, crawling around the kitchen on his hands and knees. Above him, the roof had disappeared and stars flickered in the clear night sky. The rain had stopped, and that was bad news. Rain gave them cover.

Eddie got to his feet and followed the others as they crept out into the hallway. It was dark, but he could see well enough. He could hear, too. The tank was right next to the house, so close that Eddie could feel the rumble of its mighty engine in his chest. Mac pulled Steve close.

'Take Digger and head due east, into the trees. Don't stop until you reach the fields. When you get there, stay out of sight and wait for us.'

'What's the plan?' Steve whispered.

'The plan is, we're getting the fuck out of here before they get organised and sweep back through the hamlet. If we're not there in ten minutes, keep heading east, then north, try to link back up with our guys. Got it?'

Steve nodded. Mac stood in the twisted doorway of the cottage and looked outside. He waved, and Steve and Digger were moving, turning hard right and into the darkness. Mac watched them go, then slipped outside himself. Shots rang out, but they were some way off. *Finishing off the care home residents*, Eddie guessed. And the Nine Platoon wounded, probably. The cold grip of vengeance squeezed him, and now he longed for a target. Any target.

Mac ducked back into the dark hallway. 'Tank is right beside us,' he whispered, pointing. 'How many eggs you got?'

'Four,' Eddie told him, feeling for the grenade pouches on his tac-vest.

'Okay, that'll do it.' Mac went over the plan. Well, a sort-of plan, but Eddie wasn't worried about the risk. He wanted payback.

He followed Mac outside and immediately saw the enormous tank barrel pointed to the north. The rattling engine covered the crunch of their boots on the gravel, and then Mac was around the corner. Eddie followed, squeezing through the narrow gap between the tank's treads and the wall of the house. The smell of warm engine oil and sickly diesel fumes was almost overpowering. The tracks were right by his face, rusted and ugly, and smeared with grease and oil, grass and mud, and God-knew-what else. Just ahead, Mac paused before the open ground at the rear of the tank, and Eddie heard more excited jabbering over the grumbling engine. Mac turned, gave him the thumbs up. Eddie returned the gesture, then Mac was gone.

Eddie scrambled up the side of the metal monster, using the cage armour to climb on top. He heard the suppressed stutter of Mac's weapon, saw a body below drop out of sight. He saw the turret hatch ahead, propped open. He checked the immediate area. There were figures around, but it was dark and they were moving north through the trees. Eddie tried to act casual, just in case someone looked his way. He knelt down and plucked four grenades from their pouches, laying them on the turret. Mac climbed up next to him.

'Ready?' he whispered.

Eddie nodded. A voice echoed from inside the tank. Mac leaned over the hatch.

'Ya rifaq bakhyr?'

The voice answered, the tone casual. Mac took two grenades and pulled the pins. Eddie did the same, and then they dropped them into the hatch. Mac kicked it shut, and then they were scrambling off the back end and running hard, past the shattered cottage towards the eastern side of the hamlet. The grenades detonated a moment later, a rapid series of muffled bangs, and then an enormous explosion almost knocked them off their feet.

Neither of them looked back. Instead, they kept running, dodging through the trees, Eddie following Mac's shadow, the woods briefly lit by an orange glow before the dark crowded in once more. After another 50 metres, Mac stopped and spun around, taking cover behind a tree. Eddie leap-frogged him and did the same, watching the ground behind them for signs of pursuit. Flames roared above the distant rooftops, and he heard frantic shouts, but no one was headed their way. Still, it didn't pay to hang around.

They kept moving east, the woods darker and deeper. After another 15 minutes, the trees thinned out and they saw open ground ahead. Mac took a knee at the edge of the trees and whistled. Eddie heard Steve's musical response coming from a hedgerow that stretched away in both directions.

'Did you get them?' Steve whispered.

'Are you deaf?' Mac grinned.

'Sweet,' Digger slurred, a field-dressing wrapped around his head.

'How's he?'

Steve winced. 'Concussion. Significant laceration, but ears and nose are clear of fluids. He needs to rest up. Come on, I've found a spot.'

The hedge was a tall hawthorn with vicious barbs. Steve crawled beneath it via a well-worn animal path and they all followed. Eddie was last and found himself in a vast, empty field. Steve led them north, moving quietly, keeping close to the thick boundary and the cover it offered. After five minutes of walking up the gentle incline, Mac called a halt and let Digger down gently.

'It's all right, I'm fine.'

'You've got a concussion,' Mac told him.

'Stop fussing. Where's my gun?'

'Back there, buried under that house.'

Digger swore violently. Eddie scanned the horizon with his scope. More fields stretched into the distance, rising and falling, dissected by dark hedgerows. 'We're pretty exposed here.' He pointed across the field towards a dark cluster of roofs a kilometre away. 'Looks like a farm down there.'

'I need my gun,' Digger said, an obvious slur to his words. 'I feel naked without it.'

'Forget it,' Mac told him. 'We wait here. Cover is good and we're a long way from the hamlet. We keep out of sight, then wait for our boys to catch up. Couple of hours, maybe.'

Steve turned to the east. 'Sun'll be up by then.'

'We can't get caught out in the daylight,' Eddie warned.

'And we can't move. Nipper's in no fit state.'

'I'm fine, Mac. Stop babying me.'

'Enough of your lip,' the Scot scolded, 'or you'll no get a bedtime story.'

Eddie grinned in the dark.

The smile faded as gunfire rattled in the distance.

[32]
BRIDGE OF SIGHS

Beyond the abandoned frontier settlements of Haydon Bridge and Gilsland, the B52s had transformed those heavily-defended areas into vast landscapes of mud and broken earth, scattered with twisted sculptures of metal and concrete. The huge bombs had walked their way from south to north, stamping across the earth, obliterating every-thing in their path. Minefields, barricades, surveillance systems, oceans of razor wire, SAM batteries, and sub-surface control centres had been vaporised, leaving behind a pockmarked, desolate moonscape beneath the leaden night sky. Operation *Rolling Thunder* had opened the door. Now it was up to others to keep it open.

As the last of the mighty aircraft had emptied their bomb racks and climbed back towards the North Atlantic, huge convoys of British and American engineering teams emerged from woods and forests and raced towards the broken, smoke-filled landscape, rumbling down the tracks and approach roads in their specialist vehicles, safe in the knowledge that the enemy troops defending the ground to the south had been temporarily neutralised. Time, now, was of the essence.

At Haydon Bridge, the first troops into action were the US Army bulldozer drivers, their giant blades pushing mountains of grey stone down into the shallow South Tyne River, strengthening the banks for the bridge-layers behind them. After they'd spanned the waterway, British Trojan engineering vehicles roared to the opposite bank and began carving a wide path across the frontier with their dozer blades. The road layers followed with their high-density polyethylene panels, quickly forming the first hundred metres of a four-lane highway that would eventually link both sides of the frontier.

The engineers worked furiously, knowing that combat units waiting in staging areas behind them were desperate to enter the fray and support the spearhead forces now pushing out from the city centres of Newcastle and Carlisle.

In the low, damp cloud above the engineers, attack drones circled the sky, their wings heavy with Hellfire and Sidewinder missiles. Far above their combat counterparts, surveillance drones swept the ground below, their multi-band sensor packages watching and listening for the reappearance of enemy forces.

As the new roads stretched across the breaches in the frontier, surviving caliphate SAM units registered aerial activity to the north. Knowing that they were prime targets for the infidel missiles and bombers, the mobile SAM launchers kept their engines running, moving every 15 minutes, desperate to stay one step ahead of the forces they knew were hunting them.

They also knew something else; the SAM envelope that

had protected the skies over the frontier for so long had been torn open.

At Edinburgh airport, four Fairchild Republic A-10 Thunderbolts took to the pre-dawn skies and headed south on full power. In service since the 1970s, the 'Hog', as the A-10 was affectionately known, remained one of the most effective weapons platforms in the US military's inventory, and the four black aircraft – each decorated with sharks mouth nose art – were carrying some serious ordinance.

Primary weapons were their Avenger 30-millimetre auto-cannons, a nose-mounted gun that fired 4,000 armour-piercing rounds a second. They also carried four GBU-42 precision-guided bombs, each with a 250-pound warhead. The Hog moved fast and low and carried a lethal punch. The flight of deadly aircraft from the 76th Fighter Squadron out of Moody AFB in Georgia were on their way to deliver that punch.

They thundered low across the frontier, banking toward the bright pulses of light that flared and faded in the skies south of Newcastle, where British troops desperately needed some serious close air support.

Zaki watched a man in blue overalls mopping the floor of the operations room, saw him sweeping the head back and forth beneath the console where most of the blood had spilt. There was also a reddish-brown streak that meandered all the way to the door and was being studiously ignored by others as they crisscrossed the room. He recalled the operator's face, the slight turn of her head, the spark of alarm in her eyes as he'd aimed his pistol at the back of her head. Then the deafening bang, the cries of shock that were quickly stifled, then the stunned silence, broken only by the faint buzz of radio traffic.

Oh, how he'd enjoyed that moment. Not the shooting itself, although that came with its own distinct pleasure. No, it was the fear in the eyes of those around him, even in Mousa's face. He knew the general didn't respect him as a soldier, or as a leader, especially after the debacle in Ireland, although that wasn't his fault. His officers had proven themselves to be incompetent cowards, but the stench of that failure still lingered. He could see it on the faces of his Ops Team, their noses wrinkling whenever he was with them as if he'd walked a dog turd into their presence. The same officers whom Mousa had urged him to consult. Zaki's instinct was to bait them with veiled threats, but the voice told him to listen instead, to encourage them, and feed them enough rope to hang themselves if the failures of Ireland were repeated. *That* was the kind of practical advice that Zaki took heed of.

'General Zaki?'

He blinked and refocussed. The room buzzed with feverish activity, and the man with the mop and bucket was now erasing the bloody path to the ops room door. An air force major stood a respectful distance away, his face a study of trepidation.

'What?'

'Sir, Alliance forces have established a significant beachhead on the Cumbrian coast, and enemy aircraft are running sorties into caliphate territory. There are reports of engagements all along the frontier.' He paused, then said, 'Sir, we need orders.'

Zaki tutted and got out of his chair, snapping his combat

jacket tight and sweeping his shoulders back. He waved his hand. 'Lead the way.'

He followed the major to the tactical display table. The Ops Team were grouped around it, pointing and debating, all of them senior officers from the caliphate's land, sea, and air forces. They lapsed into silence as Zaki approached, quickly making room for him at the table. Zaki leaned over it, his hands gripping the rim, his eyes wandering across the digital map of northern Britain and its dizzying array of live-feed information. He looked at the faces gathered around him and spread his hands.

'Is someone going to update me or do I have to guess what's happening?'

'The situation is fluid,' blustered a white-haired colonel with sagging jowls.

How many times have I heard that phrase? 'Are you trying to tell me you don't know?'

The relic's eyes flicked nervously to the pistol on Zaki's belt. 'I'm saying there are many moving parts and more are coming into play as we speak. The Alliance is launching a full-scale invasion, of that there can be no doubt now. Scores of aircraft and ships are now heading towards northern Scotland, and the localised border skirmishes have escalated. We're now looking at a major conflict.'

Zaki clapped his hands slowly. 'Bravo, colonel. You clearly have a talent for stating the obvious. I take it we have battle plans for just such a scenario?'

The red-faced colonel nodded. 'Of course, but the loss of Ireland was unexpected, and the enemy's military build-up accelerated so rapidly we...er...'

Zaki's eyes narrowed. Mentioning the Irish debacle in his presence was a risky game, as the colonel had just realised, but he decided to let it go. *Put them at their ease,* the voice counselled, *gain their trust. Remember, patience is a bitter plant that bears sweet fruit.*

'So, the old plans are useless. Recommendations?'

'Not useless—'

'Proceed,' Zaki snapped, wondering if those sweet fruits were worth the trouble. He listened as they unveiled a new defensive plan. The men around him spoke of multi-element deployments, of position strengthening, and the destruction of enemy naval forces in the Irish Sea. Zaki liked the sound of that one. A decisive victory would go some way to bolster his professional reputation. Uncle would be pleased, that was for sure, and his was the only approval that Zaki truly sought.

'Where are these reinforcements?' he demanded.

'Four divisions are heading north from Leeds and Manchester as we speak, general. The lead elements will reach the combat zone in the next four hours.'

Zaki nodded. 'Very good.'

The discussion continued, but after a short while, he lost focus. He was bored and tired. He silenced the tedious drone of voices in mid-flow.

'If you need me, I'll be in my quarters.'

He ignored their confused expressions and left the bunker. Up above ground, he headed back to his sizeable apartment, flanked by his bodyguards. The air was cool and still, and in the east, the horizon had paled a fraction. He needed time alone, to think and to sleep.

Inside his bedroom, he dropped his uniform to the floor and climbed into bed. He lay in the darkness, eyes open, staring at the shadows on the ceiling, his chest rising and falling as his mind began to drift. His eyes fluttered and closed. They snapped open as he felt the mattress dip by his feet. He lifted his head and saw the figure sitting at the end of his bed. He heard the shallow wheeze of its breath, the ancient voice that spoke his name.

'Rest, Kalil. You will need your strength. War is upon us.'

Zaki's eyes returned to the ceiling. He didn't want to look, just in case the curtain shifted and the light fell upon the face that turned towards him. Something told him he didn't want to see that.

'Yes, war,' he echoed. 'One we must win. One that *I* must win.'

'How far are you willing to go?'

Zaki thought about that as he stared at the ceiling. 'To the gates of hell itself.'

The voice rattled in the darkness. 'Then we shall travel there together.'

[33]

HAMMER TIME

'Take your clothes off! All of you, now!'

Bertie stripped, tugging his t-shirt over his head, dropping his trousers and underwear at his feet. He cupped his privates with both hands, but it was so cold that one would've done the job. He did a quick head count and saw there were at least 20 of them standing in a long, naked, guilty line.

'Take three paces back and turn to your left,' the head screw yelled.

His voice boomed around the reception hall. Bertie did as he was told, stepping back and facing left, discarded clothes on one side, a mob of screws on the other, surly bastards in black combat trousers and fleeces, crossed swords emblazoned on the left breast. And they each carried a long club, not dangling from their belts but gripped in their hands, ready. They were more like bouncers than professional prison staff, Bertie observed, but that didn't surprise him. Before the invasion, the men and women who now ran the prisons would've been banged up themselves.

The one doing all the shouting was called Durkin, a 40-
something black man with a bald head and a thick beard, a
man who clearly spent most of his downtime in the gym.

'Left!' Durkin screamed. 'Left, left, you fucking moron!'

The target of Durkin's rage was the man in front of
Bertie. He was short, pale, and skinny, no more than 20
years old, and he trembled like a terrified animal. He threw
himself around, but Durkin was already on him. The head
screw towered over him, arms and shoulders rippling as he
berated his victim.

'Don't you know your left from your right?'

'I'm sorry, I—'

'You're what? Stupid? A dumb fucking infidel?'

'No, I—'

Durkin punched him, a short right hook that caught the
kid square on the jaw. His knees gave way and he went
down hard, unconscious before he hit the wooden floor.
Durkin looked down at him as if he'd just spotted a turd.

'Get this thing out of my reception hall.'

Two of the screws ran forward and grabbed the kid by
his ankles, his limp body squeaking as they dragged him out
of sight. Bertie kept his eyes front. Durkin stared at him, and
for a second, Bertie thought he might have a crack at him
too, but then he walked away and bellowed again, pointing
to a door across the hall.

'That way! Single file, eyes front, no talking! Move!'

The naked line rippled forward, and Bertie followed on
as the last man. He heard the screws behind him, muttering,
sniggering. He felt the sharp jab of a club in his spine, but
Bertie didn't react, he just kept moving, kept his mouth shut
and his eyes front, just like Durkin had told them. It was all
about being invisible now. About survival.

The hall was vast, with coloured lines on the wooden

floor and iron girders high above, but there were no signs anywhere, not even for a fire escape or a toilet. Bertie had no idea where he was, but he knew it had taken almost two hours to get there. They'd passed through a few checkpoints on the way, and the sirens had wailed for most of the journey, but later they'd faded to nothing, which made Bertie think they were a long way out of London. North, south, east, or west, he had no clue.

He'd seen the bright lights of the perimeter fence, and he'd heard the rattle of the roller shutter as the van was driven into a courtyard of high, grey stone walls. Then they'd marched him straight into the hall where Durkin and the other prisoners waited. Bertie had been the last to arrive.

'Hurry up! Move!'

Bertie felt the painful jab of a club up his arse. The screws sniggered again, and Bertie winced. It was common knowledge that the penal system in England and Wales now tolerated all kinds of abuse, and he wondered how long it would be before they came for him. When they did, he wouldn't make it easy for them, but they'd get their way. And that was the irony; in a land where homosexuality was punishable by death, the authorities turned a blind eye to the wholesale rape and torture of its prisoners.

He passed through the double doors into a much smaller hall. A row of chairs waited for them, each with a smiling screw stood behind it. He watched his hair fall in clumps around his bare feet as they shaved his head, and then they were on the move once more, through another door and into a cold, dark corridor. Durkin bawled again as they lined up along the wall. There was a square of light up ahead.

A storeroom, Bertie realised, watching the men ahead of

him stepping into orange overalls and dressing quickly. He shuffled along the wall until it was his turn. He stood in front of the half-door cum serving hatch. The grey-haired, tattooed screw standing behind the counter snarled at him.

'Name?'

'Payne. Albert Payne.'

He ran a stubby finger down a printed sheet, then ticked his name off with a pen. He reached underneath, then slapped a set of coveralls on the counter.

A yellow set.

'What's this?' Bertie asked, and then his face exploded in pain as the screw slapped his face. Bertie reeled, then stood up straight and obedient before the others piled in.

'My apologies, sir.'

'You learn fast, Payne. Not gonna do you any good, mind.' The screw laughed, a humourless bark that made Bertie's skin crawl. Not the laughter, but the implication.

Durkin marched towards him. 'Get fucking dressed!' he bellowed.

Bertie did so, quickly. The garment was rough against his skin, and he still had no underwear or shoes, but it was a start. Another jab in the back and he was moving again, following the others. Shouts, threats, and curses chased them along the corridor until they spilt out into a large rotunda that rose for several stories to a glass roof. On the floors above, Bertie saw barred doors and unlit corridors that stretched away from the central core. A Victorian prison, Bertie knew from experience. He'd served his time in Pentonville, and this place looked similar.

It didn't sound the same, though. There was no cat-calling, no doors slamming, no standard-issue boots squeaking on the floors above, no keys and chains rattling. This wasn't the prison environment he knew of. This was something different. And that wasn't all he noticed – he was the only one wearing yellow overalls.

'You, step out,' Durkin ordered, pointing at Bertie.

He obeyed, taking a pace forward. He could feel all eyes on him as two screws grabbed his arms and escorted him out of the rotunda and down a brightly-lit corridor. Grey steel doors lined the whitewashed walls. They dragged Bertie to a halt outside one of them. The door was unlocked, and he was shoved inside.

It wasn't a cell. It was more like an interview room, with a metal table and two chairs on either side. It wasn't until they forced Bertie into one of the chairs that he noticed the thick wire loops screwed to the tabletop. His hands were threaded through them and the loops drawn tight. Bertie couldn't help himself.

'Oi!' he cried. 'What the fuck is this all about?'

A screw slapped him around the head. 'Keep your mouth shut.'

The other one knelt down and clamped his ankles to the chair that was bolted to the floor.

Not an interview room, he knew now. *An interrogation room.*

Fear churned his stomach. The screws left the room without another word. Bertie sat there in silence, his breathing shallow and rapid, his arms stretched across the table, his wrists and ankles bound to the chair. His body was frozen but his mind was racing.

You've just made a terrible mistake, Bertie. One you'll live to regret. Of that, I'll make certain.

This was her doing, of course it was. He was getting special treatment, the full package. Bertie was terrified, more frightened than he'd ever been in his life. And then the door opened, screeching on its rusted hinges, and he heard people enter the room behind him, maybe three or four. He couldn't be sure because he wouldn't turn around. He kept his eyes forward, facing the empty chair. A figure crowded his peripheral vision, and a man walked around the table and sat in the empty chair opposite. Bertie had no choice but to look.

Oh shit.

Not a screw, not one of his own, like Durkin and the others, traitors for sure, but at least there was an understanding between them. Screw or con, they all spoke the language of the street. The man who sat in front of him was not like that at all. He was Middle Eastern, and he wore a black suit with a gold, crossed-swords lapel pin and a white shirt buttoned to the neck. His beard was neatly trimmed and his unblinking eyes gave Bertie nowhere to go.

'My name is Colonel Al-Huda.'

He left his name hanging in the air. Bertie didn't know how to respond, so he kept his mouth shut.

'The governor sends her best wishes.'

'Who?'

'Governor Spencer. Your former employer.'

'*Governor* Spencer?'

'There have been some administration changes. Nothing to concern yourself with.' He inspected his fingernails for a moment, then looked at Bertie. 'Your only priority now is helping me with my inquiries. There isn't much time, you see.'

Bertie swallowed, his stomach bubbling like lava. 'I know nothing about—'

He heard a rustle behind him, and then a man leaned over him and clamped his right forearm in an enormous hand. In the other, he held an ugly claw hammer. Bertie's eyes widened as the man raised it over his head.

'Wait, please—'

He brought it down, once, twice, a third time. Bertie screamed, long and loud as he felt the bones in his hand break. Tears of pain ran down his face as he watched the broken skin turning purple.

'It will only get worse,' Al-Huda told him. 'Once they break your hands and feet, these men will take the nails from them. Then they'll take the hammer to your testicles, and then your teeth. Doctor Chowdhury will ensure you remain alert and coherent throughout.'

Bertie glimpsed at the man through his tears, older, bald, with round glasses, standing against the wall to his right, a battered leather bag at his feet.

'What is it you want?' Bertie asked.

Al-Huda stood and placed his hands on the table. He leaned over Bertie, his voice cold, his eyes like a mantis about to devour its prey. Bertie shrivelled beneath that soulless, inhuman gaze.

'I want to know everything, Albert Payne.'

He stepped back and folded his arms. The man with the hammer raised it again, high over his head.

Bertie screamed.

[34]

FARE THEE WELL

The wind picked up, rustling through the hedgerow. Eddie was lying prone, tucked in close to the roots of the hedge, allowing the darkness to wrap itself around him. Steve was a few metres away to his right, Mac and Digger on his left, all of them just vague shadows in the dark. His rifle pointed out across the empty field. Nothing moved, nothing close anyway. To the south-west, white flashes lit up the sky, and the thunder of heavy combat rolled across the countryside.

'That's Birtley,' Mac whispered. 'The New Yorkers are getting stuck in.'

'While we're hiding in a hedge like a bunch of pussies,' Digger sulked.

The blow to his head had done nothing for his attitude, Eddie noted. The wind gusted again, rattling along the hedge, and he swept the field with his scope. White-tailed rabbits bobbed across the hard, stubby tufts of some unknown winter crop.

'It'll be light soon,' Steve whispered in the dark. 'If we get caught out here, we're dead.'

As if to reinforce his point, heavy guns boomed to the west of them, and tracers arced across the sky. Mac fiddled with his radio.

'Anything?' Eddie asked him.

'Switch 'em off,' Mac ordered. 'We're out of range anyway, and if the Hajis are scanning for signals, they might just ping us here.'

Eddie switched his off, then turned to tell Steve to do the same. His eyes narrowed, searching for the inky shadow that was there only a few seconds ago. He brought his rifle up and swept the field. He found him on the third sweep. 'Steve's gone walkabout,' he told the others. 'Three o'clock, heading for the farmhouse.'

'What the fuck?' Mac said, seething. 'Get after him, Eddie, drag his stupid arse back here. And do it quietly.'

Eddie was already up and moving, keeping low and tight to the hedgerow. His boots slipped on the muddy fringe, and he slowed his pace, snapping his NVGs onto his helmet.

Night became green day. He glimpsed Steve disappearing into the farmyard beyond the field. He thought about cutting across but decided against it, unwilling to leave a fresh trail of military boot prints behind him. Instead, he kept to the hedgerow and worked his way around.

It was several more minutes before he stepped onto the hard standing of the farm itself. To his left were a row of single-storey outbuildings, most of them housing rusted machinery. To his right, 50 metres away, stood the farmhouse, with a muddy pickup parked outside. Eddie moved real slow, gun barrel up, watching for Steve, watching for potential targets. Any moment now he expected to hear the rattle of a chain, the desperate scampering of a guard dog as it charged out of the darkness. He loved dogs, didn't want to shoot one, but he would if it came to it.

The house was quiet, no sound at all from inside, but a soft light flickered in the downstairs window. Farmers got up at the crack of sparrows, Eddie knew. He also knew that no sane person would be sleeping through the thunder of battle that raged a few klicks away. So this farmer was up, probably cooking breakfast, and the sudden image of bacon and eggs sizzling in a pan made Eddie's mouth water. He moved towards the window. A low whistle stopped him.

Steve was crouched behind the pickup, a gloved finger pressed to his lips. Eddie went to his side. Steve's voice was low in his ear.

'Hajis are inside. I counted three of them, ransacking the place.'

'We should bug out,' Eddie whispered.

Steve shook his head. 'No chance.'

He raised himself up and pointed his weapon across the back of the pickup. Eddie did the same. He heard voices inside, then splintering wood and coarse laughter. He glimpsed one of them through the window, a big guy with olive skin and a straggly beard. He wasn't wearing a helmet, and the guy had his AK slung across a chest rig stuffed with magazines. He was in no hurry either, and that worried Eddie. The front line might've shifted further north than he thought. The man turned as another voice barked, then he moved out of view.

'They're leaving,' Steve whispered. 'Wait until they're all outside.'

'Rog.'

The farmhouse door opened and Eddie saw a different man step out into the green world of his NVGs. He was squat and bald, and he dipped his head and plopped his lid on. He strolled towards the pickup, his AK-12 assault rifle held low in one hand. Two more men followed, one of them the big lump he'd seen through the window. Baldy had a radio in his hand, and he lifted it to his mouth...

Steve opened up, and Eddie was firing too. He heard the thump of rounds hitting body mass, the grunts of pain and surprise. Boots skidded on the gravel drive, and bodies buckled. A rifle clattered to the ground.

Eddie moved around the pickup and advanced slowly, eyes flicking between the Hajis and the farmhouse. He fired again at his targets, putting a bullet in each of their heads. They stopped moving, breathing. Baldy was still alive, though. He rolled on the ground, moaning and clutching his stomach, his helmet lying to one side. Steve broke cover and stood over him. The man saw him and stopped moaning. Steve jammed his suppressor into Baldy's eye and pulled the trigger.

They entered the building and listened. There were no footsteps, no creaking doors or floorboards, but that didn't mean there was no one else there. Using NVGs and hand signals, they cleared all the rooms, upstairs and down. They found no more enemy troops, but they discovered the bodies of the farmer, his wife, and their dog in the back parlour. Steve left them where they lay and closed the door.

In the kitchen, Eddie blew out the candle and rounded on him. 'What's with the disappearing act? Mac's going ballistic.' Steve turned and left the room. 'Hey! Don't just walk off. What the fuck's going on?'

'Go back to the others, Eddie.'

In the hallway, Steve plucked a hat and coat from the hooks on the wall and stepped back outside. Eddie followed, watched him kneel and rummage in Baldy's pockets. He straightened up, a key fob in his hand. And suddenly it all made sense.

Eddie caught him up and grabbed his friend's arm. 'Don't do this, mate. You'll never make it.'

Steve shook his hand off and opened the driver's door. 'I've already checked the map. If I stick to farm tracks and walking paths, I can make a few miles cross-country before sun up. I'll lie low for the day, then head south on foot when it gets dark. There's nothing strategic between here and home, no major roads, nothing.' He gave Eddie a tired smile. 'I nearly died back there, we all did. I won't risk that again, not when I'm so close.'

'You're not going anywhere.'

Eddie spun around as Mac loomed out of the dark, his camouflaged face dark and furious. He got straight up in Steve's face.

'You've put us all at risk, ya selfish bastard. Lose the key, now. We're heading back to the lie-up.'

'No,' Steve told him. 'This is something I have to do. If you had a family, you'd understand.'

'Don't play that fucking card with me. Half the battalion is in the same boat as you, so don't think you're a special case.' He nodded down at the bodies. 'Search these jokers for intel, then dump 'em out of sight. Move.'

Steve didn't.

'Are you fucking deaf?'

Eddie tried to get between them. 'C'mon guys, that's enough. This is stupid.'

'Back off,' Mac said. He pulled his pistol from his tac-vest and held it by his leg. 'Last chance, Palmer. Stand the fuck down. That's a direct order.'

To Eddie's horror, Steve smiled.

'You're a decent man, Mac, and I doubt we'd have made

it this far if it wasn't for you. You've got a nose for trouble, an instinct, one you've always trusted, right? Well, my instinct is telling me that my girls are in trouble, and I can't ignore it anymore. I have to go to them, Mac, d'you understand? I *have* to.'

Mac stared at him long and hard. Eddie looked on, worried that someone would get hurt, then suddenly Mac deflated. He stepped aside, tight-lipped. Steve gave him a nod and headed for the pickup.

Mac turned around, looked over Eddie's shoulder and cursed. 'Jesus Christ, I told you to stay put. Doesn't anyone fucking listen round here?'

Eddie saw Digger appear out of the dark and kneel by the big Haji. He dragged the AK-12 rifle from his body, then helped himself to the dead guy's magazines.

'Quiet!' Mac whispered.

Eddie heard it then, the low roar of jet engines, getting louder, rolling across the fields towards them. The ripping sound that followed a moment later was unmistakable.

'A-10s,' Mac said, and then a series of orange flashes lit up the sky beyond the rising ground to the west. 'They're hitting that Haji convoy.'

'Beautiful,' Digger smiled. He got to his feet and watched the sky, his helmet missing, a bloody bandage wrapped around his head, an enemy weapon cradled in his arms. He grinned as the Hogs pounded the unseen, distant highway. 'That's it, fry the bastards, Chop 'em to pieces.'

Mac stepped towards the pickup. 'Listen to me, Steve. If they stop that convoy, it might open up the route south. Another 24 hours and it could all change.'

'Could change for the worse too.' Steve climbed into the driver's seat. 'I can't take that chance.'

Mac nodded in defeat. Digger looked confused. 'Where's he going?'

'Home,' Mac said.

Digger screwed his face up. 'Really?' He marched over and leaned in the driver's window. 'Hey, Stevo, you'll never make it, you daft twat.'

'So they keep telling me.' The engine fired up and settled into a low rattle.

'Got enough juice?' Mac asked him.

Steve checked. 'Enough.'

Mac headed around the back of the Nissan. He flipped his rifle over, smashed out the light clusters, then walked back. He looked at their surprised faces and said, 'It's still dark, and I'm not gonna sit in this thing while Palmer pumps the brakes every two minutes and gives away our position.'

Steve stared at him. 'You're serious?'

Mac shrugged. 'We're MIA, anyway. We'll see you home, make sure your girls are all right, and then we head back – *all of us* – and find our people. That's the deal, take it or leave it.'

Digger beamed and climbed into the back of the pickup. Eddie shook his head.

'I don't believe this. This is mad.'

'Stop your whining and grab some more civvy coats,' Mac told him.

Eddie ducked back inside the house, grabbed everything off the hooks and dumped it all in the back of the pickup. Digger scrambled on top and made himself comfortable.

'Lose your lids,' Mac told them, snatching his own off his shaved head. 'I'll ride shotgun. Eddie, you take the seat behind Steve, cover the right flank. Digger, stay out of sight, just in case we need an ace up our sleeve.'

'Got it, boss.'

'What about the bodies?' Steve asked.

Mac climbed in and shut the door. 'Just drive before I change my mind.'

Steve dropped the vehicle into gear, and then they were moving. He kept the lights off, crawling around the driveway before pulling out onto the main road and heading east. As they crested a hill, Eddie saw a distant wall of fire. *The A-10s,* he guessed. They must've chopped up that convoy good and proper. Further south, the battle was still raging at Birtley, but the flashes and the thunder weren't as intense as they were before. *Maybe we're winning,* Eddie thought, but it was crazy to assume anything so early on. It hadn't even been 24 hours yet, and London was almost 400 kilometres away. Wazir would fight for every inch of land in between, that's what he'd promised in so many of his wild-eyed, finger-wagging speeches. That being the case, the fight would be a long and bloody one.

A few minutes later the Nissan slowed, and Steve turned onto a narrow track. He drove slowly for a bit, then stopped.

'I'll need my lid on,' he told Mac. 'I need my NVGs.'

Mac nodded, and after a moment they were moving again, bouncing slowly and steadily along the track, the hedge whipping and scraping past Eddie's window.

'I feel like we're running away,' Eddie said.

'This is my call,' Mac told him, his eyes fixed on the world outside. 'If it makes you feel any better, you didn't have a choice.'

'You say so.'

'I do.'

'Still doesn't feel—'

'Shut the fuck up, Eddie. Please.'

Mac was troubled too. Steve had other priorities, but Eddie knew that when the dust finally settled, he'd struggle with that same guilt. They'd cut the cord from the Second Mass, abandoned their unit, and now they were on their own.

It wouldn't be long before they were recorded as MIA, but with any luck, they'd link up with the battalion before his folks were notified back in New London. If they were told, Eddie had zero doubt it would rip their world apart. The thought of that pain troubled him deeply, and he now regretted taking Steve's advice. He should've written the letter he'd wanted to write, should've told his mother and father how sorry he was, how selfish he'd been. He'd cared only about avenging his brother's death and had never spared a thought for the fear and uncertainty he'd left behind.

He made a promise to himself, that if he got through this, he'd make it up to them somehow. Stay at home, take care of them, be a good son and not the memory of one framed on a candle-lit mantelpiece.

He took a breath and tried to clear his head. There was no point in stressing about things he couldn't control, nothing he could do other than try to stay alive. He owed his folks that much, at the very least.

And they were doing a good thing, he decided. They were helping a friend, a brother, one of their own. All four of them had survived this far by sticking together, by good fortune and the bad luck of others. The union they shared, the invisible bond between them, it was keeping each one of them alive. If that bond was broken, then so were they.

Mac had known it back at the farm, and now Eddie knew it too. They had no choice but to see it through, to stand together as a team.

Or fall, divided.

Eddie banished the thought from his mind and gripped his gun a little tighter.

The Nissan headed south across the countryside, the darkness that cloaked its passage slowly yielding to the thin band of gold that stretched across the distant horizon.

Did you enjoy ***Invasion: Uprising***?

I hope you did.

If so, would you mind rating ***Uprising,*** or leaving a
review?

It would be hugely helpful.

And many thanks for your time.

.

ALSO BY DC ALDEN

Invasion: Downfall
Invasion: Uprising
Invasion: Frontline
Invasion: Deliverance
Invasion: Chronicles
Invasion: The Lost Chapters
The Horse at the Gates
The Angola Deception
Fortress
End Zone
The Deep State Trilogy
UFO Down

Please visit the official website at:

www.dcalden.com

Printed in Great Britain
by Amazon